THE TREE

CHIP RICE

PUBLISHED BY FASTPENCIL

Published by FastPencil
307 Orchard City Drive
Suite 210
Campbell CA 95008 USA
info@fastpencil.com
(408) 540-7571
(408) 540-7572 (Fax)
http://www.fastpencil.com

Printed in the United States of America.

First Edition

To Bill Rice.
Beloved gardener, woodworker,
fisherman, historian, and most of all father.

ॐ

ACKNOWLEDGMENTS

Above all, I thank God for the ability and opportunity to write. I also thank you, dear reader, for taking a chance on this debut novel by an unknown author. I am truly grateful, and welcome your opinion at www.chiprice.net.

To my wife Shari, thanks for your love and support. Will and Andrew, my amazing sons, thank you for keeping me young at heart. And to my sister Mary Ann, thanks for contributing your medical knowledge.

This book was made substantially better by the insight of proofreaders Scott S. Robbins, Brent Lecheler, Bill and Judi Rice, Shirley Zeger, and Delores Wingert. Thank you all for such wise and constructive feedback. Additional thanks to Scott S. Robbins for a signature cover design.

I thank Pastor Bob Kapp for helping me clarify and embrace my calling to write. Many thanks also to Pastor Shane Wilson and the men of Christian Life Assembly. Your encouragement means more than you know.

1

CHAPTER ONE

From his leather bucket seat in a posh Mercedes Benz, Daniel Crawford said nothing. Conversation with his father was a risky endeavor, and it always had been. Behind the wheel, Russell Crawford adjusted his Ray Bans, punched the accelerator, and passed a small convoy of out-of-state vans. Then he eased the car right as onward they traveled, father and son, at peace amid the whirr and drone of highway traffic. Until Russell asked about the Bell-Knarr Packaging Company.

"We're fine," Dan said, aligning words in his head with rapid precision. "There's another acquisition brewing. A company in Rhode Island. I've been swimming in due diligence. Now there's a consulting firm involved; closed-door meetings, the usual tension." He tugged his seatbelt, looked at his father. "How are things in the Charm City?"

"Margins are down, you know that. But we'll do what needs done. It's the nature of the beast." Russell checked his blind spot, and changed lanes again. "Your execs about to clean house?"

"People are certainly nervous."

"Well, that's the way it goes. Like I've told you many times, Danny Boy: It's just business."

Just business. Dan pondered the idea for a silent mile, until his father's phone rang. Russell stuck it to his ear with a coarse greeting. Dan watched the speedometer touch eighty-five. "I thought we closed the book on that issue?" Russell's voice was a buzzing saw blade, ripping commands, coercing a red-eye flight. "Listen," he said, finally slowing the car. "I'm driving home from an Orioles game; let me call you back." He closed the phone, slapped it to the console.

"Another crash and burn?" Dan said.

"Oh, those idiots in Boston can't nail down a simple outlet chain. We just golfed last week. They assured me the deal was well in hand. Now they're coming back with legal snafus, wanting to delay everything. Man, I could use a drink." He drew a deep breath, turned on talk radio.

Suburban asphalt surrendered to farmland as the car sped north, approaching the Mason-Dixon Line. For several miles Dan stared out the windows, except for one inconspicuous moment when he let his eyes drop, searching and evaluating. An aggressive bite of a third-inning hot dog had dropped ketchup on the pocket of his red plaid shirt. His father had yet to notice, and hopefully wouldn't.

"That schmuck you told me about," Russell said. "Keith or something; does he still work at Bell-Knarr?"

Dan chortled. "You mean Kevin Clark?"

"Yeah, that's him. Got tanked at a holiday party? Almost lost his job?"

"He should've been canned. Everyone calls him KC Masterpiece, like the barbeque sauce. The guy owns no clothing from this decade. And that ridiculous comb-over! We had him so ticked at a meeting last week that he shook loose some of the combed-over parts. Hair was arching out from the side of his head, defying gravity or something."

Russell's huffs of amusement comforted Dan, but only in part and with a measure of uneasiness. For unlike the CEO driving the car, Dan wasn't bullet-proof. He was one wrong decision, one failed attempt, one ketchup stain away from becoming the brunt of his father's ridicule. "You know, Kevin's actually one of my direct reports," he said, keeping Russell focused on the more deserving schmuck.

"You're kidding me."

"Nope. Happened when I grabbed that promotion a couple years back. He had seniority but they passed him over, gave me the position."

"Ouch," Russell said. "How'd he handle that slap in the face?"

"Surprisingly well. He even congratulated me, claimed to be content in his current position." Dan shifted his weight, cracked a few knuckles. "Sure makes working with him easier."

"Another guy resigned in place." Russell shook his head. "They're everywhere."

A few miles into Pennsylvania, they exited the highway and drove to Russell's house of stucco and stone, built in the newest phase of a gated community. He parked his Mercedes in an empty, cavernous, four-car garage, and the engine fell silent.

"So how long have you been in this place?" Dan asked.

"Two years in August. Come on in."

Dan thrust a smooth stick between his thumb and forefinger. Colorful balls scattered and clacked in all directions, but none dropped. He replaced the stick with a bottle of lager, rested his arm on a glassy slab of granite, and scanned the room. Olive walls were adorned with Americana and topped with creamy crown molding. Behind the bar, a panoramic photo of Camden Yards hung above a flat-screen television. He climbed on a stool, watching Fox News flicker to the sounds of smooth jazz, playing on a nearby Bose.

Russell placed his scotch on the bar. "Now you're in trouble."

"You've got a billiards room in your basement. How can I compete?"

Ignoring the question, Russell took aim, sunk a solid...and another... and another. "You anywhere closer to buying a wooded lot?" He circled the red felt table. "You've been talking about it for years." He made another shot, and then finally missed.

Dan tipped his lager, slid down from the stool. "No, not really. It's not possible yet; not with Robyn at home full-time." He pressed the edge of the table, hoping to locate a shot, but his eyes felt compelled to trail Russell instead; to watch him walk toward the bar, swirl his scotch, take a long swallow.

"You know," Russell said, his back to Dan. "They do have day care centers."

Dan blasted the cue in an open side pocket. "Robyn's determined to do the stay-at-home mom thing. She doesn't care about building a new house. Not anymore."

Vertical creases splayed from Russell's squinting eyes. "What do you mean, Danny? You're the man of the house; you want to move the family to a bigger place, that's your prerogative. You've been married what, seven years?"

"Nine."

"Okay, nine. And you're still living in a cookie-cutter? You want a new lot, get it. Why would she not want a bigger place?"

"Okay! Drop it already."

"Hey! You disrespectful twit." Russell clanked his glass on the granite, returned to the table. "All I'm saying is: I don't understand."

Dan swigged some lager. "I don't either," he confessed. "I really don't."

Russell recovered the cue and hammered it on the table. Then he drove in the remaining solids, including the eight. Game over.

Dan chugged what was left of his beer. "I have documents to review."

"Labor Day," Russell said. "We'll make a fire out back, teach your boy to toast marshmallows." He chalked his stick, and then extended a hand in Dan's direction. "Good luck on the Rhode Island deal."

Dan shook hands and thought, albeit fleetingly and for no specific reason, about sinking a left hook into his father's leathery cheek. Instead he offered thanks to which Russell only nodded, turning toward the bar and fishing a phone from the pocket of his gray tweed slacks. Then he poured another scotch, took a long swallow, and barked something in the phone about Boston and outlets and idiots.

Like the one still anchored to a vinyl three-bedroom?

Dan climbed the basement stairs and stepped onto cherry hardwood, perfectly matched to ornate moldings and built-in cabinetry. Elegant rooms were set apart by white pillars, and beneath a vaulted ceiling, a brownstone fireplace climbed two stories like a rocky cliff. His footsteps echoed as he passed a grand piano, flanked by two palm trees in thick copper kettles. Overhead, a crystal chandelier captured beams of evening sunlight, streaming through two arched windows. As the front door opened, humidity shoved him, almost forcing him to pause and look back at a hallway lined with rooms his father hadn't shown him; private, personal rooms. Were they full of secrets, or as empty as the garage? For nearly a minute he gazed down the hall with a troubling blend of curiosity and indifference, until Russell's voice exploded from below: "Close the door!"

Dan adhered the command before walking to his leased BMW. The sedan's engine purred as classic rock filled the interior. Flexing his fingers in a rush of cold air from the dash, he gazed in the rearview at his sun-tanned face and cadet blue eyes. A smug grin parted his cheeks until he looked at his bangs, dark and draped upon his forehead…concealing a seldom-seen scar. His lips drew tight, his gaze fierce, and after slamming the shifter back three notches, Daniel Crawford drove away from a castle not his own.

2

CHAPTER TWO

Eight years, Dan found himself thinking. Eight years had passed since he'd left public accounting to join Bell-Knarr Packaging. And though he still sat enclosed in a slate gray cubicle, he had achieved middle management, become a licensed CPA. His personal analysis was now integral to Bell-Knarr's financial reporting, and the company had yet to impose a pressing deadline he couldn't meet. Last year he attended a private luncheon at the West Shore Country Club, rubbed shoulders with corporate controller Jason Middaur and Jonathan Clauser, CFO. They presented Dan with an engraved tambour clock, named him Accounting Associate of the Year, and left little doubt that a private office would soon be labeled with the name Daniel Crawford.

His pulsating phone displayed: Robyn Crawford. He reluctantly answered the call from his wife. "How was the game?" she asked.

"The O's lost again. Dad's suite was awesome, though."

"So, when will we see you?"

"I'm on the highway now but I need to swing by the office. There's a ton of stuff to review by tomorrow. I'll try to make it home by bedtime."

"You've been gone all day. Can you at least work from home?"

Dan tensed. There was no way; not with four-year-old Evan climbing all over him, shouting out every couple of minutes. "I'm neck deep in paperwork, and I'll never get through it with all the distractions at home."

"Distractions?"

"I'm sorry, babe. I didn't mean you or Evan, necessarily. I just—"

"I'm looking at a baseball game, Dan. Colored for you. And guess who's hitting the grand-slam? That's right...*you* are."

"Honey, listen—"

"No, you listen! Don't take being a little boy's hero too lightly, because you're not going to be one much longer."

Dan's cheeks burned. "What do you want from me?"

"Nothing. Go to work."

Silence.

With dampened adrenaline, Dan thought of going home, offering a genuine apology, taking the family to dinner. But papers were eight inches high on his desk, and he couldn't risk falling behind, not with so much at stake. Crossing the Susquehanna River on the George Wade Bridge, his speedometer hit eighty-five, prompting him to think about the man who'd just kicked his butt in a game of pool. The man who'd been kicking it for years.

He took the Front Street exit, toward downtown Harrisburg. Evan's drawing would have to wait.

Robyn stood in the dark hallway, watching.

Dan entered the kitchen with files in his arms and a soft briefcase slung over one shoulder. After unloading it all on the table, he connected his laptop, slipped off his sneakers, and grabbed a diet soda from the fridge.

She walked barefoot onto the cool tile floor. "Get through everything?"

He twisted to face her. "What? Oh, yeah, yeah." He leaned toward the table, and pecked a few keys. "Yeah, I'll never get it all done," he told the computer. "But working tonight sure lightened the load. I just have some e-mails to wade through; the usual drill."

Robyn, dressed for bed, leaned on a counter, pretending to read. A straight, brown pony tail brushed her upper back. "It's nine-thirty."

Dan nodded, moved toward her. "I know," he said, eyes posed with remorse. "And I understand why you hung up earlier. I probably deserved it."

She broke eye contact, drummed her burgundy nails. He'd played this card a hundred times: soft words, a sexy little grin. "Save it, Dan. I don't give a rip."

He gripped her arm. "Excuse me? I try to apologize, and you—"

"Apologize!" Her head snapped left, engaging his riled expression. "You're just trying to smooth things over 'til next time!"

"Next time what!" He released his grip, flexed his forearms.

"The next time you abandon your family for a stack of unfinished paper-work. I'm sick of it! I'm… I'm going to bed." She took three quiet steps.

"Robyn, wait."

She stopped, turned. "I've been waiting, Dan. For a very long time." A tear rolled down her cheek. Dan stepped forward to wipe it away but she dodged his hand, wiped it herself.

"You've got e-mail," she said, returning to the darkness.

3

CHAPTER THREE

Assistant Director of Alumni. That was her title, and she would have been director, eventually. Still, hers was a decent income with abundant perks, like those private dinners for schmoozing alumni, feigning interest in Sinatra or Manheim Steamroller. Robyn had been a darling on campus, adored by the influential. But then she got pregnant, insisted on staying home…

Staring at fabric walls, Dan slouched in his rolling arm chair, and tried to refocus.

On the quarterly report!

He checked his watch, slapped his desk, scooped some files, and blazed a trail across speckled industrial carpet. Papers shuffled when he stormed in the conference room, ten minutes late. Three accountants watched with pensive expressions as he sat at the end of a long table. "Please tell me we've made progress on the Q."

Senior accountant Megan Brandt responded. "We've gotten two changes from the folks in inventory. They upset everything."

Dan's jaw became a vice grip. "Tell inventory to book their entries next quarter."

"Those changes came directly from the VP, Dan. You want to make it a fight, get Middaur involved."

Dan shifted and grimaced. He hated taking lip from a subordinate, but Megan had a valid point. Jason Middaur never ceased to accelerate deadlines without calling other departments to task. "I'll speak to him this afternoon. Where do we stand on expenditures?"

Kevin Clark adjusted his glasses. "Just need a few more breakdowns. I'll have them on your desk in an hour."

"Good enough. Now, there's a couple—"

"But Dan…"

Dan bit his tongue, acknowledged Kevin with an open palm.

"I'm supposed to meet with PRS at two."

A hush fell over the room. Eyes sagged, a pen clicked. Dan maintained a stern expression. This was, after all, just business, the nature of the beast. "No problem, KC. Just let me know when you're out. We'll touch base then."

Kevin's announcement was hardly a surprise. And Dan was not about to let this critical staff meeting digress into a somber discussion of Penchack, Ryder, and Sachs, the consulting group hired to evaluate multiple aspects of the corporate structure in light of continuing economic decline (according to the official memo). Everyone knew their consultation was tied to the Rhode Island acquisition, and that PRS was prepared to streamline or downsize or flatten the organization. Whatever term softened the reality of firing people.

"It's going to be another late night," Dan said with locker-room pep. "Keep the coffee pots full. Pizza's on me."

For thirty minutes she'd peered through a sliding-glass door, watching Evan's attempt to furnish a box with dirt, leaves, and sticks. And he still wasn't finished. She slid open a pane, and through a dusty screen said, "It's time to feed my little zoo keeper."

"But mom, I'm not done!"

"I'll give you ten more minutes, but then it's lunchtime, mister. Aren't you hungry?" Evan stuck his head in the box. "I'll go make your sandwich."

"Okay," the box mumbled.

Soft music streamed from a slender radio, mounted under Robyn's beige cabinetry. The air smelled of Lysol and overripe bananas. She reached for a loaf of whole grain bread but hurried to the window when her phone began ringing. Outside, next to the box, Evan had squatted with his knees in his armpits and his chin at rest in both hands. She grinned as the phone touched her ear.

"Hey, what are you guys up to?" Dan asked.

"Caring for our new pet."

"Yeah, right. A new stuffed animal?"

"No, much more fun. We found a toad in the mulch and decided to put it in a box. Evan's been arranging dirt, sticks, leaves, you name it. Looks like a regular zoo exhibit."

"You're gonna get warts."

She ignored the joke. "We'll keep him around for you to see. Ev named him Wendell."

"Well, I won't be seeing Mr. Wendell tonight. We're absolutely slammed. Inventory hit us with changes, and I'm down a person because of the consultation. I'll try to make it home by bedtime."

Robyn pictured Dan at his desk, skimming e-mail, barely hearing his own voice, let alone hers. "But I've made plans to go out tonight. I'm meeting friends at Starbucks and then hitting the mall. I'm sure I told you."

"Well, I guess I forgot about that, but…."

She held her ground in silence.

"Look." His tone was sharp. "We've got deadlines to meet. I've required my team to work late. I can't…" He sighed. "I need to be here."

"But I made these plans two weeks ago."

"Plans to what? Sip lattes and browse through stuff you don't need!"

Again, silence. But now her chest tightened, her eyes misted. Who was he to talk about needs?

"Alright, fine, I'll log in from home."

"I need to leave by 6:30."

"I'll be there."

The mist in her eyes became tears on both cheeks. She brushed them away with a quivering hand, and Evan got more than ten minutes.

4

CHAPTER FOUR

Dan slouched above a plate of warmed-up spaghetti. At the end of the table, his laptop dinged. It was all he could do not to look.

Evan's fingers were flared over his cheeks. The tip of each pinky stretched his eyes into slits, and his hair lay in waves on his forehead. In front of him, on the table, a straw was inserted in a small, shiny pouch. Twice he'd asked to squeeze it…*pleeeease!*

Dan blew on his spaghetti, twirled it with a fork. "You want to go outside when I'm done?"

"Yes." Evan released his eyes, folding his arms with a huff.

Dan rubbed his brow. "What would've happened if you squeezed that pouch? I'll tell you what: Juice would've shot all over the table, and I'd have a—correction; you'd have a big mess to clean up. Now, why on Earth would I let you do that?" Evan shrugged as Dan dropped his fork.

Such a harsh tone. Such foolish questions.

"I'm sorry, buddy. It's been a long day. Daddy's getting tired. Let me gobble down this spaghetti and we'll play ball until bath time."

"But I wanna play with Wendell," Evan said with a whine, leaving the table and rushing outside.

"Whatever," Dan said to himself, sliding his laptop close enough to scan e-mail, mouse in one hand, fork in the other. But a minute later he glanced out at Evan, hunkered near a cardboard box and holding a plastic baseball

bat. Moved by a shot of unexpected guilt, Dan closed his computer, abandoned his spaghetti, and walked outside to the lengthening shadow of a ten-
foot maple. Evan beckoned him forward, smiling ear to ear. And then,
crouching together in the dry summer grass, they touched the toad to stim-
ulate hops, until Wendell fled the scene. Dan's first impulse was to stomp
the defiant little hopper. Instead he ran circles around the yard, laughing
like a child at the frenetic pace and haphazard motion of the chase.

"Gotcha!" Dan shouted, the toad finally in hand. Evan smiled victori-
ously, flexing his thin, sweaty arms.

Evan emerged from the tub with wrinkled fingers and his wet hair pushed
into a sloppy, spiked arrangement. His body smelled clean and a little like
chewing gum. Bubbles perched in Dan's disheveled hair, which he also
spiked in response to Evan's prodding. Standing bare-chested in front of the
mirror, they played air guitars until their punk-rock hairdos dried and flat-
tened. Then it was snack, teeth, and off to bed.

"Daddy?"

"What?"

"Do you have to work tomorrow?"

"Yes I do, champ. Tomorrow's Friday."

In the soft glow of a Pooh Bear nightlight, Evan tucked his sheet beneath
his chin, and pushed forth a pouty lip. "I wish you didn't have to work so
much." His words were barbed wire. As a child, Dan had also spoken them.
To a gigantic man with precisely parted hair who'd sharply professed:
"That's life."

Dan swallowed a lump, kissed Evan's head.

"Good night, Daddy."

"It certainly has been," Dan whispered. And yet ten minutes later, he
stood in the kitchen, scorning the clowns in IT. The quarterly report
awaited his attention, but he'd lost his connection to the Bell-Knarr server
—again!—thanks to software upgrades riddled with bugs. He filled a mug
with coffee, carried it to the window.

And instantly forgot about work.

Beyond two fields, above a soft, rolling hill, the moon appeared full and orange in the dusky twilight. And on top of the hill was a tree. *The* tree, he called it. Tonight he saw only its silhouette, black ink penned upon a splendid parchment of moonlight. To Dan the scene was stunning, a natural masterpiece, and like so many times before, the tree had once again captured his—

Ding! A restored connection diminished the moment.

Dan entered his password to download the pressing report. Then he read and muttered. Calculated and corrected. Fired off three critical e-mails, downed as many cups of coffee. So absorbed in work was Dan that an hour passed before he thought of the tree. Looking toward the darkness that had overtaken twilight, he hoped for one final glimpse of the distant hilltop. But against the blackness of night, the window now reflected what he'd rather not see: a driven accountant, working alone.

Robyn was whistling when she opened the door.

"How was ladies night out?" Dan asked, pecking his keyboard.

She slipped out of pink sandals. "Oh, pretty good." It was a half-truth; she'd gone to Starbucks but bailed on the mall, opting instead to sit alone at Barnes and Noble, reading marital advice from the latest Ph.D. to hit the best-seller list. A much wiser use of time, she'd figured...and was about to confirm.

"How were things here?"

"Fine. I guess you noticed the toad is sticking around?"

"Yeah, what's up with that?"

"The little guy pulled my heartstrings."

"Evan or the toad?" She sounded playfully annoyed.

Dan shook his head. "Evan."

Robyn grabbed her sandals and headed upstairs. Evan was twisted in a sheet, mouth gaping. She laughed at the sight, kissed his forehead, and gently closed his door. Better play it safe; according to the book, there's no predicting how loved ones might react to I-feel statements. She entered her bedroom and replaced her floral top with an oversized tee that read: Realize Your Dreams at MCC. In the hallway bathroom, where lights still burned,

she picked up a towel that was striped with toothpaste. Then, drawing close
to the mirror, she picked biscotti from her teeth while looking in her own
nervous eyes. "You've got this," she whispered, turning off the light.

Returning to the kitchen, she filled a kettle with water, and said, "Looks
like you two had a bath-time party."

Dan continued typing. "I forgot to cleanup. Sorry."

"That's fine." She sparked the stove, then searched the cabinets for
vanilla decaf. "I'm just glad you two finally had some fun together. He really
misses you."

"Yeah, Evan mentioned that." The keyboard fell silent. "Well, kind of."

Robyn's heart fluttered. She pulled tea from the cabinet, and looked at
Dan. "What did you tell him?"

"I…" She watched his shoulders rise and fall. "I just kissed him good
night." He typed again as the kettle tinked and rumbled and finally whistled.
Robyn turned off the burner, poured a steeping mug, and carried it and
Dan's carafe to the table.

"Need a warm-up?" She filled his cup before taking a seat and listening to
a minute of clickety sounds from his fingers. "You'll be up all night if you
keep drinking coffee."

Dan's eyebrows rose. "You just poured me—"

"I know, I know." They shared a fragile smile.

The moment has arrived.

Robyn breathed deeply. "Dan, I feel neglected by your long hours, and
hurt by your indifference. I wish you would realize… I mean, I wish you
would put your family first and realize how much we miss, I mean, need
you." She almost vomited. A high school expression (gag-me-with-a-
spoon!) sprung to mind.

Dan pressed the table, his jaw firmly set.

Robyn twisted her wedding ring, drew another breath. "Okay, that didn't
come out quite the way I intended. But we're in trouble, honey. And we'd
better fix things before it's too late." She looked at his face, awaited his eyes.
"Dan, I keep trying to convince myself that someday something will click in
that stubborn heart of yours, and we'll just…I don't know, just… Oh
c'mon! I've been thinking for hours about what to say, and I still sound like
a bad fairy tale!" Her elbows hit the table, her face in her palms. She heard

Dan moving, heard a long sip of coffee, and lifted her head when his mug thumped the table.

"Do you even get the pressure I'm under?" His brow was pinched, his nostrils flared. "Managerial accounting is very stinkin' hard, Robyn! I oversee a department of fourteen people with three direct reports. And I could work around the clock and still not get done what's expected of me. By Jason Middaur and every other executive slave driver! But I'm home to see Evan every night, am I not? Maybe later than you'd like, but what am I supposed to do! I need this job. We need it."

"Oh what a bunch of crap!"

So much for the textbook approach.

Dan thrust back his chair, causing coffee to slosh and spill on the table. Then he stood, crossed the kitchen, and pounded the door of an overhead cabinet. "Don't take that tone with me." His words were methodical, spoken toward the cabinet. "I'm the man of this house, and I will not be spoken to that way."

"Excuse me?" Robyn stood, rounded the table. "Is your name Dan or Russell?"

He wheeled and rushed toward her, his finger stopping inches from her lips. "SHUT UP!" His chin quivered. "You have no clue how hard I work! NONE! And you don't appreciate any of it! I'm sick of living in this cookie-cutter house! And I'm sick of you! You've derailed my life!"

Robyn trembled, her eyes spilled tears. Dan lowered his hand and removed his laptop from a path of creeping brown liquid. His printed pages were already spotted and wet.

"Mommy?"

They froze in silence.

Stay in bed, baby. Please stay in bed.

Robyn wiped her cheeks. "You're fighting a battle you don't need to fight." She paused, whimpering, unsure what she'd meant or if she even cared. She felt hollow. A fatalistic resolve echoed deep in her soul. Then a door knob turned upstairs.

"Mommy?" Evan's voice was louder, clearer.

Robyn moved swiftly to the stairs as Dan said nothing, did nothing.

Nothing.

The idea haunted her all the way to Evan's arms.

Dan switched off the lights and sought comfort in the darkness. He could once again see beyond the kitchen window, to where thickening clouds now blotted the moon. The tree, consequently, was shrouded in blackness.

His hand tipped a glass of something stronger than coffee. It burned his chest but did little to soothe the ache in his heart. They'd had many fights, but none like tonight: *I'm sick of living in this cookie-cutter house! And I'm sick of you! You've derailed my life!* In nine years of marriage, he'd never sounded more like his father.

And it scared him half to death.

As a boy he'd hidden under covers, his head compressed beneath a tear-soaked pillow as the walls of his house seemed to quake with rage. More than once, he'd peed his pants at the thundering sound of approaching footsteps.

He took another sip, and a yellow light appeared. A lightning bug? No, something far away. He sipped again. A window in the farmhouse, beyond the tree?

Has to be; there's nothing else there.

Sip after fiery sip, with inexplicable curiosity, Dan stared at the bright yellow rectangle until, as quickly as it had appeared, the light vanished.

5

CHAPTER FIVE

Dan shuddered awake in the family room recliner, sweaty and tormented. Rubbing bleary eyes, he looked in the kitchen. The table was askew and topped with brown paper towels. On the window sill, a glass tumbler held the long pour of whiskey he'd decided not to finish. And thank goodness for that; it was Friday morning, the last day of quarterly close. He'd be a ticking time bomb, even without a hangover.

Thoughts of last night became wispy cobwebs as he squinted to read the inscribed tambour clock. Then he kicked closed the chair and raced upstairs, fifteen minutes behind schedule. An hour later, Gucci tie on his neck and his hair parted with laser precision, Daniel Crawford was ready for work.

His day began with a drive through Fieldcrest Acres. And like every other morning, he loathed the monotonous expanse of vinyl-wrapped houses. His lot, thank goodness, was in the development's final phase and bordered by farmland interspersed with forest. A spectacular view, but he'd be out of that shack soon enough. Exiting the neighborhood, Dan matted the throttle.

Overnight thunderstorms pushed away in the eastern sky, allowing rays of sunlight to pound his tired eyes. Steam hovered over the wet, winding roads near McKinley, where he bought iced coffee from a strip mall Starbucks and chugged it to the sounds of Springsteen, playing louder than usual on his satellite radio. This was sure to be a demanding day, and he'd just had one whale of a night.

Robyn awoke to stale-smelling puffs from Evan, snuggling close. No surprise; he'd asked countless questions about Daddy's mean words before drifting off, well after midnight. He scrunched and rolled over as she dislodged her arm. Tucking blankets around him, she kissed his cheek, and then quietly left.

Downstairs, tension lingered like an offensive odor. Dan's caustic remarks looped in her mind like recorded messages, over and over and over, triggering memories from…Who knows? Who cares? For years she'd stepped around his anger, indulged his fake pleasantries, done anything and everything to prevent another fight.

I deserve better. Evan deserves better.

She hated to think of divorce. Yet Dan didn't seem to recognize or understand or God-forbid care that their marriage was failing. Perhaps he wanted out? But what about Evan?

A divorce will crush him.

As if on cue, mattress springs creaked overhead. She listened to the whispery sounds of stocking feet descending the stairs, shuffling through the kitchen. "Mommy, you made a mess!"

Rage swelled in her chest. *We were up half the night because of your thick-headed father! He made the mess!* But she kept her mouth shut, walked to the kitchen, and hugged her messy-haired boy. *Please… not a divorce.*

She spotted Dan's whisky, and dumped it before Evan could ask.

6

CHAPTER SIX

Printed pages were fanned like playing cards, their suits denoted by color-coded Post-its, their margins defaced by scribbled red ink. But at least the quarterly report was in Middaur's office awaiting comments, perhaps even final approval.

"Did you hear anything yet?"

The sudden question jolted Dan from his paperwork. "No." He blinked his eyes into focus. "But I just submitted it an hour ago." He turned his chair toward the opening of his cube. Kevin Clark wore gray slacks with faded knees. A mug in his hands read: BEWARE of ACCOUTANTS, THEY MULTIPLY!

"You guys did a great job last night," Dan said. "I'm amazed you got through everything."

"We were here 'til almost ten."

"Well, maybe you can cut out early this afternoon. Let's see if the report goes through. And hey, while you're here, how'd it go behind closed doors yesterday? Things got so frantic we never talked. Is everything okay?"

And why in the world are you still employed?

"Oh, you mean with PRS? It was okay." Kevin put a hand on Dan's cube. "I don't mind telling you I was scared. I thought I was being fired, you know what I mean? But they just asked a bunch of questions about the department. Who does what? That sort of thing."

"That's good," Dan lied, his desk phone ringing. He threw Kevin a catch-you-later gesture, and answered the call.

"Have you heard about Karen?" Megan asked.

"No, I haven't. What's up?"

"Fired. Just a few minutes ago. I swear, Dan, it's waterworks over here."

Dan's mouth dried. He curled forward, talked quieter. "You're kidding. I never would have expected."

"You're telling me. She might not have been the most pleasant person, but she sure-enough produced."

"Who dropped the bomb?"

"Middaur and Clauser. Oh, and some twerps from PRS. They've eliminated the position."

Dan lifted a pen, picked at its cap. *A young mother sent packing?* Emotions swirled but he swallowed them whole. After all, this was only business, the nature of the beast. He'd get the scoop from Middaur, once the dust settled.

"You still there, Dan?"

"Yeah, I'm here. Let me wrap up a few ends. I'll swing over to say goodbye."

"Well, you'd better hurry. She gets escorted from the building in an hour."

The call ended, and Dan sensed he wasn't alone. He spun to face the persistent little schmuck who'd doubtless overheard. "Karen's been fired. They eliminated her position. She's got an hour to clean out, if you want to stop by."

Kevin stared at nothing as color drained from his face. "But she was a hard worker."

"Well, that's how it goes KC. We all knew a restructuring was in the works. PRS has been poking around the office for six weeks now. It's nothing personal; the economy's tanking, Rhode Island's coming online, which will help margins as long as we establish a more efficient organization. It happens all the time; positions get axed. Like I said, it's nothing personal."

"Are you telling me that a struggling mother losing her job is not personal? And with unemployment rising?"

Dan white-knuckled his armrests. "I'm not saying I don't care, Kevin. I hate that people get hurt by the process. I'm just saying that some firings are simply based on which cog an employee represents within the machi—"

"Oh, whatever, Dan! Of course *you* can tow the corporate line."

Dan stood, puffed his chest. "What's that supposed to mean!"

Kevin wrapped both hands around his mug. "We're not stupid. Everyone knows they're grooming you to be the next Middaur. I knew that the day they gave you my promotion. So go ahead and talk shop, but don't push that stench at the rest of us."

"Don't you dare speak to me like—"

"Fire me, Dan! Kick me to the curb! Laugh at my hair when it falls everywhere! Do you honestly think I don't know how you feel about me? You know what; strike that. You *feel* nothing. I hope you do get a private office; it's exactly where you belong."

An hour had passed, and Dan sat alone in his cubicle, his mind spinning like tires in mud. How dare that detestable, mediocre accountant mouth off like that?

But Dan's conscience had also been pricked. Kevin Clark had been married at twenty-four, divorced at twenty-nine. He'd fathered two children but now saw them only during supervised visits. His house was a downtown rental, close to Second Street, the heart of Harrisburg nightlife. Dan was never with him during the "thrill of the buzz" or "the agony of the hangover," but he understood that Kevin's words were a play on the legendary opening to ABC's Wide World of Sports. And he often wondered: Does Kevin feel like that infamous skier—broken, defeated, misery on display for the world to see?

Killing emotion was only proper form in the corporate world, according to Russell Crawford. But Dan was not his father. And despite Kevin's accusation, he did feel. For years he'd sloshed mortar on bricks but with little avail; for behind the walls his heart still beat and bled and sometimes cried for the boy he used to be.

His desk phone rang again. Middaur's Administrative Assistant. *Of course he has questions; so much for leaving early.* Dan answered, listened, and almost stopped breathing.

At the end of a reddish-brown table, Dan folded his hands to prevent them from shaking. To his right sat Jason Middaur and Jonathan Clauser. Opposite them sat an unfamiliar man and woman, looking toward Dan but never at him.

Middaur spoke first: "Dan, I'm sure by now the entire office is aware of what's taking place in here today, so I'm not going to delay telling you that your position at Bell-Knarr is being eliminated. We've been evaluating the corporate structure, along with consultants from Penchack, Ryder and Sachs, to determine the best course of action under these difficult economic times, and in light of our pending acquisition, as you well know." His words sounded rehearsed. They always had.

"And Dan," he continued. "The positions that we are retaining at your level are presently filled with more experienced personnel, both here and in Rhode Island. I'm afraid there aren't any opportunities for a lateral move." He leaned forward, elbowed the table. His fingertips touched. "There's never an easy way to say this, Dan, but we believe the best course of action is to let you go at this time, to let you make a fresh start elsewhere. I'm terribly sorry."

Absolute silence.

Dan's teeth felt cemented together. His knuckles unexpectedly cracked.

Then Clauser took a turn: "You've served us well, Dan; there's no question about that. And per company policy we're prepared to give you a six-month severance package. You'll find it outlined in here along with a formal letter of termination." He reached for a folder, slid it toward Dan. "You can extend benefits, too. You'll receive instructions in the mail, and you can do it all online. The folks in HR can guide you through that process. Oh yes, there's also some information in there about Bell-Knarr's outplacement services, should you choose to utilize them."

More silence. Throats cleared, papers were arranged without cause.

"Dan," Middaur said. "Our company policy dictates that we give you one hour to clean out your cube of any personal belongings. At that time, or sooner if you're ready, Paul from security will be around to escort you out of the building. He'll collect your key-card and ID badge as well. There are plenty of empty boxes in the copy room. Take as many as you—"

"Company policy," Dan managed to say. It wasn't a question, hardly a statement. "I can't believe this is happening. I was accounting associate of the year. Remember the clock, gentlemen!" He lifted his hands with a facetious smile. "That was only a year ago, Jason! I've poured my life into this place, and you're cutting me loose, just like that? What should I do, go graciously? Is that what you expect? That you'll just recite this jargon and wait for me to stand up, shake your hands, and say, 'These things happen, no hard feelings.' I mean, come on! You've got to be kidding me." Middaur and Clauser stared at Dan and then each other. The PRS puppets shifted in their seats. "So you have nothing else to say? I'm officially fired?"

"We're sorry, Dan. The decision's been made."

7

CHAPTER SEVEN

A canopy of leaves shaded Riverfront Park, where Dan sat sulking on a green painted bench. The air was thick, the temperature stifling. From across the Susquehanna came the rumble of freight trains, working in the Norfolk yards.

For more than an hour he'd watched the rough, brown water. And several times he'd reached for his phone. But what would he tell Robyn? And when? He could fake things a while, maybe secure an interview and pitch the whole scenario as some kind of self-initiated career move. But what about Russell? He'd see right through it.

I should break Middaur's double-talking jaw! Knock his teeth down his throat!

Fists clenched, Dan stood, and saw a stone half embedded in the muddy earth. With rage trumping reason he aggressively dug, clawing the stone free. After pausing long enough to study its form, he reared back and threw it, watching it rise and fall and blurp in the river. Gone in an instant. And in spite of his anger, Dan wondered with a gentle curiosity where the stone would eventually hit bottom. Or if it ever would, in the murky depths of such a swollen river.

His elbow throbbed, his fingers were scraped, and mud was now caked beneath his well-groomed nails. But still Daniel Crawford only cursed his pain—physical, emotional, every last, lousy bit of it.

What to pack when you're leaving…forever? Such an enormous word; she'd thought the same on her wedding day.

One suitcase was full, a second underway. "A vacation," she'd told Evan, which was partially true. He would revel in the surf and sand, allowing Robyn time to reflect and to plot their next move. Dressed only in Spider-Man swimming trunks, he rushed into the bedroom. "When are we leaving?"

"Who told you to change?"

"But you said we were going to the beach!"

"We are, after a seven-hour car ride."

"How long is that?"

"You know what, don't worry about it. Just grab a shirt from your dresser, something red or blue." Evan ran toward his bedroom. "And try the bathroom!"

An hour ago she was angry, offended, and brimming with confidence. Now every folded piece of clothing squeezed sadness and doubt through the hairline cracks of her splintering resolve. But they needed a break, a time of separation. That she could stomach; divorce felt in league with death.

Dan had never played lacrosse or held any claim to fame at Towson State. But with dark hair, arresting blue eyes, and a smile that prickled her skin, he was her big man on campus. On their first date they'd strolled the Inner Harbor and dined at Phillip's Seafood. She ordered coconut shrimp, too nervous to eat them. He dismembered crabs and palmed beers, his protruding fingers smothered in seasonings. Late that night near the water's edge, Daniel Crawford kissed her lips. She went home a woman in love.

For weeks things were bliss between them, until Dan's drive to succeed advanced like rust upon her shiny new prince. By month three it might as well have been stamped upon his forehead, beside the scar she eventually noticed. She almost ended the relationship. Almost. But a lust for money can dull gut feelings, shred intuition. His father was a wealthy big-shot, she'd prompted herself. Why not Dan? *Go ahead, princess; take the ride! Take the—*

"You foolish little girl," Robyn whispered, zipping the second bag closed.

She'd packed enough clothing; more than enough. And a paisley-printed bag beside the bathroom sink was filled with toiletries. Only one need remained: an envelope for Dan, placed somewhere downstairs.

Evan returned in a lime green shirt. "I'm ready, Mommy!"

"I'm ready too, babe."

Robyn picked him up, kissed his cheek, and masked the truth of their departure with a smile full and wide. "Mommy's ready, too."

Dan was new to Bell-Knarr when he'd last attended happy hour. Oh, the irony.

"What can I getcha?" asked a prissy tender in a skin-tight tee. His hair was messy and rock-star cool.

"Yeungling bottle. On second thought, make it a scotch."

"Straight?"

He has to mean the drink!

"Yes. I mean, not mixed. I want ice… On the rocks, I guess."

The tender arched an eyebrow. A minute later he returned with a drink. "Here we go; one scotch, straight-on-the-rocks."

Dan placed a five on the bar, forcing himself to say, "Keep it." Then he took a long sip, felt the burn, and looked around the room. To his right, a group of uniformed men gripped micro brews and called everyone dude. A fat one held a draft, some smoked cigars. In a far corner, a nerdy guitarist drew rounds of applause and ear-piercing whoops. And above the bar, televisions sparkled in rows of bottles and racks of glasses, much like those in Russell's billiard room. Dan's father had always claimed there was a point at which ice melted just enough for a man to savor the fleeting perfection of scotch-on-the-rocks. But Russell said a lot: *It's only business, the nature of the beast. You're the man of the house; aren't you, Danny?*

Dan finished his scotch, crunched ice with his teeth. "Next one's on me," said a voice from behind. Dan looked over his shoulder at combed-over hair and bloodshot eyes. Kevin Clark placed a ten on the bar, ordered "two of whatever Dan's drinking." The bartender smirked but obliged.

"If it makes you feel better, they canned me, too."

Dan remained silent. His gut roiled, his mind stirred. *Drowning sorrows with Kevin? I'll take a bullet to the head.* The drinks arrived.

"Kevin, look, I've gotta drive, and I haven't eaten a thing all day."

"I was out of line this morning, Dan. It was the tension. I knew I was on the way out. Hell, everybody did." He shook his head, took a long drink. A tear slipped onto his cheek. "Freakin' smoke." He rubbed his eyes.

Dan put a hand on Kevin's shoulder, and tried for another escape. "You gonna be okay?"

"Yeah, I'll be alright. But what are you gonna do now?"

"Go home," Dan said.

"No, that's not what I meant. What are you—"

"I have no idea, KC."

Their eyes met, and a shock of empathy seemed to transcend judgment. Perhaps it was fatigue, the emotions of the day, or the likelihood he'd never see this pathetic man again. Regardless, for reasons beyond his control, Dan realized he and Kevin now stood ankle-deep in the same mud puddle, if only for a day. He lifted his Scotch. "To the thrill of the buzz!"

The fatso beside them raised a frothy mug as he chimed in, "Hear! Hear!"

"And to hell with hangovers!" Kevin added, smiling like a fool before chugging his entire drink.

Dan felt almost naked; no briefcase to plop in the corner, no laptop to connect or documents in need of his immediate attention. What's more, Robyn's car was gone and he didn't know why. Thunder had been rumbling ever since he got home, and strong gusts now pressed the back of the house. A neighbor's wind chime clanked in the gathering blackness.

Standing in front of the sliding glass door, he opened the drapes and looked at the tree. From this distance, its clusters of leaves appeared to shake like pom-poms in the face of impending danger. Scraggly trees along the field's old fence row thrashed in the wind like disgruntled toddlers. But not the tree. Alone on its hillside, it gripped the earth like an iron claw, refusing to be moved.

Dan closed the drapes, turned to check the time, and noticed an envelope on the fireplace mantle, leaning on the face of his trophy clock. His name was scrawled in black ink, underlined twice. He rushed to it, opened it, and found two folded pages. One bulky and white, the other gray and more formal. He began with the latter:

> *Evan and I are at Aunt Marsha's beach house.*
> *I'm not sure how long we'll stay or what the future holds for*
> *our family. But if anything in you still values our marriage,*
> *you'll respect my need to be away from you for a while.*
> *I don't want to hear from you or see you until I'm ready.*
> *You push, I file.   ~ Robyn*

Dan covered his mouth, sat on the loveseat, and re-read the note until Robyn's words became distorted in his moistening eyes. Folding the stationary, he stared at nothing as his muscles tensed and self-control leaked from his body. The paper crumpled in his fist, and then took flight across the room.

Rising to his feet, Dan grabbed the tambour clock and smashed it on the hearth. Splinters of wood and shards of glass nipped at his pants. The brass plaque landed by his shoe. Daniel Crawford: Accounting Associate of the Year. He picked it up, zipped it toward a wall where it sliced and stuck like a well-thrown hatchet. Thunder clapped again as heavy drops plunked the glass door. And then he remembered the second, bulky piece of paper.

A baseball game?

It was colorful and disproportionate, with a dotted line trailing the ball right out of the park. The bases were loaded. Stick-figures cheered. The batter was larger than life with dark scribbled hair and an ear-to-ear smile. Like a little boy's hero.

Evan's drawing floated and flipped to the loveseat as Dan broke apart like a drying sand castle. He dropped to his knees, pounded the floor. Like red paint, blood from his hands dripped amid the shattered glass and wood. His lips snarled, his stomach clutched, and after sprinting to the bathroom, he hovered over the toilet, cursing Bell-Knarr with every heave.

8

CHAPTER EIGHT

The Monday morning air was already oppressive. Dan stuck to the edge of the field, where a brushy fence row provided necessary cover. Dirt and pebbles invaded his sneakers while gnats, flies, and other winged combatants took shots at his glistening flesh.

He hadn't spoken to Robyn since Thursday night. And although his firing was likely to stir in her a remnant of compassion, calling just wasn't an option. On that point her note had been crystal clear. *Still...* Dan stopped, pulled out his cell, flipped it open, and dialed five digits.

Oh, forget it!

The phone clapped shut, and onward he walked. He wouldn't want Robyn home anyway; not today. The family room was still littered by shards of smashed clock, now replaced by a pyramid of amber bottles, standing tall upon the mantle. The recliner was all but re-upholstered in corn chip crumbs. Dan had eaten little else, watching ESPN and commiserating with the Orioles, basement-dwellers of the AL East. He'd called them losers before but this weekend not so much.

The fence row stopped in a sunken corner where the tree was lost to sight. It was time to risk a climb into open territory, or simply abandon the stupid idea. Dan pinched the brim of his cap, pulling it tight to his unwashed hair. Sunlight seared the back of his neck. Sweat streaked his dusty legs. He took a bottle from the pocket of his cargo shorts, guzzled water, and looked back at his now distant village of vinyl.

I've come this far…

Shoving the bottle back in his pocket, Dan walked up a hill filled with colorful weeds from which grass hoppers launched in every direction. He spotted tufts of green leaves on the horizon, every step revealing more. But he likewise saw shingles and bricks and windows. The farmhouse was closer than expected, as were a few small sheds, several gardens, and a barn. All around him, atop patches of pink clover and clusters of wild daisies, butter-flies peacefully perched. But inside Dan they seemed only to gather in a large, unceasing flutter.

There could be a Rottweiler… a double-barreled shot gun.

A car door shut, an engine started.

Dan hunkered in the weeds, adrenaline spiking, feeling a fool. He heard the crunching sound of tires on stones, diminishing gradually. Pushing to his knees, he straightened his neck and saw a cloud of bluish dust in the dis-tance. Over a long, stone driveway? Rake's Mill Road was in that direction; it must be how the owners accessed the property.

And they'd just left.

Old brittle acorns cracked underfoot while clusters of new ones dangled from the tree's twisting masses. Dense yet orderly, complicated yet precise, with craggy, gray bark that resembled an aging crocodile.

"You *are* a masterpiece," Dan said, standing in shade, soft breezes cooling his torso.

"A masterpiece, indeed." The man's voice was behind him, and it jolted Dan like an unexpected gunshot. A cool, moist snout began sniffing his legs. "Quercus Alba," the man added, closer now. The leg sniffing stopped as a rusty-brown mutt rushed forward and circled the tree.

Turning left, Dan breathed again. "Beg your pardon?"

"Quercus Alba." He was pudgy and dressed in tan coveralls. "White Oak, if you prefer." Wispy hair topped his head, grew thicker near his ears, and his entire face seemed crafted to display a white, carpet-thick mustache. His eyes brightened as he lifted a hand. "Walter Benning."

"Daniel Crawford." He shook Walter's weathered palm. "That thing you said...?"

"Quercus alba: Genus. Species. Latin."

"Impressive."

"I know a little Greek, as well."

"Really?"

"He owns the best deli in McKinley!" Walter's booming laughter was a home-cooked meal. And for the first time in days, Dan laughed, too.

"I apologize for trespassing. I just—"

"Nonsense; there are no signs posted here. It's nice to have a visitor. And one interested in my favorite tree, no less."

"I live in that development." Dan motioned. "I can see this tree from my kitchen window. Been admiring it for years. Thought I'd finally take a closer look."

"Well, I'm glad you did. It's to be appreciated, for sure."

Dan looked at the tree as the dog bee-lined the yard, slowing near the barn.

"So, you've got the day off?" Walter said.

Dan's heart sunk. "Yes."

"Me, too." Walter chuckled. "I'm retired. Spend my days tinkering around this old place. And you, Daniel?"

"Accounting." He sounded professional while looking at his feet. "For Bell-Knarr Packaging."

"Bell-Knarr?"

"In Harrisburg, right off—"

"Yes, I know the company. It's just... Well, you must have known that poor fellow. Friday night, was it?"

Poor fellow? He can't mean...

An ambiguous dread inflated Dan's chest. He'd watched nothing but sports since Friday. Three newspapers, stuffed in orange plastic, still lay in the driveway. "I'm sorry, Mr. Benning. I have to go."

"I've upset you, overstepped my bounds."

"No... No, it's okay. I just..."

To hell with hangovers! That's what Kevin shouted. And nobody chugs scotch!

Acorns cracked, grasshoppers scattered, and that yapping brown mutt chased Dan half the way home.

9

CHAPTER NINE

Robyn sat on a blanket beneath an overcast sky, back arched, toes in the sand, arms wrapped around bent legs. A pony tail swung from her soft-yellow cap, its brim pulled low against gusty breezes. Seagulls shrieked.

Such a lonesome sound.

Evan played in the heavy wet sand, close to the ocean, dodging its frothy advances and laughing when his footprints washed away in the surf. "Just let the water hit your feet, honey!" Aunt Marsha had said this a dozen times, squeezing her hips and shaking her head, her voice sounded spoken through a pipe.

To the rhythm of breaking waves, Robyn closed her eyes. She'd been a big shot Friday night, bending Marsha's ear until one in the morning, sipping champagne, shredding Dan like a block of moldy cheese. But three days had passed, along with her cavalier spirit. She'd demanded he not push. And he hadn't...but why? Respect? Her feet twisted deeper in the sand. Or is he sleeping with another woman, consummating his new found freedom? It wasn't the first time she'd entertained the notion, not with two perky females in Dan's department. Both married with children, but so was he.

Just call him, already!

She opened her eyes, fumbled through a beach bag, gripped her phone but then dropped it again as raindrops spotted the sand. Evan sprinted toward a covered deck while Marsha, lumbering behind him, said, "The little chicken's gonna get wet now!"

Forsaking the phone call, Robyn gathered toys, folded the blanket, and lowered her head against the wind-driven rain as she hurried for shelter in a house that wasn't home.

Dan unrolled the Sunday edition of the Patriot News. His eyes locked on a slender column.

Fishermen Discover Man's Body

While police and rescue workers continued to search the Susquehanna River near City Island on Saturday, the body of a man who leapt from the Market Street Bridge was discovered several miles south, by two unsuspecting fishermen.

"It's something you think will never happen. Maybe in a nightmare. The water wasn't great, but we was hoping to land a few fish. Now I'll be seeing [a man's] body every time I think of taking the boat out," said one fisherman, who asked to remain anonymous, about discovering the male body wedged beneath a tangle of tree roots along the west bank, close to Goldsboro.

Police have identified the deceased as 43-year-old Kevin Clark of Harrisburg. Witnesses saw Clark standing near the edge of the Market Street Bridge around 10:30 Friday night. Several motorists stopped and attempted to console Clark, who was described as "tipsy and boisterous" by one witness. Clark apparently yelled several obscenities before breaking a bottle on the pavement. Witnesses say he then lifted both arms and jumped backward.

"The look on his face, the gasps, that eerie splash. I don't know if I'll ever get over seeing this," said Brandon Sharpe, one motorist who attempted to talk Clark out of jumping. "It was clear what he was planning to do," Sharpe added. "The people who stopped; we all knew, and we did all we could. It happened so fast. Such a shame."

Helicopters wielding spotlights searched the river until late Friday night but saw no sign of Clark. Police and area rescue workers began a more extensive search early Saturday morning, but their efforts were hampered by high water levels from a line of heavy thunderstorms that drenched the mid-state earlier in the week.

"I was surprised to learn that Mr. Clark's body had washed so far south, but storms have really swollen the Susquehanna," said Harrisburg Police Chief Roger Marsh. "We were very limited in what could be done. These [rescue workers] have done an outstanding job, given the conditions as such, but we've had to keep safety foremost in our minds. Those [fishermen] should never have been on the water. I'm glad they're okay, and we're all thankful to have ended this recovery mission."

The Patriot News has also learned that Kevin Clark was fired Friday from Harrisburg's Bell-Knarr Packaging Company. Bell-Knarr has offered no comment, but company spokeswoman Laura Shellenberger says an official statement concerning Clark's death will be forthcoming. Please see **BODY A7**.

Dan's hunch was confirmed, compressed into journalistic detail. The typeface became a swirl of gray as he pictured Kevin's body, pallid and swollen and trapped beneath a muddy gush of water. He imagined the fall, wondered if Kevin had closed his eyes or stared at the starry night in the few, peaceful seconds before a skull-crushing thwack ended his life. Or sent him gurgling and choking for God knows how far.

Dan's chin touched his chest. A warm tear traced the bridge of his nose. Pressure throbbed in his temples as sadness receded in a gripping, red undertow. Scanning the garage, he crumpled the paper, ripped it to shreds.

Just kick me to the curb! Laugh at my hair! You feel nothing!

He rushed to his golf bag, slid out a three iron, and swung it like an axe. The club head punched through the windshield of his BMW. Glass marbles fell in the car as a cadence of squeals drowned the cry of his heart.

Dan felt a baby's breath away from collapsing on the kitchen floor. But he'd finally remembered Walter's last name, and found a listing for W. Benning on Rakes Mill Road. Staring at the tree, he dialed … waited. A woman answered.

"Hi, yes." Dan cleared his throat. "May I talk to Walter?"

"Who's calling, please?"

"It's Daniel… Dan. The guy who walked over there today. I mean, maybe he mentioned me." He sat down at the table, on a chair he'd almost missed. "Whoa…" He teetered, grabbing the table's edge with his free hand.

"Walter's out at the shop. You'll have to leave a… Well, hold on now." The woman paused. "I think I hear him. Walter! There's a Daniel Dan on the phone. Says he took a walk with you?" Seconds passed in silence. "He'll be right with you."

Dan heard muffled noises, then a familiar voice. "Walter Benning."

"Mr. Benning, this is Dan Crawford. We met by the tree th'schmorning."

"Ah, yes! The former track star, I'm now assuming."

Dan laughed, way too long. "I…" He drew an audible breath. "I left quite a dust trail, didn't I?" Laughter surfaced again, like a nasally hissing.

"And you've called me because?"

"I'm sorry. I just…" Dan laughed again. "That's exactly why I've called. To apologize that I'm sorry."

"For running away?"

"For running away," Dan echoed. "You were very kind to me. And said nothing wrong." His stomach felt like a vat of carbonated vegetable oil.

"You've hit a rough patch?"

"You, sir, have no idea."

"But you're home? You won't be driving?"

Dan ignored the question, staring out the window. "I've never seen the tree move before. Can I just tell you that?"

"Alcohol has deceived many a man, Daniel."

Dan's consciousness darkened in chunks, like banks of lights above an empty stadium. "My windshield is shattered," he mumbled.

"How interesting." Walter paused. "Are you off tomorrow?"

Dan huffed a few times, then swallowed hard and squeezed his eyes closed. "I'll be off all week."

"Meet me at the tree?"

"Better make it late morning." Dan's words had softened to mush.

"I'll keep an eye out for you. Good bye, Daniel."

Dan's forehead touched the table, until a pulsating jingle grew progressively louder. Half-conscious, he opened his phone, saw 'Dad' on the screen, and dared not answer. Instead he crawled through the darkness, until his stomach finally spilled by the bathroom door. Lying fetal near the mess, he breathed its stench and cried himself to sleep on the floor of a tilt-a-whirl house.

10

CHAPTER TEN

He'd eaten no breakfast, sipped soda as he shaved, and his abdomen ached from dry-heaving. Now, cascading water seemed to finally awaken his senses as Dan lathered, rinsed, and massaged his back with hot pulsations. And though his stomach fluttered time and again, it heaved no more. The hangover, thankfully, was fading. Of greater concern was the voicemail bolted to his brain: "Monday night and you don't take my call… whatever. I see comb-over got his fifteen minutes. Caught a blurb on the evening news. What was he thinking? Anyway, Labor Day's not gonna work but I have this Saturday open. Let me know." *Saturday; only four days away. And yes, what was Kevin thinking?*

At exactly 10:27, Dan started his journey across two fields. His tee shirt grew damp and dark in the usual places, and dusty air turned to mud on his tongue.

Upon reaching the tree, he pulled his fingers through channels of bark until Walter emerged from the barn, brushing dust from his light blue coveralls, a navy cap resting high on his head. His gait was slow but spirited, and his moustache turned up when he lifted a hand to wave. "You're alive and well," he called, sounding short of breath.

"I'm alive." Dan said, walking toward him.

Shaking hands, Dan watched a bead of sweat enter Walter's left eyebrow. Flecks of wood were nestled like insects in the white forest on his upper lip. His cap was small and unbranded.

"Another scorcher," Dan said.

"I'll say." Walter rolled his eyes, contorted his face. "Care for lemonade? We'll sit on the porch. You can meet my wife."

Although still wary of his tender guts, Dan consented. The men strolled toward the farmhouse, which today appeared more rusty than red. Beside every window, black shutters hung like bookends. Dirty white paint blistered and peeled from soffits and porch posts. "You've got quite a green thumb," Dan said, passing a vibrant flower garden.

"Nonsense," Walter said. Slender boards creaked as they stepped onto the porch. "Margaret deserves all the credit. Just wait 'til you see her vegetables."

Dan sat on the striped cushion of a stained wooden swing from which he could see bird nests tucked above every porch post. Fat-bodied bees buzzed and stopped…buzzed and stopped…near hanging pots of pink flowers. A long, gravel lane bent gracefully toward a distant ribbon of asphalt.

"Margaret?" Walter said through a screen door. "There's somebody here I'd like you to meet." He pulled off his cap, ran fingers through his thin, white hair. "Margaret!" He glanced at Dan, gave his head a small shake. "Excuse me, Daniel. I'll grab the lemonade."

The screen door screeched as it opened, swept most the way closed, paused, and snapped tight behind Walter. Dan lifted his feet, allowing the swing and his mind to sway. The patchwork fields he'd stared across for years looked strangely altered. To look upon them from here felt much like coming home to a house full of rearranged furniture—new lines, new spaces, swatches of fabric moved from shadow to light, everything familiar yet realigned in an overall dissonance that in time would become the new normal, unnoticed as before.

Might the same be true of people?

The screen door opened. Walter held two glasses. Behind him a woman stepped onto the porch, a smile on her unadorned face. Silvery hair capped her head like popcorn, and her frame was slender, hardly discernable beneath a soft yellow polo and relaxed-fit, acid-washed jeans.

"Honey," Walter said. "Meet Daniel Dan."

She slapped his shoulder. Ice clinked as Walter shook with silent laughter. Dan stood as she approached. "I'm Margaret Benning. So nice to meet you." Her hand felt like bones in a pouch of moistened leather.

"You as well." Dan released her hand, took a cold, wet glass from Walter.

"I'm sorry I called you Daniel Dan."

"Think nothing of it," Dan said. "I wasn't myself when we spoke on the phone." She nodded, still smiling.

You were a drunken idiot, that's what she's thinking.

"Well, I'll leave you two alone," Margaret said. "Enjoy the—"

"I'm sorry, too," Dan said. "To call here when I'd had too much to drink; it was out of line."

Margaret looked at Walter, then smiled at Dan. "Forgiven." She winked. "Enjoy the lemonade." The screen door screeched and snapped. Dan took a long swig that sweetened his pasty tongue.

"Why don't I show you 'round the farm?" Walter said.

They walked the perimeter of several small gardens before strolling along the gravel drive, toward the barn. To their right, a vein of limestone punctured the sod like a row of eroding tombstones. And behind the stones was an overgrown field in which three towering pines (Norway Spruce, Walter informed) seemed to guard the entrance to a forested path.

"My pride and joy," Walter said near the barn, stopping at the base of a grassy ramp, sandwiched between wedges of weathered stone. "It's a German bank barn. Over a hundred years old."

Dan studied the building, cruddy red in the places where paint still clung. Walter ascended the ramp and opened a door twice his height. The yapping mutt burst from within. "Rockler!"

"No, it's okay." Dingy paws pressed Dan's thighs and clawed at his shorts. "Rockler? Is that your name, boy?" He scratched the dog's limp ears until Rockler's paws plopped back in the gravel. "The barn's a lot bigger up close," he said, unsure if Walter heard him.

High on one side, near the barn's tin roof, Black swallows darted like little stealth bombers from star-like patterns of inlaid brick. "Come have a look-see," Walter called from within.

Dan climbed the ramp and entered the barn. "You're a woodworker," he said as the dark interior gradually took form.

"You bet'cher bippy. Been working wood my entire life, in some manner or another."

Dan walked the wide-planked floor, running his fingers over dusty machinery. Lumber spanned the rafters overhead. The dog sniffed and puffed small piles of sawdust, as if playing a treasure hunting game. "I was in junior high the last time I used power tools," Dan said. "And I have no idea where that crappy birdhouse is."

"I don't use them much. Hand tools; that's the way of an artisan. The smooth slice of a finely sharpened blade. There's nothing like it."

Dan placed his glass on a workbench, in front of a dirty window.

"So tell me about your family," Walter said.

Dan peered through the window, searching for his house through strands of cobweb and a smattering of glossy-brown spots. "My wife's name is Robyn. We have a four-year-old son. His name is Evan."

"A bundle of energy, no doubt."

Dan bit his bottom lip. "Yeah, well…they're away right now." He turned toward Walter. "Visiting family at the beach while I get some things done around the house."

"I do hope you'll bring Evan over to see me some day. Every farm needs a youngster to explore its wonders." The floor creaked as Walter walked toward Dan and sat on an upended crate. "This old man can't take the heat."

Dan sat on the workbench, twisted the handle of an old iron vice, and looked at Walter. "What am I doing here?"

Walter's chin rose to meet his arching moustache. "Let's see: you run away, call me drunk as a skunk, and I invite you over." His statement hung until laughter erupted from both men, causing Rockler to bark and run in circles. Their composure returned incrementally, working its way between lingering chuckles. "You've hit a rough patch," Walter finally said.

Dan's lips compressed, his chest tightened. "But I barely know you." For several seconds he heard skittering claws and the thumping buzz of trapped, desperate flies. His stomach gurgled, and a sensation like helium inflated his skull. "I'll make things smooth again."

Walter looked far from convinced. "This man who jumped from the bridge, was he a friend?"

Dan stood, brushed the seat of his shorts, and watched the dust dance in a bar of afternoon sunlight. "No," he said. "We just worked together."

Walter drew a breath, nodded on exhale. Then he slapped his knees, and also stood. "Well, I'd better get on with things. Got a to-do list as long as my arm." His thick palm patted twice on Dan's shoulder, then took his glass.

At the bottom of the grassy ramp, Dan stopped and motioned toward the Norway spruce. "Does that path lead anywhere?"

Walter rubbed his chin. "I suppose all paths do." He cleared his throat, smiled faintly. "Of course, that one doubles back eventually. There's not much forest there. Enough for a pleasant walk and some firewood. We catch uninvited hunters occasionally, too."

"I see. Well, thanks for having me."

"You're very welcome, Daniel."

Dan's stomach growled again as he walked toward home, his body now clamoring for proper nourishment. And despite careful steps in a hardened tractor tread, gritty dirt once again found a way into his sneakers. Lifting his eyes, he saluted the sun, identifying his house and Robyn's Toyota… backing out of the drive!

11

CHAPTER ELEVEN

Robyn slapped the steering wheel. "Stupid! Stupid! Stupid!"

She'd made a bold move—threatened divorce, left him alone for three days, secured the upper hand. Now he was supposed to listen. Honestly listen. They may have even made love.

But a shattered clock and soiled carpet! Beer bottles! Vile odors! A golf club in the windshield of his precious BMW!

With tears about to spill, she took the next exit and pulled into Dunkin Donuts. Minutes later, shielding her eyes at a corner table, she stuffed her face with glazed Munchkins. Evan's favorite. She cried harder at the thought. Thank goodness he'd stayed with Aunt Marsha.

She wiped her fingers, took a swig of iced tea, threw away her trash, and returned to the car. From there she dialed the beach house and spoke to the answering machine: "Marsha, hey, I'm on my way home—back, I mean. Anyway, maybe we can shop for a few things tomorrow morning? I think we'll be staying for... Well, I think we'll be staying." She keyed the ignition, and drove away.

Cold air pushed from the dash, chilling her skin and drowning out the radio. And though she'd finally stopped crying, her mind was awash. Nothing about her discovery made sense. She'd envisioned a breakthrough, a turning point, a delightful moment of groveling in which Dan apologized, pleaded for her return, and promised family over... everything!

He's a prick; not a prince. I'll call a lawyer first thing in the morning.

She stomped the throttle, reclaimed her place on the busy interstate.

Shivering, Robyn poked off the AC, sharpening the voice on the radio: "…was recovered near Goldsboro after jumping from the Market Street Bridge late Friday night. Police have ruled the death a suicide. The Bell-Knarr Packaging Company, in an official statement released today, said that while they deeply regret the loss of life, the corporation is standing behind its decision to fire the mid-level accountant, adding that the termination was one of several aimed at flattening the organization. We'll have more news next hour, right here on Harrisburg's best mix of—"

She silenced the radio, then tightened her grip on the wheel. Blood drained from her head, and her lungs retained a breath taken somewhere near mid-level accountant…or was it death?

Pull over! Stop the car!

She drove a mile in silence before spotting blue signs with colorful logos. An exit ramp; a place to pull over. She steered toward the shoulder, way too fast. Cinders crunched and pelted the wheel wells. Her heart became a piston. Her arms locked, her feet pressed the brake pedal. The car turned sideways, backward, and suddenly dropped.

The shimmering letters on the red van's door read: Zimmerman's Auto Glass. Standing beside it, Dan signed a clipboard for a lanky young man in a flat brimmed cap. "Just let us know if you have any problems," the man said. Dan smiled and nodded at the seemingly prophetic remark. The red door clunked shut, and the van pulled away.

Entering the house, Dan instantly sensed the fruits of his labor—two hours of sweeping, picking-up, vacuuming, and scrubbing. He'd lit every scented candle he could find. A greasy box sat open on the table, exposing two Hawaiian slices and the crusts of six others.

He grabbed a soda, looked long at Evan's baseball drawing (now on the refrigerator door), and sat down in the family room recliner. The TV brightened and flipped like a visual rolodex as he searched for a ballgame, but it was only 4:30. He turned off the set, dropped the remote, and brooded over questions that had stomped upon his mind since seeing Robyn's car: When did she arrive? Was Evan with her? What did she do ... or take? And why did she leave?

Because she walked into a puke-infested disaster!

"Well, it won't happen again," he whispered, looking around the restored room, smelling harvest spice and lilac and who knows what else. The aroma was pleasing and eclectic, like the memories now lifting from somewhere deep in his soul. He thought of gasping cries from a tiny, folded body, gripped by a surgical glove. "It's a boy," said a female nurse, her mouth covered by a swath of mint-colored fabric. Dan recalled the feel of dainty fingers wrapping his; and a diapered bottom perched in his palm; and a drooling face resting soft upon his shoulder. But for every such memory there was much Dan could not see, much he had never seen. His eyes squeezed closed in search of first smiles, first steps ... first anything? Instead he saw kites he'd refused to fly, really-useful engines he'd hated to watch, and 'I Love You, Daddy' cards that he'd somehow misplaced.

Dan opened his eyes, chugged his soda, and directed his thoughts toward urban twinkles, spread atop the rippling harbor where he'd strolled hand-in-hand down a Baltimore pier, arriving at the sweetest kiss he'd ever known. He remembered a chapel filled with daisies, a row of young ladies in tufted, yellow gowns, and a knock-out brunette, clothed in white lace, sliding gold on his finger. He recalled honeymoon nights, nervous pulls of intimacy, and ... *SHUT UP! You have no clue how hard I work! And you don't appreciate any of it! I'm sick of living in this cookie-cutter house! And I'm sick of you! You've derailed my life!*

His body clenched and his head hammered until a scream erupted, deep and guttural. The recliner kicked closed. The remote sprung from his lap to the floor. He snatched it, took aim at sliding glass ... and saw the tree. Twice, Dan reared to throw. Instead he sucked in his lips and bounced the remote on a loveseat cushion, huffing and hurting and staring across fields.

Between panting breaths, Robyn recalled skidding down the grassy embankment. Her arms were still locked at the elbow. Her feet still held the brake pedal firmly to the floor. She looked straight ahead but sensed movement around her—speeding traffic on the interstate, cars slowing on the exit ramp, and a gangly man, approaching from a parked cement mixer.

His hand rapped the windshield. "Put her in park and kill the engine!"

She rehearsed his words until they finally registered. The shifter clunked forward, the key rolled back, and a sudden silence seemed to amplify the highway.

"You okay, Ma'am?"

Feeling like a specimen, Robyn looked left and nodded. A mud flap of black hair dropped from the redneck's tattered cap. His chin was a wiry mess, but his smile was comforting. She moved the key forward, and cracked the window. The smell of baked asphalt rushed in like hot breath.

She caught movement in the rearview, and turned to see the man, circling the car. Then he knelt out of sight. To check the wheels, she reasoned, relaxing her arms, breathing more naturally. Running fingers through her hair, she tried to recall details: skidding, spinning, radio news about—

I have to get out of here!

She swung her head right…left…right. The man was nowhere. She looked up the hill, hoping to discover other stopped vehicles, but saw only ripped sod and a rotating mixer. She triple checked the locks before unbuckling. With her palm pressed against the seat, she leaned slowly right, reaching for the grab handle above the passenger door. Her body twisted. She put a knee on the console. Her forehead touched glass. And she peered down at…nothing? Where in the—

"It's only minor damage." His scratchy voice shot through the cracked driver's window.

Gasping, she twisted and maneuvered to an awkward position, seated on the console. She drew a deep breath, and chuckled. "I'm sorry, my nerves are just…"

"I hear ya. It's a hell of a thing to go slidin' off the road. But the car ain't bad. I pulled a clump'a dirt out the tailpipe, probably upset the muffler and all like that. And I'd get them tires aligned and balanced. You live close?"

"Yes." She almost choked on the word.

"Just drive across this here, onto the hard road. That's what I'd do, 'fore the cops show up. I'll set in the truck 'til you get her back on the road. Sure you're okay, now?"

"Yes, I'm fine, I... I just don't... Wait, hold on a second." She reached behind the seat, lifted her purse.

"That ain't necessary, Ma'am." He clucked his lips. "The view you gave me a minute ago was thanks enough." He winked, then jogged up the hill.

Stunned and still gripping her purse, she watched him climb in his truck. Then she smirked at his cheap remark, imagined him waiting for sexual gratuity, some kind of triple-X encounter with the desperate housewife he'd saved from roadside distress.

She slid back in the driver's seat. The engine fired, the window zipped closed. Backing away from the embankment, she swung the wheel right. And over clods of weeds and litter, Robyn bounced her way to freedom.

12

CHAPTER TWELVE

"Thank God, you're alive!" They were the last words Dan expected when he'd answered Robyn's call.

"Wait a minute," he said. "Calm down. Of course I'm alive. What's going —"

"I heard about a body and a suicide and that it was an accountant from Bell-Knarr and I'd left you and so I thought—"

"Robyn! Stop. Breathe. Where are you?"

"In the car. In a Target parking lot."

"Is Evan with you?"

"No; he stayed at Marsha's. Dan, I've been in an accident, and—"

"What! Are you okay?"

"Yes." She sobbed. "But not really... I just..."

"Robyn, which Target?"

"The one in Carlisle."

"Don't leave. I'll be there in twenty minutes. Promise me you won't leave."

The Beamer slowed, exited the highway, and rolled through a couple of intersections before entering the complex. Robyn's forest green Camry was parked in the lot's far corner. Dan stopped close to her car, turned back the key, and hopped out.

Robyn emerged, hair loose and flowing around large white sunglasses. Her sandals flapped to her quickening pace. Dan embraced her, felt weeping on his shoulder.

"I don't know where to begin," he said in her ear. "Come home with me."

Robyn's grip tightened on the small of his back.

"Can we at least talk in the car?"

She pushed away gently, and nodded. Dan removed his sunglasses, wiped his eyes with his shoulders, and opened his passenger door.

"Wait," Robyn said, sliding a finger under her sunglasses. "Wasn't there a golf club...?"

"Zimmerman's. You've heard the commercial: new glass, ultra-fast."

Her head shook as she settled onto the two-tone leather. Dan closed her door, rounded the vehicle, and took his place behind the wheel. "It was Kevin Clark."

"What?"

"He went on a binge after Bell-Knarr fired him. Ended it with a dive off the Market Street Bridge."

Robyn covered her face.

"I was fired, too." The words came faster and sooner than intended, like an errant slip of the tongue. Hisses pushed through Robyn's fingers, followed by a large and gasping inhale. She peeled away her sunglasses, looked at Dan. Her eyes were streaked and swollen. "I'm sorry, Dan. I had no idea."

He reached for her hand. "What about this accident you were in?"

"I heard about Kevin's death on the radio, only I didn't know it was Kevin so I panicked. I pulled off the highway too fast, and backed down an embankment. Some guy stopped and checked out the car. He said it seemed okay, but when I got on the road, the steering wheel shook. And the car keeps pulling to the right."

"But you weren't hurt?"

"No. Just scared."

Their fingers laced as their eyes drifted. Silence filled the interior. Dan heard muffled thumps from closing doors and the distant outburst of an angry mother. Releasing Robyn's hand, he started the engine. "Relax...I'm just running the AC." Another minute passed without words.

"It happened last Friday," Dan finally said, placing his hands on the leather-wrapped wheel. "The quarterly report was on Middaur's desk. We were just hanging loose, you know; waiting for his remarks. And then I get a call that people are being fired. Soon after, I get word that Middaur and Clauser want to see me. I knew what was up before I even entered the room; the back-stabbers." He lifted a hand, massaged his eyes. "Anyway, they cut the position. Offered no options for staying, just six months of severance pay."

Dan glanced right. Robyn's head was tilted forward, and she was picking her nails.

"I ran into Kevin at a bar that afternoon," he continued, picturing the untidy schmuck. "He'd been fired, too. So when Walter hinted that something tragic had happened to a Bell-Knarr employee, I knew right away, deep down, that it was—"

"Walter?"

Their eyes met, and Dan laughed. "Yeah, he's another story. You see, Monday morning I walked to the tree, the one I've always—"

"Yes, I know the tree, Dan." Irritation simmered in her voice.

"Okay. Fine. Anyway, I get there, and this guy, an old man, startles me from behind. Turns out it's his farm. But instead of running me off he strikes up a conversation, cracks a joke. So here I am, trespassing, probably looking half-dead after all I'd been through, and this old fellow is treating me like an invited guest. His name is Walter Benning."

"Walter Benning? You mean *Doctor* Walter Benning, the biology professor?" Her eyes brightened above rising cheeks.

"Well, that's not what he called himself. He just said he was retired. I didn't ask."

"Walter Benning was one of the most popular professors at MCC. He retired during my last year there. Students loved him. Everyone did. Kind of a husky man? Bushy, white moustache?"

"Sounds like the guy."

"I can't believe this." A full-blown smile spread on her face. "Dr. Benning lives across those fields?"

"You bet'cher bippy," Dan said, using Walter's intonation.

They laughed until their eyes broke contact, as if some rule of engagement had been circumvented. Dan grabbed the wheel again as their spark of joy melted, and said, "I told him I had the day off. When he heard the name Bell-Knarr, he started sputtering about something in the news. I knew in my gut that Kevin was involved. And I lost my senses, I guess. Ran away like a frightened child. To make matters worse, I called him that night…after way too many beers."

Dan's eyes fixed on the dash. He sensed Robyn's head turn, then drop. But she wasn't crying; at least, he didn't think so. Rather she was waiting, listening, and still picking her nails. "I ended up back at his place the next day, but invited this time. I met his wife, and he showed me around, took me in the barn." He looked right. "There's something about the guy, Robyn. I don't know…he's just…larger than life or something."

Their eyes met again. "You trashed our house."

A twinge of anger took hold in Dan's chest. "Because I was fired. My wife and son were gone. And…" He exhaled forcefully. "Okay, I'll admit it; Kevin's death also hit me like a sledge." He awaited her response. She only looked away. "Look! I'm not proud of what I did, Robyn. And I'm certainly not defending it. It's just…" He scrunched his brow. "Whatever."

"Don't whatever this Dan!"

"I cleaned up!" He twisted in his seat. "You walked into a nightmare; I get that. But things are better now. I finally unboxed the shop-vac you gave me for father's day. I scrubbed the carpet, lit every smelly jar of wax in the house. Now cut me some slack. I'm trying, okay?"

Robyn's tongue traced her teeth. Her eyes, now red and determined, darted left.

"I'll find another job," Dan said, his ribcage percolating. "I'll reach out to a few head hunters, get my resume in shape. The market is down, but let's be honest: I bring a lot to the table."

"You bring a laptop to the table. Every night."

Like prison bars, Dan's teeth locked against a gang of harsh words. And for once, he kept them contained.

"You said you were sick of me," Robyn said to her knees. "I've known that for a long time now. Evan needs a father to…" Her tone softened, she swallowed hard. "To play with him, and spend time with him." She looked at Dan as a tear escaped, tracing the contours of her cheek. "He needs you to love him more than work."

A doleful lump lifted high in Dan's throat before pulses of anger rammed it back to the depths. "I'll find something with better hours."

She looked away. "You need to find your heart." Her words seemed to pounce, as if they'd been lying in wait. Dan straightened his posture, glared out the window, and despite a swarm of adrenaline, he listened. To a minute of silence…two minutes. "I didn't walk out on hours," she finally said. "They were insane. But…" He heard her shifting in her seat. "Work absorbs you, Dan. It means more to you than anything else. Including your family." Her words lacked inflection, like the deflated verbiage of a resignation speech. "You've become like your father. I can't live with that, and I refuse to let Evan."

Dan stepped to the pavement and clutched his hair before slamming the door. The passenger side immediately unlatched, and Robyn's sandals snapped like machine guns. Within seconds she'd dropped in the Camry and started the engine.

Stop her, you fool!

Dan ran behind her car, smacking his hands on the trunk. Reverse lights brightened, the engine revved, and the car thrust backward. Side-stepping, Dan thumped the passenger windows. "Stop! STOP!"

She braked, climbed from the car, and stood with fists on her hips. "Did I mention your anger!" Her idling car grumbled like an upset stomach.

Giddy with adrenaline, Dan almost laughed in her screwed-up face. "I'm sorry. I just… This is all so hard to deal with."

"Tell me about it!"

The Camry burped a few times, then shut off. Robyn opened her fists to catch her falling head.

"I still love you," Dan said.

She turned from his confession, and leaned upon her dead, scalding car. "Ouch! Dang it!"

"Take mine."

She whirled to face him. "You've got to be kidding."

"Take the BMW, Robyn. Go back to the beach. I'll have the Camry towed and repaired."

"You're serious?"

"Just be sure to bring it back with a full tank, young lady."

She lifted both hands. "Dan, I'm not sure I'm coming—"

"Take it."

After swapping necessities from their respective cars, Dan watched Robyn settle into his seat. "Any questions?" he asked, standing beside the driver's side door.

"I don't think so." She looked over the gauges, adjusted the mirrors.

"Robyn, I'm…" He knelt on the pavement, folding his arms over Robyn's open window. "I'm not sure where to look." Sunlight burned the back of his neck. His heart ached with uncertainty and a dreadful hint of finality.

"For what?" she said, studying his expression.

"My heart." He leaned in, tilting his head, but she only turned away, starting the car with a hasty goodbye. The rising window clipped Dan's elbows. It might as well of chopped him in two.

13

CHAPTER THIRTEEN

Dan sat with his father on a massive patio; part flagstone, part pavers, with built-in benches and a tall fireplace. Their chairs were positioned near a crackling blaze. The sky was dark, the air moist.

"I just couldn't get away. There's too much going on at the office," Dan said.

"So they just decided to play in the sand without you?" Russell asked.

"Yeah, well, her aunt had everything arranged. So it didn't seem right to bail on her. And besides, I'll get a lot more done this way."

"Is that what you told your old lady?"

"Not exactly."

Russell laughed like an evil Santa, and pulled deeply on his cigar. "Where's the Beamer, again?"

"I told you, the dealership. It needs plug wires or something. They couldn't get the problem squared away before closing time. I'll get it Monday night."

Russell stood and walked to an ice chest. He grabbed another green bottle, dried it with a towel, and twisted the cap. "So you drove them halfway to ... " He lifted a finger as his cheeks filled with a belch that he blew toward the sky. "You drove them halfway to the beach, then stopped here on the way back?"

He's playing me! No... relax. He's just getting drunk, running his mouth.

"Well, it seemed to make sense." Dan tipped his beer. "Marsha was willing to meet us, and I was planning to come here anyway."

Russell threw a log on the fire, sat again, and took a long swig. "You know what I can't believe?"

"What's that?" Dan eyed the flames.

"I can't believe that moron jumped off the bridge. It's a job; they come, they go."

Off the hook at Kevin's expense... again.

Dan swallowed every brusque response on his tongue, excused himself to the bathroom, and a minute later stood looking in the mirror at his blood-shot eyes and blotchy skin. He hadn't gone for a run in days, or consumed anything of nutritional value: pizza, soda, microwave dinners, a few too many beers. He flipped off the light and returned to the patio. Russell's face looked ghostly in the pale blue light of his open phone.

"You got a call at this hour?" Dan said. "Blonde or brunette?"

"It's not my phone." Russell stood, a cigar flashing red in his lips. He blew away smoke as the phone light vanished. "A text arrived while you were inside, Danny Boy. I thought it was mine, until I grabbed it." He took another drag. Flames hissed in the fireplace.

Dan reached for his phone. "Sorry about that. I'll just—"

Russell jerked the phone away, clicked on its backlight. "Let's see here... ah, yes... Thanks for lending your car. It was a noble gesture that meant a lot to me. I know there is love for you still in my heart, and I hope that with time it can be recovered." His cackling laughter ended with a cough and another long pull on his cigar.

"Alright, you've had your fun. Now give me the phone!" Dan fought to keep fear off his face. His eardrums pounded, his arms tightened, his nails dug into his palms.

"But there's more," Russell said, blotting his cigar in an ash tray. He picked up his beer, took a long swig, and pulled his forearm over his drip-ping chin. "So sorry to hear you were fired. But there is hope. For you and for us." The phone snapped closed. "Now, isn't that touching?"

Dan stepped forward, thrust a hand toward the phone. "Give me the—"

Plastic smacked his cheek, forced his head sideways. He heard clacking on the flagstone, close to his feet. Stinging pain numbed to puffy tingles, and he tasted blood. Hands thumped his chest, scrunched his shirt, and stood him up straight. "You sat here and drank my beer and fed me a load of crap!" Russell's face was stubbly, his breath sour.

A neighbor's back yard flooded with light, and the sound of jingling metal turned their heads toward an Irish setter, tail wagging, crossing the patio. Releasing Dan, Russell squatted to pet the intruder. "Who's a good dog? That's right; who's a good dog?"

Dan's knees trembled, his stomach was in knots. By the light of the flames he located his phone, and stuck it in a pocket.

"How goes it, Russ?" said an elderly voice from a distant balcony.

"Quite well, Arnie. Yourself?"

"Well, I shot an 84 this morning. That's enough to keep me ticking another day, I suppose. C'mon girl! Get over here!"

Russell grabbed the dog's collar. "You weren't invited to my party. No you weren't." He led the dog to the neighbor's yard.

Without hesitation, Dan rounded the house, opposite his father. He dug keys from his pocket. *Almost there… Almost there…* Wet grass licked his toes through open sandals. And then a bird squawked and flew from the pitch black depths of a cypress tree. Dan threw up his hands, and the keys! Heart racing, he dropped to the ground. Mower clippings stuck to his hands and legs.

"Danny?"

He'll look inside, first. Hurry! Find them!

"Danny!"

He patted furiously—left, right, everywhere. His hands began to shake. Tears welled. *Wait a minute!* He shoved his hand in a pocket, pulled out his phone, and cast an LED glow on the glistening ground. Bingo! Keys back in hand, he ran to the driveway, and with trembling fingers, he pressed the fob.

Deafening whines erupted from Robyn's car alarm. Lights flashed on both ends, causing Dan to drop the keys again. Falling to his knees in the strobe-light effect, he studied the fob. The markings had worn from the buttons; it was anyone's guess. He scrunched his eyes, pushed bottom center.

The alarm silenced. Standing, he pushed top left. The locks thunked open, and the interior glowed.

Windows brightened in nearby houses as Dan hurried into the driver's seat. Warm liquid streamed down the side of his throbbing knee. He cracked the door, casting dim light upon a nasty scrape which grew instantly, shockingly painful. Then he raised his eyes and saw his father marching down a long brick path toward the driveway.

Just suck it up and drive! GO!

Dan fired the engine, threw on high beams. Russell covered his face with two waving arms, and stumbled over a row of round boxwoods. He landed on his rump in the wet, black grass.

Throttle touched floor, tires chirped.

Don't get up, Dad! Ever!

14

CHAPTER FOURTEEN

The sky was pale and yellow to the west, plum to the east. Crickets fiddled from inky places in the brushy fence row, accompanied by the distant sounds of children and lawn mowers. The evening breeze was refreshing, like those off the ocean. Like those kissing Robyn? Dan bit softly on his bottom lip as his eyes scanned the edge of the field for the specific patch of thistle in which he'd dumped Wendell, the neglected, garage-baked toad.

His bare feet twisted in the dew-laden grass, another reminder of last weekend's slippery escape. The entire debacle had looped through his mind for days; days Russell doubtless spent barking orders and spewing hackneyed one-liners at executive mouthpieces. Roughing up his son was a faded recollection by now; a scribbled sticky note peeling from the back of his one-track mind.

The welt on Dan's cheek had finally disappeared, but his knee was still bandaged. His phone, thankfully, continued to function despite myriad scratches. He'd read Robyn's message countless times...without responding. She needed time, and he intended to give it.

A brush of cool air seemed to beckon for coffee, and Dan rose to brew a pot, until something caught his eye. *There it is again! Movement, near the field.* He stared at the cornstalks as they swayed in the dim light of dusk. "Huh, I could have—"

"Bark! Bark! Bark!"

A sandy brown mutt emerged from the corn, sniffed the ground, and disappeared again in the leafy rows. Dan stepped into his athletic sandals, walked toward the field, whistled twice, and called, "Rockler! Here, boy!"

No response.

He glanced up the fence row, into murky shadows cast beneath a canopy of twisted trees, and saw more movement. Larger, upright movement. A husky man, moving toward him. And then a voice: "Getting dark before I expected."

"Walter?"

"You bet'cher bippy."

Dan heard footsteps on the soil. "What brings you this way?"

"Two tired legs!" Walter's laugh was a light in the darkness. At the sound of it Rockler burst from the corn and sniffed Dan's ankles. Walter limped to the lawn, the waning light of day reflecting beads on his forehead. Today's coveralls were olive green. "I thought I'd walk this direction for a change." He stopped several feet from Dan, leaning on his favored leg while clutching a hip with one hand. He drew a deep breath. His moustache fluttered. "Thought I might get lucky, catch you and the youngster—Evan, I believe it was—out shooting hoops or something."

Dan wanted to hide in the corn with Rockler. But part of him wanted a hug. The impulse startled him almost as much as Rockler's sudden toe licks. He jumped back and out of one sandal. Walter roared with laughter, and this time Dan joined him; his first real laugh since imitating this... *Oh yeah!* Dan recovered his sandal, and said, "My family is still on vacation... *Doctor* Benning."

Walter smiled. "My reputation has betrayed me."

"Not many people identify trees in Latin."

"I suppose not." Walter stepped closer. "I retired a couple years ago. Been busy as a bee ever since, keeping up with that old farm. We love the place, though. Keeps us young at heart, I guess." A minute passed as they watched the dog. "I see you're a wounded warrior."

"What?" Dan followed Walter's eyes. "Oh... The mower kicked up a stone yesterday, of all things. Gashed my knee pretty good."

"Might be cause for a new blade? You want me to take a look—"

"No, that's fine. I've been meaning to get a new one. Maybe this mishap will finally get me to Home Depot. What about you, Walter? I don't remember a limp when we toured the farm."

"Arthritis; some days are better than others. It flared up about halfway here."

They both flinched when a bat flittered overhead, more heard than seen.

"I was just getting ready to make some coffee," Dan said. "You interested?"

"Decaf?"

"Never heard of it."

"Well in that case, yes."

As the coffee brewed, Dan retrieved another chair and positioned it near his. Between them he erected a table on which he lit a citronella candle, just as Robyn always had. The sky was gray, even darker to the east. And a half moon hung over Walter's distant house.

Dan placed freshly-filled mugs on the portable table, then sat beside Walter. A suctioning sip was followed by a sigh, and Dan wondered whether Walter's moustache was wet. Insects and frogs produced a shrill summer soundtrack while Rockler, like a clinking bandit, scurried about the yard and corn field. From elsewhere in the neighborhood, jovial voices rose and fell with the breeze.

Both men stared at the blackening landscape, which for a moment enticed Dan, made him feel as if confessions might slip like whispered words through a child's cupped hands. But the moment was fleeting.

My private life is none of his business. We can talk about the weather, the news, the—

"I don't suppose I could trouble you for a flashlight?" Walter said.

Dan strangled his thoughts. "I'll drive you home. No need to walk."

"Oh, that's not necessary."

"I'd like to."

"Well, I appreciate that, Daniel, but I've got the dog and—"

"Bungee cords. Bungee cords will hold him to the bumper."

Walter raised a curly eyebrow, clearly wise to the sarcasm.

"I'm joking," Dan assured him. "We'll just throw a towel on the back seat."

Walter grinned, nodded, and sipped his coffee. "Maxwell House?"

"Now how in the world did you know that?"

He chuckled, and said, "A lucky guess. Although, I'm surprised. Thought a businessman such as yourself might serve freshly-ground, exotic beans. But don't misunderstand; Maxwell House suits me fine." He sipped again. "If Margaret has a coupon for it, we drink it; which reminds me, may I use your phone?"

Dan pulled his cell from a cargo pocket, and offered it to Walter.

"Let's see here; I'm without my reading glasses." Walter looked down his nose at the tiny rubber buttons, glowing green. He poked them with thick fingers, held the phone to his ear. "Margaret, I ran into Daniel Crawford on my walk. We've decided to have coffee. He's going to bring me 'round home when we're finished." He passed the phone back to Dan. "Gardening in the dark is my guess, but she'll get the message."

Dan put his phone on the table, surveyed the sky, and saw only one star. "How long were you at MCC?"

"Nineteen years. It's a wonderful school. Where did you study accounting?"

"I'm from Maryland," Dan said, still looking up. "Graduated from Towson State. Landed my first accounting job with a public firm in Harrisburg. One of the big four." He made quotations with his fingers. "Anyway, my wife got hired at MCC as the assistant alumni director." He looked at Walter, smirked. "You know, she nearly burst at the seams when I told her I'd met you; said you were adored by everyone on campus."

"Hah! By the students, maybe. Dean of Sciences, other profs; not so much."

"Why's that?"

Walter took a drink before answering. "A particular theory…" His eyes met Dan's. "I held the unpopular view." Candlelight danced on his face. "Well, we've half a moon this evening."

"I can even make out the tree," Dan added. "But only its outline." He soon discovered, however, that his mind could supply the missing colors, etch the fine details. Where his eyes saw only an obscure form on a faraway hill, his mind saw greatness. A burst of distant laughter halted further pondering. "Must be some good coffee they're drinking."

"Served in aluminum cans, most likely."

Rockler stiffened and barked until Walter shushed him. Then a few minutes passed with only sips as the air became noticeably cooler.

"Are you a father?" Dan asked.

"No. We tried for many years." Walter lifted his coffee. "I always felt like my time with students eased some of the pain."

Dan's cheeks warmed. He looked at Walter, watched him push a finger around the rim of his mug. "Man, I'm sorry. I didn't mean to get so personal."

"Nonsense; how were you to know?" Walter turned, looked Dan in the eye. "But now that you do, may I offer a word of advice."

"Yeah...sure."

He leaned closer. "Love your little boy with everything you've got, from the very depths of your soul, Daniel. I'd have given anything for that chance. As would many other couples."

Dan tabled his mug, swallowed a lump, and looked away. "Need a warm-up?"

"No, thank you. At this hour, I'd do well to stick to one cup."

"Walter, I'm..." Dan's body stiffened, he could barely breathe. Confession was unchartered territory. "I'm glad you're here."

"It's been a pleasure."

Tell him. He's a teddy bear. Trust him.

"About that rough patch." Dan stared at the grass. "I haven't been honest with you." His fists clenched, his mouth dried. "I'm just not sure..."

"I understand," Walter said. "When you're ready. If you're ready. Just let me know." His wooly mammoth moustache rose high on each end. And then—*Smack!*—his open hand hit the back of his neck. "Ornery little blood-suckers!" The last of his coffee splashed on his coveralls. And both men laughed until they cried.

Because his tires had spun in the gravel of Walter's driveway, Dan's attention was set on listening for glitches in the recently repaired Camry. At least,
that's what he told himself after almost scraping a minivan, parked on the
shoulder of Rake's Mill Road. A minivan that wasn't there when he'd arrived
with Walter and his dog. But two hours had passed since then, thanks to a
batch of Margaret's irresistible cookies, which the men downed while
watching a ballgame on the grainy screen of Walter's console television.

So a van has broken down. No cause for alarm.

Dan swerved back into the right hand lane of the narrow, winding road.
A minute later he noticed headlights. Behind him and closing. Arriving at
the state highway, Dan pulled to a stop sign and checked left-right-left as the
trailing headlights tucked beneath his bumper. He squinted in the mirror, at
what appeared to be the same van. Had someone merely stopped to make a
call? The Camry accelerated. The minivan followed.

Cruising smoother asphalt, Dan's mind sparked with irrational thoughts.
Was he being pursued? Had someone been awaiting his departure? He sig-
naled right, and raised his eyes to the rearview. His pursuer hadn't signal.
Relieved, Dan pulled into Fieldcrest Acres. The headlights followed, nonetheless.

What in the… ? Oh, get a grip, Crawford!

Fieldcrest Acres was swimming with minivans. The vehicle behind him
was likely a neighbor returning home on Saturday night. Dan looked
steadily forward, mindlessly tuning the radio. And when he glanced up again
the van appeared to be slowing, backing off… or lurking? Dan wondered if
he should pull in his driveway, reveal his true address. He might do better to
simply keep going or maybe pull curbside, throw the hound off his trail, lure
him into—

It's a minivan! Just pull in the driveway!

He did. And the van drove past. Burgundy, Dan noted just in case.

15

CHAPTER FIFTEEN

A minute had passed since the garage door opened. She'd expected Dan to burst from within and welcome them home. But he hadn't...so where was he?

Evan waited in the BMW as Robyn turned the knob, entered the kitchen. *Her* kitchen. A white carafe squeaked on the counter. She loosened the lid, released the pressure.

"Dan?" No answer.

It was Sunday morning; could he possibly...? No way; Dan spent Sundays worshiping sports. But the TV was off. A car door slammed. *NO!*

She sprinted to the garage and found Evan lifted high on Dan's shoulder. Her hands covered the bridge of her nose. Tears traced her fingers, tickled her wrists. Evan's head swung toward her. "Mommy, why are you crying?"

Dan smiled, opened an arm. "Welcome home."

She ran back inside, emotion surging. Her feet pounded the stairs. She was supposed to be the strong one in this convoluted scenario, not him! *Curse that smile! I'm not here to run into his arms! I should not have brought Evan. Everything's ruined!*

"Robyn?" Dan's voice searched the quiet house as Evan's tiny footsteps circled swiftly toward the stairs. She locked the bathroom door, pulled her hair, and tried to think. She heard Dan approaching, then a rap on the door. "Robyn? Honey, I'm not sure what's going on but take whatever time you need. I was sitting outside when you arrived. If I wasn't supposed to see Evan… Well, I guess I apologize, but when he saw me he just—"

She unlocked the door, flung it open, and beheld his shocked expression. Then she gripped his shirt and kissed his mouth. Their lips parted, the kiss deepened. Dan's arms wrapped her body, drawing her closer. His strong hands slid into her hair.

Stop it! Stop him!

She pushed back. His chest rose and fell but he let her go. "I can't do this," she said. "I just came to…" Her head was a shaken soda.

He's sick of me. This is fleeting, pent-up emotion. I'll be a door mat next week!

"I'll be with Evan," Dan said, backing away.

She closed the door, pressed the vanity, and leaned toward the mirror. Eye liner looked like skid marks on her cheeks. She wet her hands, splashed her face. What now? Oh God, what now?

Ten minutes later she found them in the kitchen, eating pretzels and talking. Their backs were turned, so she leaned against a wall, grinning as Evan described every lump of sand he'd molded on vacation. Dan, in turn, talked about a farm and a goofy little dog named Rockler. Neither of them, she hoped, knew about the suitcases still in the car.

"Dan?" The room fell silent. He turned, threw an elbow over his chair. "Can I talk to you alone for a minute?"

He nodded, tossed Evan's hair. "I'll be right back, sport."

Near the staircase, out of Evan's sight, Robyn said, "We really need to talk. Do you think we can get a sitter this afternoon, on such short notice?" She kept a stern expression; the sitter was for discussion purposes only.

So why in the world was Dan smirking?

Arms extended, Evan walked a hardened tractor tread, heel to toe, as if on a balance beam. Dan watched from behind, thrilled to be taking his son to meet Walter.

Evan's body looked leaner than he remembered, more boyish. Tan skinny legs, sprigging out of denim shorts. Protruding shoulder blades. Sketchers turning gray with field dust. And sweaty black hair, tucked beneath a Phillies cap (which he chose at the beach for its cool red color). "I still cheer for the O'wioles," he'd assured Dan at the start of their hike.

"Do they have animals?" Evan asked in stride.

"They have a dog, remember? Rockler."

"I want to ride a horse."

"Well, there aren't any horses on Mr. Walter's farm, but you'll have plenty of fun. I'm sure of it."

Evan squatted to pick up a stone. With a little-leaguer's wind-up he threw it into the trees. They heard foliage tear and then a deep clunk as the stone struck a tree.

"It's a hit!" Dan said. Evan laughed and looked for another stone. "Just one more, ace. We don't want to be late." He noted the sound of bees on honey suckle.

Evan stood, kicked up a leg. His pitch was higher this time. It clacked through branches and ended with…a splash?

"What was it, Daddy?"

"Steeeerike Three!"

As they ascended the hill, Dan spotted the Bennings under the tree. Walter wore blue jeans, belted high and proud. Margaret donned beige slacks, partly hidden by a draping yellow shirt. They both smiled. Margaret picked at her tight, gray curls.

"So you do own real clothes," Dan said from a distance.

Walter seemed to chuckle as he walked toward them, Margaret at his side. "My Sunday best." He pretended to straighten a tie. They convened on the lawn, not far from the tree. Walter bent at the waist, extending a hand. "So you must be Evan. I'm delighted to meet you." Evan grinned and slapped his palm.

"Oh, bless his little heart," Margaret said, as if to herself.

"How did you grow such a big beard?" Evan asked.

Walter nearly burst with infectious laughter. "A fine question." He stroked his moustache. "C'mon Evan, let's have a look around."

Evan glanced up for Dan's wink of approval. Then he walked beside Walter, toward the barn. Dan and Margaret followed. "He's adorable, Daniel. Just adorable."

Dan shoved his hands in his pockets. "Yeah, he's a great kid."

Walter talked about tractors and barns and vegetables. Evan's red cap turned or bobbed in response. And something like sadness swelled in Dan's chest. A longing he couldn't identify, a longing that kept him trailing behind, unwilling to say goodbye. But Robyn was waiting.

"Hey sport," Dan called. "Daddy's gotta get home."

"Bye, Daddy."

Dan glanced at Margaret. "You're sure you don't mind him staying for supper?"

"Just as long as grilled hot dogs are okay," she said. They stopped and turned toward each other as Walter and Evan kept walking.

"Are you kidding," Dan said. "You'd better make him two." Margaret placed a hand on his arm, and softly laughed.

"Take all the time you need, Daniel," Walter called from afar.

On the lonely trek home, near the honeysuckle, Dan realized he'd forgotten to ask about the mysterious splash. But no way he was walking through that jagged mess. The question could wait. It was time to focus his thoughts on more important matters. Like marriage. A few strides later, when his phone rang, he assumed it was Robyn, doubtless wondering what was taking so long. He answered the call without looking.

"Can you talk?" Russell said.

Dan's heart sprinted. "Yeah."

"About last Saturday; what can I say? Never mix beer and scotch. Anyway, I was out of line."

This can't be happening. My dad doesn't apologize.

"Getting fired is rough," Russell added. "And Robyn leaving, well..."

"Thank you. I appreciate that."

"So listen, I don't know what those schmucks were thinking, but I know Jon Clauser. I'll get him on the links later this week, rattle his cage for you. They might reconsider—"

"Dad, whoa. I'm not sure."

"You don't want your job?"

"I want a job, it's just... These guys pissed down my back. I think I might prefer to explore other options."

"Yeah, well, you have a point, there. I'll keep my ears open then, go to bat for you."

This is not my father.

"Thanks, again," Dan said before closing his phone, a smile spreading wide on his face. Joyful adrenaline burst in his chest and quickened his body. Like a child, he pitched a walnut-sized stone into the trees, listening for a splash, expecting a splash. But after a series of snaps he heard only a thud and the high-pitched squeal of a retreating chipmunk.

If there was indeed water in the midst of the tangle, he'd outright missed.

"That pretty much covers it," Dan said, peeking at the time on the microwave. He'd been talking for forty minutes. His mouth felt like an inside-out sock.

Robyn stiffened in her chair and appeared to flex her eyes. She breathed deeply. "I need a shot of caffeine. You?"

"No, I'm good." The ice cubes in his drink were like glassy toothpicks, but the cup was still full. He could deal with watery soda. What troubled him was Robyn's unresponsiveness. He'd explained everything: arguing with Kevin, getting the call, and sitting at the end of that God-forsaken table, listening to the polished words of men pretending to care, men he'd trusted. He talked about sitting by the river, meeting Kevin at the bar. He'd even gone so far as to open up about feelings of regret and how thoughts of Kevin's suicide haunted him, made him wish for a second chance to befriend the man or at least show a little respect.

He watched her poor a glass of iced tea. Their eyes met briefly. "So you have nothing to say?" he asked.

She put the pitcher in the fridge, sat down again. "It's a lot to digest, Dan. My head's spinning."

"Well, maybe it's time to put your cards on the table. I know you left, obviously. And I kind of know why. But I think it would do us both some good to hear the whole story."

She looked out the window, put her chin in one hand. "I'm not sure there is a story. And I'm not sure where to begin."

Dan drank his flat soda and almost spoke. His foot tapped in the silent tension.

"I want to say that you're not the man I married," Robyn finally disclosed. "But that would be a lie. I knew what I was getting. I guess I always knew. Sensed it, anyway. That drive in you…" She turned her head toward him. "To be wealthy like your father. I always knew it would be hard to love, but I thought money would make it okay. Worthwhile, you know?" She looked out the window again. "Such stupid things we think at that age."

"So you never loved me?"

Her head whirled back in Dan's direction. Tears welled in her eyes. "Yes. I mean, no. I mean…" She closed her eyes and drew a breath. "I loved you. I still love you. *You*." She shifted her body, her chair scuffed the floor. "How can I say this?" Her hands lifted, as if behind a podium. "It's like, when we first met, when we fell in love, this drive was a seed in you. It was there along with so many other things: humor, sensitivity, maturity. Things a girl can really go for, you know? And you weren't that bad looking, either."

Dan released a breathy chuckle.

"But you've changed, Dan. I mean, that seed, that drive; it's overtaken you. It's become the only part of you that we see anymore. You make us feel like obstacles to your ambition. You didn't need to say you were sick of me. I already knew. And someday soon, Evan will, too."

A warm tear fell on Dan's cheek. He made no effort to hide it.

"If you want to live alone in some gated community, and become some hardened, jet-set father and husband, then I'll take Evan and get out of your way." She broke into sobs. Dan cried, too, until he bit a knuckle and defaulted to anger. Potential insults swarmed his brain as he stood, walked to the window, and almost punched it out. His heart was a stone wrapped in chains.

And then Robyn spoke again. "There's something else I need to tell you."

Dan found them in a meadow behind the barn, playing fetch with Rockler. "Daddy, watch!" Evan hurled a stick (all of twenty feet). Rockler retrieved it, darting and barking and pleading for more. Evan clapped and cheered.

Thunder rumbled from charcoal clouds, poised to hide the setting sun. "Glad you came in a car this time," Walter said.

"Yeah, well, thank Robyn for checking the radar. You ready to go, Ev?"

Evan threw the stick again. Rockler gave chase.

"I hope he wasn't any trouble," Dan said.

"Of course not. He's been a delight."

"Evan! Now!"

Walter put his arm around Evan. "Better get home now. There's a storm on the way."

"Can I come back tomorrow?" Evan asked. Dan rolled his eyes.

"Well, I've got quite a few chores to finish tomorrow," Walter said. "And I imagine your daddy has to work."

Oh, no; please, not now.

"There was a fire," Evan said, driving a spike in Dan's chest.

Robyn! Talking about this in front of Evan!

Walter's brow furrowed, like the remark had triggered some foggy memory. "A fire, Daniel?"

Dan reached for Evan's hand. "Fi-erd. I was fired."

"I'm terribly sorry."

"Evan," Dan said. "Why don't you run inside, say goodbye to Miss Margaret?"

Evan complied, with Rockler in tow. Thunder clapped and echoed. Sunlight waned before turning off like a switch, and both men glanced at the approaching blackness.

"We can certainly use the rain," Walter said.

Dan ignored the small talk. "There's a lot I can't bring myself to tell you."

Walter put a hand on Dan's shoulder. "Tuesday morning sound good?" Their heads turned toward the sound of crunching gravel, from a burgundy minivan, turning around at the end of the drive. Dan cocked his head and pondered the odds.

"Daniel… Tuesday?"

"We'll meet you at the tree," Dan said, still watching the van.

16

CHAPTER SIXTEEN

Alone in the kitchen, Dan finished his coffee. The house was silent and tense, like a hushed theater. His resume was sharp but opportunities scarce, at least locally. He'd tapped all his contacts, created online profiles, and scanned every listing. He'd done all he knew to do. So how could she? How dare she?

He rummaged through cabinets for a pack of new coffee filters, thinking it better to embrace a sleepless night. The internet was faster; he could search for new postings (for the third time this week). He scooped grounds, poured water in the tank.

"I know it's a lot to ask." Robyn's voice was a poke from behind. But he didn't turn around. Several seconds passed in silence, until Mr. Coffee dripped and sputtered. "I can't sleep either," she added.

Dan heard a sliding chair and whispers of fabric. Side-stepping to the stove, he sparked flames beneath the kettle and searched for vanilla tea. From the corner of his eye he detected Robyn, sitting and watching, in a purple robe that covered her shoulders. The kettle hissed, and he couldn't help but recall the last night they'd spent drinking coffee and tea. *You've derailed my life!* Had his brutish remark been proven perfectly correct?

Dan poured water into Robyn's favorite mug, placed it on the table, and looked in her eyes. "So Peter Chase finally retires, and you get the call to replace him?"

"No, that's not it." Robyn bounced her tea bag in the scalding water. "The current assistant is replacing Peter. I was asked to consider his job, the same position I used to have. It's far from a done deal, but with previous experience and social equity on my side, I think I have a pretty good shot."

Steam burst from the coffee maker, signaling the brew cycle was complete. Dan filled his cup and sat down next to Robyn. "Who called you again?"

"Peter did, actually. He just thought I might be interested."

"And you're telling me you are, is that correct?"

Robyn stood, carried her mug to the trash can, and carefully dropped in the dangling teabag. "Look," Dan said. "I'm not criticizing, I just…" He took a drink, tried to relax. "It's just that I can hardly say the words: stay-at-home-dad. It's like verbal castration or something."

Robyn placed her tea on a counter, and kept her distance. "That's your problem, Dan. Being a man is about so much more than an office title or—"

"And you know this, how!"

"Oh, here we go again! Let me tell you something: You wake Evan and we're out of here!"

"What do you know about being a man, Robyn?" His words seeped through his jaw like a line from Dirty Harry.

"I've been dreaming of a husband since grade school. That's what girls do. You don't have to be a man to know what you want in one."

"Okay, fine, so I'm not prince charming, but I've—"

"You're not prince anything. You're not. You've become a self-absorbed workaholic."

"Don't you—" Dan tucked his chin, found an ounce of composure. "You have no right to speak to me that way."

"Then who does, Dan? Who can tell you the truth? You're losing your family because of the truth I just told you. Now, you can either get it through your thick head and make some serious changes, or you can deny it all and end up like—"

"My father!"

Dan stood, paced the kitchen. "My dad can be pretty rough around the edges, Robyn. But he's the one who cared enough to support my search for a new job. Called me just this afternoon, offering to help. That's more than you can say."

Robyn looked down, and Dan returned to the table. The fridge groaned, ice cubes dropped in their bin. "And why do you think he suddenly cares?" she asked.

Dan sat, knowing deep inside that he'd wondered the same. Beneath Russell's uncharacteristic support churned a whirlpool of suspicion. And like a child in water wings, Dan could only cling to the swirling, irrational joy.

"He's selfish," Robyn continued. "Whatever your dad said today is about him, about protecting his image. Think about it: you're his son, and justified or not, you were fired."

"You're being unreasonable. Paranoid, even."

"See what I mean! You never listen!"

"Mommy?" It was a drowsy mumble.

"Now what?" Dan looked at her. "Do I leave?"

Robyn palmed her cheeks, whispered something in frustration. "No. My bad." She trotted upstairs.

Dan relaxed, rubbing his face. And of all the dumb possibilities, he thought about Walter, imagined him lying on his back, snoring like a diesel engine. But the image soon crumpled back to Robyn's proposition: work on restoring relationships, rediscover your heart, your true self. She couldn't have chosen sappier jargon, but at least she was making an effort. He massaged his temples, and thought of a classmate in college: a quirky guy named Lawrence who "got religion" at a campus crusade, freshman year. Henceforth, Pastor Larry would chastise frat houses, proclaiming words to be the power of life and death. Or were they sharp as a sword? Either seemed rubbish, and yet Robyn's words had somehow pierced Dan's heart. But so had Russell's.

Life? Death? Somewhere in between?

Robyn entered the kitchen.

"Get him settled?" Dan asked.

"Yeah."

"Listen," they said simultaneously, enough to raise two smiles.

"I'm not staying home." The smiles vanished. "I've worked too hard to step out of the game. But you should pursue the job at MCC." He watched her swallow, then added, "You might need it."

17

Chapter Seventeen

Thunderheads were already gathering, but Dan had agreed to Tuesday morning. No interviews were scheduled, and Evan had been nipping at his heels since 7:30. Margaret stepped onto the porch at the sound of their approach. At the same time Walter emerged from the barn. Pulling close to the front walk, Dan killed the engine, helped Evan from the car.

"We're figuring on pizza for lunch," Margaret said. "What do you like?"

"Doesn't sound very down-home," Dan answered with a grin. "But since you asked, pepperoni."

"There'll be a fresh salad on the side, don't you worry."

Walter arrived. "Hello, young man. Young *men*, I mean." He winked at Evan, then looked squarely at Dan. "Any news on the job front?" They shook hands.

"I'm afraid not," Dan said, looking around the property. "Rockler behind bars today?"

Walter chuckled. "Last I saw, he was chasing butterflies behind the barn. Hard to believe he didn't come running at the sound of your car. Which is quite nice, I might add."

"I finally got my own ride back."

"Well, it befits you." Walter started to kneel but winced and stayed standing. "Now, as for you, sir," he said to Evan.

"Yes!" Evan smiled from ear to ear.

"How would you like to see my model train?"

Evan clapped and jumped. Walter laughed. "I set it up this morning, just for you." He motioned them forward. "It's right inside."

The screen door creaked and snapped as they entered. "Here we go," Walter said, leading them into the dining room. A rust-colored chandelier brightened gradually above a large, chopping-block table. On the table, thick metal tracks formed an oval around an odd assortment of plastic buildings and trees that looked like overcooked broccoli. A diesel engine, silver and blue, was coupled to three white box cars and a bright red caboose. "We picked this up at a flea market years ago. Haven't had it out since."

Evan climbed on a chair, folded his arms on the table, and rested his chin. "Wow," he said. "Does it work?"

"You bet'cher bippy." Walter flipped a switch. The engine buzzed, then began to move. Within seconds, the train was whizzing around the oval, passing inches from Evan's nose, and filling the air with an aroma of hot electricity.

"Faster!" Evan said.

Walter's eyes sparkled. Margaret entered from the kitchen saying, "Make a whistle sound, Evan!"

And Evan made a wonderful sound—robust and innocent—like the noise Dan used to make while pushing locomotives through a half-open book, listening for another B&O freighter to pass through his Baltimore suburb. During those few special minutes he could pretend the authentic sounds came from his favorite toys. And that's exactly what he'd begun doing that afternoon, when his mother grabbed her purse and said, "Hurry, Danny!" He ran from his room, hopped barefoot and shirtless into the front of her running Buick. "What's wrong, mom?" She smiled. "Nothing, Baby. Nothing's wrong. You'll see." They raced to a street adjacent to the tracks, stood on its litter-strewn shoulder, waved to the engineer and then held their ears, laughing as the train thundered past. In the quiet that followed, her hand tossed his hair. "I love you, Danny Boy." Two hours later, he told his father about the train, saw fire in his eyes, listened to his pounding steps and the sickening sound of flesh smacking flesh. "Don't ever waste my gasoline like that!"

"Daniel?" Walter said.

"What?"

"Are you okay?"

"Yeah... Yeah, I'm fine." Dan blinked, forced a smile. "Just a mesmerizing little train you've got there."

"Why don't you two go on and talk," Margaret said. "When Evan's through I've got a coloring book that somehow landed in my grocery cart." She winked. "Just let me pour you some tea. Pizza should be here in half an hour."

Glasses in hand, Dan and Walter walked to the tree, chatting about the weather and the sound of a combine working somewhere nearby. "The leaves will be changing before we know it," Walter said.

"September's only a week away."

"Hard to believe."

"Is your knee well enough to sit?"

"Oh, I think so. Getting-up will be the problem. But you're here."

The grass beneath the tree was cool on Dan's legs. He flicked acorn caps like little Frisbees. Walter slowly squatted and then leaned against the trunk with his arms at rest on his knees. His tan coveralls slid higher than his boots. "You know, if it weren't for this tree we may never have met," he said.

Dan expressed agreement with raised eyebrows and a delicate nod, then he looked at the branches overhead. "So how long does it take a tree get this size? Two-hundred years?"

"I'd say that's a reasonable guess. Over a hundred, for sure. But there's more than the passage of time to consider, Daniel."

Dan shot him a look. "Time for my first Dr. Benning lecture?"

Walter chuckled. "I'll spare you." He stroked his moustache, drank some tea. "But I will say that our tree lives apart from clutter."

"Clutter?"

"Think about the trees in that old fence row." Walter motioned with his glass. "Or even in a thick area of forest. They're cluttered; you know what I mean? All twisted around each other with no room to spread out, always competing for nutrients. But not our tree." He lifted a hand, patted the trunk. "Our tree grows in rich soil, and with abundant sunlight. Because it's set apart from the rest, it grows differently. It lives differently." He took a long drink. "And therefore our tree has developed all the stunning qualities it was created to display."

Created? The unpopular theory?

Dan twisted on his rump, crossed his legs, and leaned back on both arms. "This almost sounds philosophical."

Walter grinned. "Well, biology is the study of life. You'd be surprised how much philosophy exists within biology, or physiology; any natural science, really. You see, form and function are always underscored with purpose, Daniel. And therein lies the profoundness you're detecting."

"Whoa, I'm a numbers guy, Walter. My idea of profound is a balance sheet with variances less than a hundred dollars."

"You admire the tree, don't you?"

"Yeah, but who wouldn't?"

"Enough to walk across two fields for a closer look?" Dan dipped his head, plucked a thick blade of grass. "Granted, you work in business," Walter continued. "But don't sell yourself short. There's more in you than just facts and figures."

"And how do you suddenly know this?" Dan stared at Walter. "What do you know about me?"

"Only what you tell me."

Dan shook his head. "Okay, since we're on the subject, why do you care?"

"Look around."

Dan rolled his eyes. "I don't get it."

"You're my closest neighbor; it's only right that we become friends."

Walter smiled, and though Dan wanted to feel angry, he couldn't help but smile back. "Gives new definition to next-door neighbors."

"Indeed."

They laughed a little, drank some more tea, and looked around at nothing in particular. "My wife left me a couple of weeks ago. With Evan. They weren't really on vacation."

"Well, I was a bit suspicious," Walter said.

"You would've found out sooner or later."

"But they're back now, right?"

"Yeah, *now*," Dan said. "But Robyn's got the crazy idea that I should stay home, work on relationships or whatever."

"And you can't possibly imagine…"

"There's just no way. I've worked too hard. Bell-Knarr screwed up cutting me loose, Dr. Benning. And as soon as I get hired somewhere else, I'm gonna prove it."

"And to whom will you prove it?"

"Everyone." Anger was creeping and swelling and lacing his words. "My family. My co-workers. My father." Dan clenched his teeth and aggressively exhaled.

"I apologize. I didn't mean to pry."

Yes you did. And my life is not an open book.

"Pizza's here!" Margaret shouted from the porch as a small blue car came zipping down the drive. Rockler, from seemingly nowhere, crossed the lawn like a barking arrow. Dan stood and offered Walter a hand.

"Permit me to say one thing more," Walter said, pulling and standing. He brushed off his rear, eyes shifting. "Daniel," he finally began. "I've had an office full of accolades. I've published many written pieces. And I don't mind telling you I've done pretty well financially. But I'm sixty-eight years old, and from where I'm standing—and thank God, I'm still standing—none of it means more to me than the precious lady who just beckoned us to lunch. Do you understand what I'm saying?"

Dan's body felt like a stretched rubber band.

"Now I'm not telling you what to do," Walter added. "But take it from an old guy; someone running the last lap, so to speak. If you lose your beautiful wife and that little angel…" His eyes welled with tears. "You'll regret it for the rest of your life."

I already do.

Ice clinked in Dan's glass as his arms wrapped Walter's tan coveralls.

18

CHAPTER EIGHTEEN

"Welcome back, Mrs. Crawford." Robyn shook five hands. Her cheeks ached, her throat hurt. Bottled water or not, four straight hours was a long time to talk. But she'd passed the test, endeared herself to the committee. Landed the job.

Outside the alumni office, the campus swarmed with students; energetic young adults with hearts full of dreams. It was an atmosphere in which she'd previously thrived. And come Monday morning she'd do it again. She felt like skipping all the way to the car, until thoughts of Dan moved her close to tears.

Three weeks had passed since they'd discussed her return to employment, and things between them were surprisingly pleasant. Not wonderful, but calm and cordial. He'd slept on the recliner (at her request) and spent most waking hours combing through job listings. But he'd also played with Evan, helped out around the house.

At a red light in McKinley, the grilled aroma of a corner pub snuck in the vents and churned memories of Labor Day weekend. On Saturday they'd gone to a ballgame at Metro Bank Park where, despite an uneventful pitcher's duel, they delighted in watching Evan crunch nachos and fan his burning little mouth. Sunday was an afternoon picnic at Dr. Benning's farm. Robyn and Margaret chatted like old friends while the men hiked to a small stream in which, at some point, Evan had apparently thrown a rock. She hadn't entirely grasped the explanation but felt nonetheless touched by the joy in their hearts.

And then came Monday.

Russell's pop-in had been nothing short of a nightmare; showing up unannounced, as if his presence were some sort of bestowed privilege. Her stomach turned loops when his Mercedes pulled in the drive. And she grimaced all evening at his pretentious remarks: "A lovely job you've done decorating, Robyn. Outstanding burgers, my dear; just outstanding. I've now seen the finest slugger to ever swing a bat."

After Evan went to bed, Dan and Russell sat outside, sucking down lagers and chastising schmucks. Russell's slim cigars glowed red with each pull, adding mafia flair to his prickly face. Just add a fedora and Tommy gun, Robyn remembered thinking, listening from a distance while casually gathering cups and plates. Dan shared news of two interviews, meticulously explaining why each position had been inadequate or not the right fit. But it was all a smokescreen, a wad of professional lingo to muddle the truth that he'd wanted both jobs but gotten neither. She couldn't fault him for massaging the facts; his father's response to failure was worse than salt in the wound. It was battery acid in the eyes, and always sharpened by alcohol.

Late in the evening, before finally driving away, Russell slurred his way through a boastful, off-color soliloquy about his corporate climb. And in those moments, as a mother aches for her disabled child, Robyn's heart broke and bled for Dan. But was it love? He was fighting for his life, or at least searching for it. Amid unfeeling banter, empty badges, and fleeting specks of paternal encouragement.

Was it love … or only pity?

Dan placed five chicken dinosaurs on Evan's plate, and loaded his own with a dozen. He added barbeque sauce and a handful of chips, cracked open two root beers, and sat. A few minutes later the garage rumbled opened, a car door closed, and Robyn walked in wearing black high heels and a pants suit to match. "No vegetables?" she asked.

"That's right," Dan said, wagging a finger. "I did forget the ketchup."

Evan grabbed the spotlight with a dinosaur battle in which he bit off the head of the loser. "Yikes!" Robyn said. Evan howled with laughter, then ate the body.

"Well?" Dan opened his hands.

Robyn looked him in the eye, and nodded. "Let me get changed," she said. "We'll talk when you're finished." She scurried upstairs.

I am finished.

Across the table, another battle ensued. "Daddy, look!"

"Evan, just eat." Dan chugged his root beer and wished it was minus the root. Then he looked at Evan's unhappy expression. He grabbed a stegosaurus, walked it across the table, and said, "It's on, now! Grrrrr!" Evan's eyes soon danced with delight as chicken collided and breading flew everywhere.

Ten minutes later, a lollipop in one cheek, Evan sat in the family room watching TV, and Robyn returned to the kitchen. She was casually dressed with her hair pulled back, and for a minute or longer Dan leaned against a door frame, watching her make salad and waiting for some commentary. None came. "So it's official?" he finally said.

Robyn stopped slicing and turned to look at him. "I wasn't sure how you'd take the news."

"Congratulations." He walked closer to her. "When do you start?"

"Monday morning. Since I'm not presently employed, they want me right away." She chuckled. "Not presently employed; I'm still talking interview-speak."

Dan's eyes dropped, his teeth clenched.

"Dan, I know this is awkward for you. I mean, it's a messy stage we're working through. But please don't make this a competitive thing or…" Her voice trailed, she sucked her bottom lip.

Dan walked to the table, gazing at the tree and then folding his palms over the back of a chair. Evan's laughter entered his ears like a parade of bubbles. He heard Robyn's feet on the kitchen floor, felt her touch on his shoulder. "I think I need a run," he said out the window.

"Along Rakes Mill Road?" she knowingly asked.

19

CHAPTER NINETEEN

By the time his sneakers hit the Bennings' long driveway, Dan felt nauseated. Walter silenced his lawn tractor, and climbed down from it. His blue coveralls were darkened beneath each arm. A red cap rested high on his head.

"Where do you find hats like that, anyway?" Dan said, still catching his breath. "With no logos?"

"Oh, they sell them at the Sears and Roebuck in town. There's nothing I feel inclined to advertise with my head. Just need to keep the sun off of it."

Dan put his hands on his knees. Drips slithered down his face like snakes, burning his eyes. "I hate to ask, but could I—"

"Nonsense; will water do the trick? I might have some Gatorades tucked in the fridge."

"Either one. I'd sure appreciate it."

"We'll sit on the porch," Walter said. "I'm due for a break."

Dan put his hands on his hips, arching his back as he followed Walter toward the house. He sat on the porch steps, and noticed Rockler sleeping under the tree. The corn had been harvested, and what used to be lush, green fields now looked like a colorless expanse of three-day stubble. The screen door creaked and snapped. Walter's boots clunked on the wooden boards. He handed Dan a lemon-lime Gatorade, twisted open the cap on one of his own, and leaned against a post. "You picked quite an afternoon to run."

Dan nodded, took a long drink. "I guess we don't get to choose when the urge to run away strikes." He looked beyond the tree. "They sure did a number on the corn, didn't they?"

"Well, that's what they grow it for. Margaret bought a bushel this week; good stuff." He chugged half his bottle, screwed on the cap. "Things okay with the family?"

"Yeah. Yeah, they're fine."

"And you?"

Dan took a drink, sucked his teeth, and stared at the porch railing. "Robyn got her old job back at MCC. Assistant Director of Alumni. She starts Monday. On the other hand, I've had two interviews but no offers. Severance runs through January, but…" He looked at Walter. "I never thought I'd see the day."

"That you'd stay home while your wife went to work?"

"I suppose that sums it up." Dan stood, chugged most his drink.

"Walk with me," Walter said. "If you've any legs left." He lifted his hat, smoothed his white hair. "I've got something to show you."

Stepping into the barn was like entering a furnace. Flies buzzed. The air was thick with the smell of old rafters and greasy equipment. Dan's sneakers scuffed in sawdust. "How on earth do you work in here?"

"I don't do much wood working this time of year. Once in a while, in the evenings. But even then this place is a sauna." Walter stopped near the workbench. The window above it was stained and crawling with flies. He yanked open a drawer, inch by inch, like fighting a stubborn mule. "Darn this humidity!" he growled. Dan tried not to laugh.

Eventually Walter took from the drawer a tool with a wooden handle, turned and tapered. The handle was attached to about six straight inches of metal, beveled at the end. He scraped the slanted edge with his thumb, and said, "This could use sharpening."

"What is it?"

"A chisel. Half-inch flat, to be specific."

"So you cut wood with it?"

Walter's eyes met Dan's. His mustache pushed forward. "Not cut but rather carve or slice or chip-away. It's the tool of an artisan, Daniel. Which is why it doesn't get used in most shops. Today, it's all power this and power that. Fast and efficient and predictable; that's all anyone cares about." His head rocked like a protesting parent.

"But not you, I take it."

Walter chuckled, looked at the chisel. "Well, I guess the subject does get my dander up a bit." He looked back at Dan. "But that's not why I got this out. C'mon, let's give it a proper edge." He slid a square of stone to the center of the workbench, topped it with oil, and with a circular motion, rubbed the metal against the stone's flat face. Dan watched for a moment, almost mesmerized by the swishy, grinding sound of the sharpening tool. But his eyes soon drifted to things he hadn't noticed before, things resigned to the barn's darker recesses. Ladders, lawn equipment, barrels, cans, shovels, pitchforks, ropes, carriage wheels, and many antique-looking implements he couldn't even identify. Leaning or stacked in the shadows, in no apparent order.

"There we are." Walter said, twisting and examining the edge of the chisel. Then he wiped it with a cloth, and handed it to Dan. "It belongs to you."

"You have got to be joking. I don't have a clue how to use this."

"Well, it's an antique. If nothing else it makes a fine decoration, given the proper décor. But here, let me teach you." Walter ducked below the bench and returned with a block. "A scrap of walnut," he said. "You'll find no better wood for experiencing the joy of a chisel."

Dan laughed. "The *joy* of a chisel? Aren't you taking this a bit far?"

"You decide." Walter used a pencil to trace the end of a small board on the face of the walnut. He also pulled a mallet from a nearby toolbox. Then he clamped the walnut to the surface of the bench, and set the smaller board aside. "Now, watch me." He took the chisel from Dan, rested his forearm on the bench, and aligned the tool's sharpened edge with the lines he had drawn. With his other hand he lifted the mallet and used it to strike the top of the chisel. The sharpened metal plunged into the walnut, but not far. Walter wiggled it free. "See what I've done there? Hold the chisel straight up, with the flat surface facing away from the rectangle, but aligned perfectly with its edge. Then strike the chisel, but just enough to sink the blade a small fraction. About the depth I've done." He laid the tools on the bench, and backed away. "Oh, and start beside the cut I've already made."

Dan stepped to the bench, surprised by the swirl of anxiety in his gut, and followed the directions. *Whack!* A smile lifted on his face.

"Well done," Walter said.

Dan wiggled the chisel free. "Do I just continue around the rectangle?"

"You bet'cher bibby. And be sure to keep the corners precise."

With the rectangle entirely etched, Walter patted Dan's shoulder and took back the chisel. "Now watch, again. This is the best part." Dan stepped back, wiped sweat from his brow, and noticed a fly the size of a marble, buzzing and bouncing around the window frame. Walter leaned over the bench. "Hold the chisel as such, and align your blade with the end of the rectangle. Make sure the beveled edge faces up, lean your chisel almost flat to the board, and then…" He tapped the chisel in soft repetition. "Keep some gentle pressure." A shaving of walnut lifted out of the rectangle, curling above the blade.

"That is truly amazing," Dan said. "I think you have more finesse than my wife."

"Finish it up, Daniel." Walter passed the chisel.

"I'm not sure I can. I mean…" Dan shook his head.

"Mistakes are part of the process. Don't fear them." Walter swatted Dan's shoulder like a coach.

Dan copied Walter's technique and, though not as gracefully, removed his own curling slice of walnut…then another. Then he hammered the edges another time, only to remove more curls. And after several cycles, the process was complete. Not perfect, but finished. And the pencil-sketched rectangle was now replaced by a slot about half an inch deep. Walter fine-tuned the edges, and said, "Well done, Daniel."

"Thanks. But I don't get it. I mean, it was cool tapping out the shavings and everything. But what's the point?"

"Ah!" Walter lifted a finger, then turned. "Where'd we put that… There it is." He lifted the smaller board, the one he had traced, and slid it into the chiseled slot. "A precise fit."

"So this is how furniture is made? One technique, I mean."

"It is," Walter said. He unclamped the walnut and handed Dan the assembled work. "It's also how men are made. Sometimes."

Dan rolled his eyes, then looked at his handiwork. "So we're back to Philosophology 101?"

Walter's mustache tweaked left.

Dan pulled the small board. "You know, this really is a tight fit." He placed the assembly back on the bench, in a dusty beam of sunlight.

"Listen to me, Daniel. Barring astronomical odds there is but one piece of wood in this entire barn to fit the rectangle you've carved with utmost precision."

"And again, the point is?"

"It fits perfectly because you chipped away just the right amount of material from the walnut board, and in just the right configuration. Little by little; not in one fell swoop. Our hearts can become blocks of wood, Daniel. And without proper chiseling, the things that are supposed to matter the most are unable to fit; not properly, at least." Walter gripped Dan's shoulders. "Life is full of chisels if we'll make ourselves vulnerable to their work."

Dan wriggled free and stepped back. "Okay. I appreciate your concern, Walter. I really do. But this is over the top, and I really ought to get home."

Walter's moustache pulled down on each end. He sighed, turning toward the workbench. "Well, don't forget this." He handed Dan the chisel. "I assume you're walking home."

Dan chuckled. "Never run with scissors, right? God forbid a chisel."

He gripped the tool, although he'd just as soon leave it behind.

20

CHAPTER TWENTY

He lifted Evan like a barbell, tickled some ribs. "Who's up for ice cream?"

"What's all the commotion?" Robyn said, hurrying in from the kitchen.

"Daddy said ice cream!"

Robyn raised an eyebrow. Dan lowered Evan, who giggled on the carpet before running to the garage for his Spider-Man Crocs. "We have a job to celebrate, don't we?"

Robyn smiled. "That's sweet, but it's almost supper time."

"Then we'll make it Friendly's. Just give me a second to clean up." Dan ran upstairs, splashed his face and pits, and threw on a clean shirt. He returned to find his family waiting in the car with the AC cranked.

The drive to the restaurant was quiet save Evan's repeated questions about available flavors and whether he could choose a happy beginning sundae. They parked near the entrance, requested a booth, and played tic-tac-toe on Evan's paper placemat. Minutes later, directly across the aisle, the hostess seated a man who looked at Dan and nodded once.

"Do you feel ready?" Dan asked Robyn. "For Monday, I mean."

Robyn sipped her diet soda, then folded her arms. "My head's spinning. They're using a whole new database now, and so much communication is done through social media. I'll have a lot to learn. Not to mention, new people. A couple of admins might remember me, but the alumni house is full of new faces."

"You'll do great," Dan said, writing an "X" where he was sure to lose. And then the food arrived: greasy morsels for the boys, a crisp garden salad for the lady rediscovering her professional wardrobe.

"Does he know?" Dan asked, a few bites into the meal. Robyn covered a mouthful of greens, and shook her head. "He should know," Dan added.

"Are you talking about me?" Evan said, holding three fries.

Robyn finished chewing, then looked at Evan. "Mommy got a job, honey. I'm going back to work next week. At the big college in town."

Evan shoved in the fries. "Are you gonna be a teacher?" They heard every other syllable.

"Don't talk with your mouth full," Robyn said. "And no, I'll be working in an office."

They waited for emotion but Evan only drank soda, dipped a chicken finger in barbeque sauce, and kept eating. Dan almost laughed. Robyn followed suit, with her head tipped as if to say, "Really?"

"You'll be staying home with Daddy, sport."

"Yaaay!" Evan clapped his shiny hands.

Robyn threw up her arms. "Oh, sure! You'll cheer for that!" A full smile spread across her face, and everyone laughed.

Including the man in the opposite booth.

Dan gave him a longer look, pegged him as a thirty-something. Buzzed hair, pudgy cheeks, heavy stubble. Glasses that edged toward trendy but looked more like replica horn rims. He wore a Dr. Pepper T-shirt over a torso that rippled from too many Dr. Peppers.

During dessert, conversation waned. Dan and Robyn sipped refills while waiting for Evan to scrape every bit of fudge from a wavy, glass dish. Robyn rested her left hand on the table as she looked around the restaurant, now overrun by boisterous children in burnt orange soccer uniforms. Dan stared at her wedding ring, placed his hand close to hers. Their skin touched, their eyes met, and her hand slid away to lift her drink.

Dan made fists on the table, looked to his left, and thought: what in the world is he looking at? The stranger turned his head, bit into his burger.

"All done!" Evan announced.

"Can you get a wet wipe?" Robyn said. "Dan?"

"What?"

"From my purse, beside you; can you get a wet wipe?"

Dan pulled out a wipe and passed it to Evan, who looked like he'd just eaten mud. "What did you do, stick your face in the bowl?" His words were tight and edgy. He sensed Robyn's annoyance.

"No, just my tongue." Evan stuck it out like a brown snake. Two wet wipes later, Dan took him to the men's room while Robyn paid the bill.

Stay-at-home-dad… try, Mr. Mom!

"Thanks for dinner," Robyn said, when they convened near the exit. Her playful sarcasm seared Dan's pride like a branding iron. Vulgarity rattled in his head but found no voice. "You're welcome," he muttered through a plastic smile, pushing open the door. And as his family brushed by he took one last look across the crowded restaurant, at the horn rim glasses of the thick man watching them leave.

"Is it just me, or was there some kind of weird vibe from that guy in the booth next to us?" he asked a minute later, buckling Evan.

"He just looked lonely," Robyn said.

Dan whispered a sharp dismissal. Then he got in the car and inched slowly backward, trying to see around the burgundy minivan parked beside them.

21

CHAPTER TWENTY-ONE

She'd laid out eleven outfits, hung the winner on the knob of the closet door: gray slacks and a mauve striped shirt. *But then again...* Robyn threw up her hands, walked out of the room, and heard Evan snoring lightly from across the hall.

Downstairs in the kitchen, near a steeping cup of anxiety-relieving tea, her nails drummed the counter as her eyes scanned pages of procedural and technical info. She hadn't held a job in almost five years, and a decade had passed since she'd started a new one. She'd just give the packet of documents one more look before—

"Darn it, Dan!" Strong hands had gripped her shoulders and begun to rub.

She heard chuckles of air. "You looked a little tense," he said.

She turned to face him. "You snuck-up on purpose, mister." She felt a grin forming despite her efforts to look stern. Dan took her mug, threw away the dripping bag, and stirred in a teaspoon of sugar. "I confess," he said, returning the tea.

"I suppose I am an easy target. I feel like I've swallowed a can of Play-Do." Robyn looked back at her notes, took a sip that felt scalding on her lips.

"Hey," Dan said.

"Hmmm?"

"Look at me." She did. "You'll do great. McKinley hired the best, hands down."

Robyn tilted her head, put down her mug, and allowed a sentimental smile to rise. No laptop. No e-mails. No scowl. No sarcasm. A gorgeous man making heartfelt remarks. Was this really Daniel Crawford? She stepped into his hug.

"I've been offered an interview on Wednesday."

And the secret comes out!

Robyn's heart stood still as she backed away. "What time? Where?"

"It doesn't matter."

She threw back her head, rolled her eyes. "Don't play games, Dan! I don't need this kind of crap right now."

He put a finger to his lips, and reached for her. She dodged his advance, grabbed her mug, and angrily sucked in tea. Then she volleyed the searing liquid between puffed cheeks, fanning a hand in front of her lips until, finally, she swallowed. From her laughing husband she took an ice cube, popped it in, and wondered why she hadn't just spit the tea out.

"I declined the interview," Dan said.

Robyn's ice cube clunked in the sink. "What? Why?"

Dan motioned toward the family room. "I'll show you."

Anticipation swelled with every step, until Robyn felt like a child on Christmas morning. Dan stopped in front of the fireplace, turning and lifting a hand. In the middle of the mantle was a family portrait, one she'd arranged last year. So he'd moved it from the wall?

"Do you remember what used to be here?" he asked. At once, Robyn's hands folded over her face. "That clock meant the world to me," Dan continued. "I thought it represented who I was and where I was headed." He looked up at the portrait. "I guess, I just..." He looked at her again. "I'm not good with touchy-feely talk." He put his hands in his pockets. "I love you, Robyn. Evan, too. And I'm gonna do it. I'm gonna stay home." He wrapped her in his arms, planting a kiss in her hair.

"I love you, too. But what changed your mind?"

"Wait here." He walked to the kitchen.

She heard the door to the garage open and close. Sitting down on the loveseat, she stared at the portrait, noting how Evan's face had changed. He was chubbier then, more toddler-like, and his hair had been lighter. The kitchen door opened and closed once more. "This had a lot to do with it," Dan said, returning to the family room.

Robyn's eyes fell on the old fashioned tool in his hands. "Okay?"

"It's a chisel." He handed it to her. "Walter gave it to me." She held the smooth wooden handle, ran a finger over the long steel shank. "Careful," Dan cautioned. "The end's pretty sharp."

"What do you do with it?"

Dan stayed quiet for several seconds. "You chip away," he finally said. "With precision and purpose."

She didn't understand but could nevertheless imagine those very words sneaking out from under Walter's thick moustache. And they made her feel warm and misty, as if she'd just watched Sleepless in Seattle.

22

CHAPTER TWENTY-TWO

Thank goodness for Pop Tarts! Dan's nose was tucked in his shirt to avoid the acrid smell of burnt eggs. *Mental note: never read box scores while cooking.* At least the smoke detectors were silent. Evan's bare feet clapped the vinyl floor. He rubbed his eyes, and of course said, "Something's stinky!"

"Probably your night time breath, big guy. Have a seat. You want strawberry or brown sugar?"

Evan pulled out a chair and sat. "The one with sprinkles." He yawned. "Where's mommy?"

"She's already at work, remember? Today's her first day at the new job. She promised to call us later; you can talk to her then." Dan put an untoasted strawberry Pop Tart on a small plate. "Breakfast is served." He chugged coffee and scraped saddle brown eggs into the disposal. "So what do you want to do today?" he asked, glancing from the sink to the table.

"Have a drink." Evan's words sounded stuck together.

Dan smirked. "Grab a pouch. You know where they are." Evan slid from his chair, padded over to the fridge. "I mean after breakfast; what should we do together?"

"I want to build a tree house. Like the one in my book."

Oh, for crying out loud! That's not what I meant.

"Well, that's a tall order, Ev. And besides, we don't have a tree big enough for a tree house."

"What about Mr. Walter's?"

"Now how did I know you were going to say that?" Evan shrugged and continued chewing. "I'll tell you what…" Dan joined him at the table. "Why don't we just visit Mr. Walter today? You can explore, play with Rockler. It's supposed to be beautiful weather. What do you say?"

"It's what my eyebrows are doing." He forced them up and down several times.

"Okay then, I'll give him a call."

By the time Evan was fed and cleaned and dressed and brushed and supplied with punchy answers to a million and one innocuous questions, Dan was ready for a nap. His super-dad enthusiasm had landed somewhere on the bathroom floor. And they were halfway to Walter's when he realized he'd forgotten sunscreen.

Margaret will have plenty; just relax.

High pressure had moved in overnight, rendering the sky a brilliant blue while breezes from the west carried hints of autumn. Evan was twenty paces ahead, picking up every shard, stick, or dried ear of corn he passed, flinging them in all directions. They stayed along the edge of the field, away from the harvested acres. Dan found something unnerving about the yellowish brown stubs, still aligned yet chopped at the knees, like a field of decimated soldiers. And although it seemed strange, they made him think of Kevin Clark. He loathed the mental images (however fabricated) of Kevin plunging into a reflected city, or flailing and choking beneath dirty, black water.

Nearing the honeysuckle, they picked their way through a few yards of prickly brush to a path beside the formerly mysterious stream. Walter had revealed both on Labor Day weekend. A root-rippled twist near the water connected to a wider, grassy path that led to the meadow behind Walter's barn. It certainly made for a more pleasant walk than skirting two fields and an overgrown hillside.

Evan shouldered a thin fallen branch as he scampered ahead, toward a stand of large hemlocks. Dan, finding the scene reminiscent of Andy Griffith, whistled the show's familiar tune until Evan wheeled around and shouted, "Daddy, birds don't sing like that!"

"Who goes there!" The call sounded like it came from cupped hands, and it was followed by an unmistakable laugh. Dan's cell phone beeped with new e-mail which he promptly dismissed as Evan, sneakers swishing in the tall grass, ran forward and out of sight. Dan kept walking, certain that Walter was just around the bend. And indeed he was, wearing tan coveralls, a matching floppy hat, and a smile that rivaled the midday sun. "I just thought I'd meet you halfway. Beautiful day for a walk." He motioned Evan forward. "C'mon young man; we've got a barn to explore!"

Evan raised both arms and progressed down the trail in a shuffle-step run. Reaching the meadow, he insisted on climbing the vein of protruding limestone. The men stood, arms crossed and watching, near the towering spruce trees. "What I wouldn't give for his kind of energy," Walter said. "I'd have this place fixed-up in no time."

"You do fine as it is," Dan said, noticing Margaret walking around in one of her gardens. She raised an arm and a smile. Then a brown flash rounded the barn and headed for Evan. Rockler put his front paws on the limestone. His tail was a blur. Evan, visibly delighted, sat on top of the stone to pet the dog's head.

In the peaceful moments that followed, Dan discovered himself looking at the sky, the grass; anywhere but at Walter. "About that chisel," he eventually said, sensing Walter's head turn. "I understand what you were saying. What you were trying to show me. I'm sorry for scoffing. It's just... That kind of talk. That kind of subject matter." He looked at Walter. "It's not what I do. It's not me."

"I understand." Walter waved playfully to Evan. "Learning to think and talk differently..." he flashed Evan a corny grin, then looked squarely at Dan. "It's part of the chiseling process, Daniel. A bit of a paradox, I suppose."

"Well, without going off the deep end, I just want you to know that I've considered what you said. Not only about the chisel, but also about my life. And about my family." His head turned at the sight of sudden movement; Evan and Rockler were fast approaching. He knelt, arms open, and scooped up Evan while the dog rolled in the grass near Walter. With his son on his hip, Dan said, "I've decided to stay home for a while, to be a stay-at-home-dad. I think it's best for my family."

Walter looked close to tears.

"Did you tell Mr. Walter about the tree house?" Evan said, wriggling free and bolting away the moment his feet touched grass. Rockler followed in hot pursuit.

Walter pulled Dan into a hug. "I'm proud of you." Dan tensed at first but then released inhibition, patted Walter's back, and wished for a moment he could say, "Thanks, Dad." They separated, and Dan felt lighter than air.

"Now, about this tree house." Walter said with an inquisitive expression.

"Oh, it's nothing. Evan's got a favorite book about kids playing in a tree house. He asked me to build one and I told him we don't have a suitable tree. So now he has it in mind to build one here." Dan rolled his eyes and chuckled.

Walter stroked his moustache, then his chin. "You don't say."

"C'mon, you can't seriously be considering this."

Walter put a hand on Dan's shoulder. "I believe we both know the perfect tree. And this is a wonderful time of year for an outdoor project."

"Oh my word, you're talking about the tree, the big white oak?"

"You bet'cher bippy. In fact, I've always wanted a tree house. It'll be ours. In our tree."

Walking toward the farmhouse, Dan tried to hide that he felt as flighty as a child. "Won't it damage the tree?" he said, projecting concern. "I mean, I'd hate to even think…"

"Oh, we might need to take off a few small limbs. But we'll consider it pruning." Walter looked at Dan, raised his curly brows. "Which, by the way, happens to be another beneficial process we should discuss."

They stopped at the gravel drive, close to the barn. Evan was in the garden with Margaret, losing his fingers in adult-sized gloves and giggling every time she shouted, "Noooope! Try again!" Dan wished Robyn were present to see it, to savor it.

A Papa John's car crunched onto the drive. Margaret beckoned with a mouth-gaping nod. "And lunch is served," Dan said in cool-guy rhythm.

Walter's cheeks pulled tight as he stroked his chin. "So about this tree house…are you free daytimes?" Sparkling eyes betrayed his stoic expression. Walter's moustache tweaked as he punched Dan's shoulder. "Let's discuss it over pizza!"

"I'll be right in. If it's okay, I think I need a moment alone."

Walter gave an understanding wink. "We'll save you half a slice."

The tree looked magnificent against the cloudless sky. Strolling toward it, Dan tried to envision a wooden structure in its branches, perhaps a cabin with a rope ladder and tire swing. Maybe even a balcony. But would such a thing detract from the tree's beauty? Or enhance it tenfold in the eyes of people the tree had brought together? Perhaps it would serve as testimony to lives being touched. Lives being chiseled. Walter had talked about form and function and purpose? But can a tree really have a purpose beyond earthly science?

Standing under the tree, Dan slid a hand across channels of bark and felt suddenly ashamed of such mystical contemplation. Turning toward the house, he pulled out his phone and opened e-mail. Several new messages had come through—*that's right!*—while they were walking the trail. He scanned the subject lines, opened only one message, and instantly dropped to his knees.

23

CHAPTER TWENTY-THREE

Like a chatty second grader, Robyn had talked all evening about her first day on the job. And Dan's cheeks ached from all the forced smiles and nods that masked his tension and fear. But at least he hadn't exploded, and he'd allowed Robyn time to unleash her enthusiasm. Now she, like Evan, slept soundly upstairs.

Dan sat behind the house, on cold concrete, twisting his sneakers in the grass. The sky was devoid of both moon and stars, its blackness offset only by the blinks of passing airplanes. He raised the hood of his sweatshirt, picked up his phone, and read the haunting e-mail: Danny...just got word...senior accountant for corporation north of beltway...call me before the search goes public...Dad

The Baltimore Beltway was far enough to decline the offer, blame the commute, endure a few biting remarks. Dan closed his phone and rubbed his temples, wondering if he should simply tell the whole sappy truth about Walter and chisels and family and home?

Then I can use my chisel to slice both wrists!

His stomach recoiled. He was an excellent accountant. And this position would pay a fine salary, even plug him into Russell's network.

I'll just tell her. I'll say, Robyn this opportunity is too good to—

The glass door opened. Bare feet skittered the concrete. Dan put his hood down, leaned back on one arm. "Evan, don't sit!" His tone was harsh. "Get back inside. I thought you were sleeping."

"I want a drink."

Dan stood. "Well then get in the kitchen."

Evan slipped back through the open door and scurried into the kitchen, his arms wrapped against the chilly night air. Dan followed, fists clenched, breathing shallow. He drew some water in a blue plastic cup. Evan drank slowly while his little hand gripped the counter. Nasally exhales filled the cup after every few swallows. Dan looked at the new, long-sleeved pajamas Robyn insisted Evan wear despite a forecasted low of only fifty-two. "You like the new PJ's?" The blue cup moved up and down, and Dan relaxed enough to smile. "Man, we've gotta teach you to chug." He took a knee.

Evan put the cup on the counter, and hugged Dan's neck. "I love you, Daddy."

Dan closed his eyes as his throat swelled. He'd never expressed love to his father; never. But what was to love? Favorite toys smashed for disrupting the evening news? Ears twisted for speaking out of turn? Hours of trembling upon soiled sheets, humming away the fury of stress and alcohol?

Dan pulled Evan closer, and lifted him. "I love you, too, buddy." He walked toward the stairs, convinced anew there was nothing to love about Russell Crawford.

Not behind closed doors, anyway.

Public appearances had been times for Dan to relish his father's smile and the soft, encouraging squeeze of his hands as he boasted about Dan's grades or the game-winning homers he was never there to see. The same hands that would later peel open five beers or throw a plate across the kitchen. Like that frosty evening in February, when a few drips of cocoa landed on his slacks. He smacked his wife's face; the last touch they'd ever share. The next day after school, Dan found her on the stairs in a climbing posture, a victim of severe asthma. Russell's mark still marred her face. The funeral parlor had masked the welt but Dan still saw it, peering in her coffin. She'd been the only person to ever kiss him, read to him, play with him, inspire him, and assure him that his life had value. His head all but melted on that cold winter day when he dropped like tossed laundry to the parlor floor.

Dan tucked Evan into bed before crossing the landing to his own bedroom, where he couldn't help but grin at Robyn's gaping mouth and heavy breathing. He brushed a finger across her forehead. She closed her mouth, rolled to one side, and pulled the covers tight. "I love you," he whispered.

Downstairs, he poured a cup of stale coffee, added hazelnut creamer, and sat on the recliner. A lamp set to low cast warmth across the room. Looking at the fireplace mantle, he fished his phone from a pocket, and thumbed a text: Dad…thanks but beltway a bit far…prefer something closer.

He placed his phone on an end table in exchange for coffee, wrapping his hands around the warm mug, and thinking of the chisel now tucked out of sight behind the family portrait. Then he opened the chair, closed his eyes, and willed his mind to relax…until his phone buzzed with a return from Russell: That's crap, Danny. You're just whipped!!!

24

CHAPTER TWENTY-FOUR

It was the most lumber Dan had ever seen at one time: banded two-by-fours, piles of plywood, and various stacks of who knows what. Were those roof shingles?

"Arrived this morning," Walter said, undoing a button near the top of his olive green coveralls.

Dan walked around the wood, running fingers over its grain and shaking his head at the quantity. "This must have cost a fortune." He lifted a sheet of plywood to peek underneath.

"Most mansions do," Walter said.

The plywood smacked together, blowing dust in Dan's eyes. He blinked it out. "I'll cover half. It's only right."

"Correction: You'll cover the heavy lifting and most of the labor. At my age, it's easier to throw money at a project than to throw out my back. Or aggravate this blasted arthritis." Walter pulled at the brim of his unassuming cap, and with tongue-in-cheek asked, "So where do we begin?" Then he laughed, motioning with his head. "You'll find the plans in that folder. I've been hashing them out all week."

Dan opened the folder. Inside, on the first of several pages, Walter had sketched a tree house with a pitched roof, two small dormers, windows with sills and flower boxes, and a fixed ladder coming down from the center of a wrap-around porch. "We can exercise our creative liberties as things progress," he heard Walter say. "But that gives us a vision; a good place to start."

"It's nicer than my three-bedroom," Dan said, looking up at Walter. "I can't believe you."

"Well, I hope you'll soon change your mind about that." Walter's moustache lifted, and their eyes locked.

Dan closed the folder. "Here," he said, placing it in Walter's hands. "You call the shots, I'll listen and learn." He bit off the tag on a new pair of leather gloves. "I have to protect my office hands."

"And your eyes, as well." Walter rooted through a Home Depot bag, and then tossed Dan a pair of sealed safety goggles, suitable for snorkeling.

Dan tore open the plastic, donned the protective lenses. "This is starting to feel like my middle school shop class."

Walter didn't respond. He stuck a thick brown pencil behind his right ear and rested wire-rimmed glasses low on his nose. His head tipped back as he opened the folder and flipped to the second page. For the next hour he instructed Dan in the proper use of tin snips, the name of every board on the lawn, and the proper way to separate parts onto risers. By the time the wood was organized, a gallon of iced tea and some freshly-baked cookies awaited them inside, courtesy of Margaret and Evan. Dan was glad for the break, and before he knew it they'd talked their way to lunch time. So Margaret whipped-up sandwiches and pulled open a new bag of pretzels. Near the end of the meal, the steady crush of gravel announced Robyn's arrived.

Iced tea in hand, everyone moved to the front porch. She stepped from the car, smiling at Evan as he ran to her, holding a plate of cookies. "Thanks, Ev!" She took the plate, and walked toward the porch. Her pony tail was pulled through an MCC cap. "Margaret, you've outdone yourself. Thank you so much."

"Oh it was nothing, honey," Margaret said. "And that little rascal did most of the mixing."

"That means me!" Evan tugged on the leg of Robyn's capris.

Everyone laughed, Walter loudest of all. Robyn's eyes sparkled when they met Dan's. "I thought you'd be a ball of dust by now."

Dan put his tea on a small wicker table. "Not yet…" He reached in a cargo pocket, strung his head with the owlish safety goggles. "But I am making a fashion statement."

"I should've brought my camera." She turned to Margaret. "Any chance you two can join us for dinner? Nothing fancy, just casual simple."

A knot of nerves cinched tight in Dan's chest. They had nothing to offer; scratched plates, a cheap dinette that barely sat four.

"We'd be delighted," Margaret said, making eyes at Walter.

"Then it's settled," Dan said with a snip, pushing the goggles back into his pocket. "Why don't you ladies work out the details while we get back to work?" He chugged his tea, put the empty glass in Margaret's waiting hand, and high-fived Evan. By the time he reached the makeshift lumber yard, he heard car doors closing. "What's next, Boss?" he asked toward Walter's approaching footsteps.

Robyn's car rumbled back down the lane, and Walter said flatly, "Pruning."

Dan walked the field for the sake of time. He'd spent the afternoon cutting branches and framing the tree house floor, all while enduring an incremental lecture about pruning and life. He had ninety minutes to get home, shower, and prep for the Bennings' arrival; the last thing he needed was a pudgy stranger meandering up the driveway, jotting notes on a clipboard.

Dan jogged onto his lawn, catching the man's eye, stopping him from proceeding to the front walk. The man flashed a smile and waved. Dan slowed, stepped onto the macadam. "Can I help you?"

"Well, I hope so, sir." The stranger extended a hand that Dan reluctantly shook. He wore a Ford Racing cap. His face was pale with flushed, full cheeks. A coral polo hung loose around his bulging midsection. "I run a landscaping business in McKinley. And I was just out today to see if I can interest folks in some discounted services we're offerin'. Just tryin' to get our name out there, you know."

"You look familiar to me," Dan said, ignoring the landscaping pitch.

"Well, it's been a few years since I played for the Phillies…" He burst into laughter that became a hacking cough. It ended with a sigh and one final chuckle.

Dan tried to grin. "That must be it."

"No, I don't believe we've ever met," chubby said. "Name's Butch Hake." He pulled a shoddy card from his pocket.

"Well, Mr. Hake, I appreciate the offer, but we're just not in the market for professional landscaping right now. I'll file your card away, though, and if…"

Butch Hake had turned his head, smiling and making little finger waves toward the house. Dan glanced right to see Evan plastered in a window. "Isn't he somethin'," Mr. Hake said, still wiggling fingers in Evan's direction. "Got one at home about his age. What's he; five or somethin'?"

"Four," Dan mumbled as Robyn showed up at the window, dressed for company.

Butch Hake's wave became more mature, as did his smile. He turned to Dan. "Now that is one fine-lookin' family you got there, Mr…?"

"Crawford, okay? Daniel Crawford."

Now walk away to wherever it is you came from.

Robyn patted Evan's shoulder in a let's-move-away-from-the-window kind of way. Then, lifting eyebrows at Dan, she touched the top of her wrist a few times.

Mr. Hake removed his cap and pulled a meaty forearm over his glistening buzz-cut. "They might call it fall, but it still gets hotter 'n blazes in September." He put the cap back on. "Well, I appreciate you takin' the card, Mr. Crawford. Now if I can just leave you this paper as well. It outlines what we do and so forth."

You're a landscaper; I know what you do! Go bug the neighbors.

Butch Hake pulled a green piece of paper from his clipboard. "That your folk's place way over there?" He nodded toward the tree.

"Now why would you ask me that?" Dan folded the paper, furrowed his brow.

"I'm sorry. Didn't mean to pry. I been coverin' this street for the past hour or so, noticed you workin' with that older gentleman. Least ways, I thought it was you. And then I saw you comin' home through the field."

Dan folded the paper a second time and creased it repeatedly. "He's a friend, not family. Now Mr. Hake I need to end this conversation; I'm running late as it is. Thanks again, and best of luck to you."

Butch Hake formed an unnerving grin. "You have a wonderful evening." Then he strolled down the drive, scuffing the heels of his grass-stained Nikes.

Dan walked quickly into the garage, trashed the green paper and business card, and kicked off his sneakers on a scrap of beige carpet. Inside the house, he ascended the stairs two at a time. Robyn was primping in their bathroom. He passed behind her, turned on the shower, and threw his tee shirt in the hamper.

"Sign your life away?" Her face stretched as she blinked in the mirror.

"Nah, it was just some landscaping guy. A real weirdo. I'm glad he's gone."

"You said that the last time we saw him."

Dan pulled off his socks. "What are you talking about? I thought he looked familiar at first but…"

Robyn shoved her make-up in a drawer. "I couldn't place him at first either, not without his glasses. Don't you remember that guy next to—"

"You've got to be kidding!" Dan's heart pounded. "That guy from Friendly's?"

"I'm pretty sure," she said with a giggle.

Dan turned off the shower and ran to the window in Evan's bedroom. He looked in the neighbor's empty driveway. He looked in every possible driveway.

Mr. Hake was nowhere in sight.

The recliner felt like a hug to Dan's tired body. Between an afternoon of tree house labor and an evening of desperate attempts to somehow aggrandize baked pasta served on decorative cardboard plates, he was physically and mentally fried. Robyn was upstairs, hustling Evan through his bedtime routine, an hour later than usual.

But the Bennings visit had been wonderful. Simply seeing Walter's stocky frame in a pair of plaid shorts and a creamy seersucker shirt made the invitation worthwhile. And even now, the entire house seemed enlivened by their presence, as if the walls had absorbed their smiles and heartwarming laughter. With Robyn and Walter in the mix, conversation had revolved around tales from McKinley Community College, like the time Walter became so engrossed in an outdoor lecture that he stumbled into the campus pond. Around dusk, Margaret insisted on helping to clean the kitchen while Walter went outside to pitch wiffle balls. Dan played center field and pretended to miss Evan's longest hits, using his announcer voice to declare them homeruns. And despite what he'd said to the stranger in his driveway, on this occasion Walter and Margaret indeed felt like family.

His eyes slowly blinked as he reached for the remote, clicked on the television, and flipped through channels. *Weather... Infomercial... Baseball!* He checked the score, the inning, watched a few pitches. But even to a fan like Dan, late night baseball could be quite a sedative. And he wanted to stay awake, to process the evening with Robyn, and thank her for initiating it. *News... Nature... Seinfeld...* What the heck? An Asian man in grungy jeans, pacing a carpeted stage, speaking with an Australian accent. A pastor? Dan sat up straight, befuddled. Pastors were old guys with oversized hair, waving Bibles behind ornate, wooden barricades. This guy looked cool enough to drive a BMW.

Robyn walked in, holding a glass of wine, and sat on the loveseat. "What'cha watching?"

"Nothing, just flipping channels." He looked at her, then nodded toward the set. "Did you ever hear an Asian man talk that way?"

"What, about God?" She took a long drink.

"No, I mean the accent. It's not the face I expect to see when I hear Aussi-speak, you know?"

"Well turn it up a little; Evan's zonked."

He did, and together they listened to the hip young pastor: "So he says to his mates, right there in Gethsemane, 'I am the vine, you are the branches.' Now think about that, Church. If He is the vine, God the father is the gardener. And God will deal with you, branches of Christ, just as any conscientious gardener tends his own vineyard." He was walking briskly, and almost shouting.

Robyn laughed, pulling her legs onto the loveseat. "You can change it; I'm lost, already."

"Hear the words of our Lord, mates," the pastor continued. "'He cuts off every branch in me that bears no fruit, while every branch that does bear fruit he prunes so that it will be even more fruitful.'"

"Honey, are you having a religious conversion?" Robyn giggled.

Dan looked her way, muted the television, and watched her drink. "No, it's just…" He turned off the set, joined her on the loveseat. "The stuff that guy was saying, about branches or whatever; it reminds me of something Walter was trying to tell me this afternoon." He looked away, lost in thought. "I'm just tired, I guess."

From the corner of his eye he saw Robyn take a long, last swallow. And as she stood to place the glass on a nearby table, he snuck a look at the curves in her silky pajamas, and felt a flutter in his chest, a warmth in his cheeks. She'd had wine, and her auburn hair, typically pulled back by now, was loose and flowing. They hadn't made love since before the separation. And even then, with daggers between them most nights, he could hardly call it making love. But there was something in the air tonight, perhaps the lingering energy of time spent with friends, or repressed passion slipping back into their struggling marriage.

Robyn sat again, closer this time. Dan looked in her eyes and tried to restrain himself.

"So you're a branch?" she said through a playful smile, pushing fingers through his hair.

"No… I mean, I don't really know." Dan's pulse quickened. "Walter was just talking about pruning, about cutting off branches for the overall… or was it long-term… health of the tree, or…" Robyn moaned an "um-hum" as her lips touched his neck, igniting 50,000 watts of get-up-and-go. Dan scooped his wife, carried her upstairs, and for the first time in months, locked the bedroom door.

25

CHAPTER TWENTY-FIVE

It was the first of October, and autumn winds rushed across the fields the way Dan used to hustle to meetings. Never, of course, had he done so wearing faded jeans and a shirt of loose flannel, or with a five-day push of black whiskers on his face. But today, perched inside a partially-finished tree house, such things seemed appropriate if not absolutely perfect.

"Sixty-four and an eighth!" he called, peering between the studs of a newly-framed wall. Below on the ground, Walter clenched the handsaw he insisted on using, and began the laborious, push-pull process. Dan listened for the shorter, quicker strokes that came near the end of the cut. Then he leaned down to receive the sawn board. They were building roof trusses, and hoped to be finished by late afternoon.

The tree house construction had been ongoing for almost two weeks. The floor was framed with two-by-six joists and sheeted with plywood, and though it rested snugly in the tree's massive branches, it was also, like a raised house deck, securely fastened to four wooden posts, anchored in concrete. The posts were Walter's idea to not only enhance safety but also minimize any damage to the tree. A wooden ladder was mounted to the edge of the floor, just in front of a door frame. And all of the two-by-four walls were erected but still in need of sheathing with either particle board or plywood;

Walter had yet to decide. The wrap-around porch and fancy windows had been scratched from the initial, ambitious plans, and yet even in its current state, the tree house looked remarkable. So much so that Dan found himself questioning whether anything, including his professional achievements, had ever filled him with such pride or instilled a greater sense of purpose.

Walter had agreed to the use of a power driver, but only to fasten the buckets of galvanized screws he favored over nails. Otherwise, it was hand tools only. Dan felt certain he'd added girth to his arms and probably shed a few pounds, although the latter was quite debatable; Margaret kept him well fed. She also provided Evan with a crash course in the proper care of mums (bee stings, too, unfortunately) and countless other autumn chores. And when the men weren't working, she delighted in pushing Evan on the sticker-new tire, suspended by a rope from the tree house floor.

Dan positioned the sawn board and secured it with a clamp. He fished screws from his shirt pocket and sunk them with the driver. Then he glanced down at Walter who was standing with his hands on his hips, just above an old leather tool belt. Sweat darkened his coveralls in the form of two crescents, low on his chest. And though he wasn't exactly smiling, his face held a look of satisfaction.

"Go ahead and make another one the same length, I guess," Dan said. "And we need to charge the battery in this driver."

"I need to charge my own battery!" Walter sorted through lumber. "Let's put up one more, then take a break." He pulled a board to his nose as if sighting a rifle. Then he clunked it down on top of two saw horses. "Not the straightest piece in the bunch, but we'll make— "

Rockler burst from his peaceful bed on the weedy hillside and ran toward the barn with a flurry of barks. He stayed left of the building, then entered the woods, where his barking mingled with the sound of scuffling leaves. "He's not the best deer hunter," Walter said. "But he'll run himself sick, trying to be."

Dan shook his head, searching for the battery charger. Rockler's barking subsided for only a few seconds. When it began again, he sounded closer, as if running toward them.

And then he shrieked.

Walter dropped the saw and jogged toward the woods. Dan climbed halfway down the ladder, and jumped to the ground. He caught up with Walter about fifty yards from the tree line, where they both stopped at the sight of Rockler, crossing the meadow in their direction, and clearly favoring his left, rear leg.

Grimacing, Walter took a knee as Rockler cowered near him, panting hard. "What in the blazes?" Walter's thick fingers caressed the dog, searching for signs of injury. "I don't see anything." Heavy, fast, crunching steps resounded from the nearby woods, fading rhythmically into the distance. Walter scratched Rockler's ears. "There goes your deer, boy." The dog gave no chase, not even a bark.

"Is everything okay?" Margaret called. Dan turned to see her walking toward them with Evan close behind, a glistening pouch of juice in his hand.

"Something's happened to Rockler." Walter said. "When he took off after a deer or something."

Rockler moved from Walter to Margaret, and his limping seemed more pronounced. His head hung low as she knelt, pulling him close. "Well for pity sake, Rock. You step in a hole? Should we get him to a vet, Walter?"

Walter stood with Dan's assistance. Then he stroked his moustache, and stared at the woods. "I suppose we'd better." He looked back at Margaret. "Take him to the house. You and Evan put a little ice on his leg." Margaret scooped up the dog. Rockler whimpered as they walked.

"You go along with Margaret," Dan told Evan. "Help her take care of Rockler's boo-boo." Then he turned back to Walter, who was staring at the trees. "Are you all right?"

"I've seen that mutt charge into the woods a hundred times." Walter looked at Dan. "Never once has it ended this way." He limped toward the trees, muttering something about blasted arthritis. Dan followed, unsure what else to do. "Where did he go in, Daniel?"

"Just past the barn." Dan pointed. "Right about there."

The men pushed through thick brush and into open timber. Although some of the plants had begun to turn brown, leaves still hung on most, allowing little visibility. But Walter and Dan walked on nonetheless, toward an undefined end, hearing only leaves underfoot and the occasional snaps of buried twigs. Dan lingered a few steps behind, allowing Walter to forge ahead despite the obvious pain in his legs. When they finally stopped, Walter drew a deep breath, exhaled audibly, and turned around. "I'm sorry, Daniel. I guess seeing my little buddy get hurt… Well, I suppose I felt the need to defend him or something. He probably just twisted his leg."

"I can't imagine why." Dan kicked a fallen branch from beneath the leaves, releasing an aroma of a moist decomposition.

Walter smiled. "Well, my knees have had enough. Let's cut straight through here." He tipped his head. "We'll come out close to the tree house. I'd better clean up a bit before heading to the veterinarian's office. No telling how long we'll be."

They picked their way through about thirty yards of forest. The underbrush seemed to thicken with every step. Dan's forearms were scratched, his jeans were snagged, and from the back of Walter's coveralls he'd flicked a couple ticks, inducing a mild paranoia of the parasitic dots.

"You can just see the house from here," Walter said. "This is the same path poor Rockler must've taken when…" His voice trailed. He held a hand behind him, motioning Dan to stop. "Do you smell that, Daniel?"

Dan drew a breath. "Cigarette smoke?"

They pushed ahead, into an area of thinner brush from which the tree house was easy to see. So, too, was a kicked-out circle of bare earth, positioned beside a scraggly pine and littered with cigarette butts; one still smoldering.

26

CHAPTER TWENTY-SIX

The teardrop tickled her nose, almost triggering a sneeze. But Robyn stopped it with the same finger she'd used to caress Evan's sleeping face, after working until nine every day this week. Turning to leave, she saw Dan in the doorway.

"I tried to keep him up," he whispered. "But he played so hard at the farm, and..."

Robyn wiped her face and fell into his hug. He kissed her hair and then left for the kitchen to make her some tea. She changed into flannel pajamas, and joined him downstairs. Sitting alone on the family room loveseat, she pulled up her feet and wished for Dan to rub them. But he was already making tea; she thought better of pushing for more.

"Sugar?" Dan called from the kitchen.

"A teaspoon."

He served her tea in a stainless steel cup, and then plopped, seemingly fatigued, into the recliner. "Need to vent?" he asked.

She sipped though a slot in the cup's plastic lid. "No playoff game tonight?" She winked.

"Pretty perceptive for such an exhausted lady." He stood again, crossed the room, and sat beside her on the loveseat. "The game was on this afternoon."

Robyn stared at her cup, fidgeting with its lid.

"The mugs are all in the dishwasher," Dan said.

"It's fine." She sipped again, looking at their portrait on the mantle.

"Seriously; what gives?"

"I feel like I'm breaking. I mean, the work is stressful, but not seeing my baby…" She clenched her teeth, blinking back tears.

"Hey…" He put a hand on her shoulder. "Homecoming's Saturday. Just three more days. You'll make it."

She looked briefly in his eyes, knowing he was right; she would indeed survive the impending swirl of insanity: the parade, the concert, the luncheons, and the barrage of reunions that all rested at least partially in her lap. Such was Homecoming; she'd been through it before. But as a younger woman; a newlywed with a husband who lived at the office. She'd never been through it as a mother. "You're right, I know. It's just, the more run down I become…" She looked up at nothing in particular. "Emotion's really getting the better of me."

Dan slid his arm fully around her as she moved her feet to the floor, allowing him to draw close. "If it makes you feel any better," he said. "Your long days have made it easier for us to spend time at Walter's. We've got the tree house almost finished, and Evan's having a blast. You should see him swing on that tire."

Robyn shot him a look. "I would *like* to see him, Dan. You're not helping." She watched his jaw take a crooked set, felt his arm slide away from her shoulders. He put his hands on his knees, and stood. "Dan, wait." She leaned forward, touched his lower back. "You didn't deserve that." Her throat tightened, a tear slipped onto her cheek. "See… This is what I mean…" She cried as he walked away.

Minutes later, her composure mildly intact, she listened to Dan preparing for bed. He'd done so much to support her new job, and to become a better father and husband. When the water turned on, drawn by the shower, she thought about sneaking upstairs, ditching her PJ's, and surprising him behind the wet curtain. But she felt planted in the loveseat, able only to suck tea from the slotted lid of a corny cup, attempting to wrestle her emotions into some sort of plausible explanation.

Why did I snap at him like that? I've been snapping at work, too. Do I really belong in this job? I'm an emotional wreck, and for what? I've been through stressful times at MCC before, but I haven't felt this hormonal since….since…

She sat up straight, her skin nearly crawling with tingly adrenaline.

The blindfold was Evan's idea. He pulled his mother's hand, leading her across the farmhouse lawn. Walter, Margaret, and Dan followed, watching her take slight, tentative steps, as if nearing the edge of the world.

"Okay… Stop!" Evan said.

Dan untied the paisley bandana. Her head tilted up, her hands covered her mouth. "Told you I'd have a mansion in the trees, someday," he whispered in her ear.

"It's awesome! I mean… Holy cow!"

"Come on, Mom!" Evan was halfway up the ladder.

Robyn turned to Walter and Margaret. "You guys are amazing." She took Dan's hand. "He helped to build this?" She smiled big in Dan's direction.

"You bet'cher bippy," Walter said.

"Mom! Get up here!" Evan's head emerged from a tree house window.

Dan watched his wife climb the ladder and crawl through the four-foot door. Soft voices echoed in the tree house, and to Dan it might as well have been glowing.

Walter had selected plywood walls, now painted with three coats of forest green. The trim around the door and windows, as well as the entire soffit, was antique white. And the roof, which did, in the end, include the two small dormers from Walter's original plans, was covered with dark brown shingles. It was the finest tree house Dan had ever seen. And Walter had said the same.

"You know, for years I worked in a space about that size," Dan said. "But the walls were made of metal and fabric." He looked under the tree house, at the muscular arms of the aging white oak, holding up his family.

"Will you be joining us for supper, Daniel?" It was Margaret's voice.

Dan turned to face her. "Well, maybe just me. Robyn wants to take Evan for a new pair of sneakers for those feet that won't stop growing. And it seems to me she promised a Happy Meal."

"Well that's a promise that ought to never be broken." Margaret smiled, saluting the sun as it inched from behind a monstrous, white cloud.

"Chicken it is, then," Walter said. "And Daniel's on the grill."

"Living dangerously today, old friend?"

Walter patted his arm. "Hardly. And watch who you're calling old." He walked toward the house. Rockler, who had been lying beneath the tree house, pushed to all fours and walked gingerly behind.

"Sure glad it was only bruising," Dan said, watching the gimpy dog.

"Oh, me too." Margaret rolled her eyes and pushed her hands in the pockets of her acid-washed jeans. "I just can't for the life of me figure out how that crazy mutt bruised his backside chasing a deer." Dan nodded, looked away. Was she not informed about the smoking hunter that might have punted poor Rockler?

He diagonally folded the bandana in his hands, and then tied it, pirate style, over the top of his head. "Aarghh!" Evan's head shot through the window, squealing with delight as Dan, one eye pinched tight, trudged to the ladder and started up.

27

CHAPTER TWENTY-SEVEN

"Keep your head down, Crawford!" Russell grabbed another golf ball and placed it on a mat of artificial turf. As if controlled by gears, he methodically pulled back his wedge. In a flash, metal scuffed turf. "That's more like it." The ball poked the practice green, about two feet from the pin. "Top that, Danny Boy."

Dan was behind his father, leaning against a support beam, silently bemoaning the fact that no other golfers were present at the Willow Hill Driving Range. So much for Russell's public persona. "Dad, I didn't come here to compete, okay?"

"C'mon, humor me. Put a ball inside of mine, and dinner's on me."

"It's already on you." Dan slipped a wedge from his bag. From a wire basket, he picked up a ball, and placed it on the mat. He heard Russell's lighter, followed by the sound of a cigar being stoked. The smell of singed tobacco reached him as he lined up his body. *Nice and easy. Don't kill it.* He wagged his rear, adjusted his grip. The club rose and fell, swiping beneath the ball, lifting it high but a shade to the right. It landed on the fringe. He pulled on his shirt collar, drew a deep breath.

"Not bad," Russell said. "You need to get your unemployed butt out here more often, though." He laid his cigar on a pad of concrete, near a no-smoking sign, and stepped to another mat. "Pass that bucket down here. I like the look of this tee." He gripped a driver this time, and launched ball after ball beyond the three-hundred-yard marker. Dan, on a good day, could barely reach two.

An hour later, they sat together at a small table in a Harrisburg bistro; an out-of-the-way place that served fifteen-dollar martinis and fancy plates of nothing for twice that amount. The entire place smelled of aging leather and expensive cologne. Dan couldn't decide if it was romantic or mobster or both. Well-dressed people talked in dim lighting. In large stone pots, tropical greenery swayed beneath patina fans. The walls were papered with burgundy stripes and trimmed in cordovan-stained oak. And a black-and-white print of some major urban skyline hung above every table. Theirs was Seattle.

Why can't he live there; three thousand miles away?

"Have a scotch," Russell said. It wasn't a question. Minutes later, the waitress brought two on-the-rocks, and Dan couldn't stop himself from thinking of Kevin Clark, or envisioning his fatal plunge.

"So you've found nothing?" Russell said.

"No." Dan's first sip of scotch felt like fire in his chest. He tried to say more, but nothing came out.

The waitress returned, flipping a page of her notepad. "Are we ready to order?"

"Shaved Mignon Panini," Russell said. "You want the same, Danny?"

Lips pursed, the waitress looked at Dan.

She hates him already.

"I'll go with the Balsamic Chicken Salad," Dan said. The waitress took their menus and fled to the kitchen.

"I just don't get it. You've got the CPA and the experience. Sure, you're a hacker on the fairways, but who can hold that against you?" Russell cackled, finished his scotch like it was Kool-Aid. "Seriously, what gives?"

"Nothing gives, Dad. I'm not going to jump at just anything. I have severance coming in, and ... "

And we went through this twice at the driving range. Just give it a rest!

"That job I emailed you, north of the beltway. It was a great opportunity."

"It was also a lot of time on the road."

"That's crap, and—" Russell smiled at a passing waitress. "Excuse me, miss. Another on-the-rocks." Ice rattled in his empty glass. The waitress nodded before turning away, and Russell faced his son again. His forehead crimped, his jaw pushed sideways. "That's a load and you know it."

His pulse drumming in his ears, Dan squeezed his glass and looked up at Seattle. "I'd like to be a better family man, spend some more time at home," he told the Space Needle.

Russell's drink arrived. He pushed a thank you through gritted teeth. The waitress turned to Dan. "Anything for you, sir?" Dan looked from Seattle to her, his eyes stopping nowhere in between. "Maybe an ice water." She walked away.

"Better family man than who? Me?"

Dan looked at the hardwood floor. "No, I'm talking about me. This isn't about you, Dad. I'd like to do a better job...." The waitress was approaching. "Thank you," Dan said as she delivered a tall glass, topped with lemon. He drank some water, giving her time to walk away. His mouth turned pasty, so he drank again...then again...and finally looked at his father.

"Well just start by being a man, Danny." Russell gulped scotch, rapped his glass on the table, and opened a hand. "Provide a better life, for cryin' out loud. What do you think I was doing all those years?"

Dan's head dropped. His jaw clamped tight. *You were shouting! Beating my mother! Beating me! Breaking things!* He shifted in his seat. "Providing," he said, head still down, feeling like a lousy ventriloquist.

"You're damn right, I was!" Russell shook his empty glass, breathing audibly through the moments of silence that followed; moments that felt like an eternity. "Men provide, Danny. Work comes first; that's just the way it is. I mean, these pans..." He leaned forward, his hushed words riding an aroma of whisky and cigars. "These pansies nowadays, turning down promotions to spend more time at home, they don't have a clue. All this modern day, liberal crap. Trying to tame men, make 'em all relational." He shook his head, finished Dan's scotch. "And then you've got the guys staying home all day, doing the work of a woman, letting their wives make the money. I mean, what's this world coming to when a man cleans house and wipes butts all day?"

Dan looked up enough to see his father's pompous expression, and watched his fingers lace behind his head. "Be a man. Tell your head hunters to expand their search, and get back in the game."

"Shaved Mignon Panini." The waitress put a plate in front of Russell.

"Outstanding," he said, lowering his hands, straightening his place settings. His eyes appeared glassy, unfocused.

"And Balsamic Chicken Salad."

Dan moved his glass to make room for the meal, which was enough for a rabbit at best. "Thank you. This looks delicious," he lied.

"Can I get you gentlemen anything else?" It was a token question; she was tense, going through the motions. Russell ordered a draft, applying the brakes. The waitress walked away.

Dan forced in a bite of the spiciest Balsamic he'd ever tasted. Then he swallowed twice, and said, "Don't you think a man needs to provide more than money?" The bite of spicy chicken almost returned to his plate.

Russell finished chewing, sucked his top teeth. "I don't need this." His head began shaking. "I swear to you, Danny; I do not need this—"

"Dad, I just think that a man should be responsible for more than—"

"You're gonna lecture me about being a man!"

"I'm just saying—"

"What!" Russell's arms opened, his palms raised. "C'mon, what! You know more than your old man, now?" The waitress stepped cautiously forward, placed a frothy mug on the table. Her face was timid, she'd clearly overheard. Who hadn't?

Russell wiped his mouth, threw his napkin on the table, and stood. He towered over the waitress; over everything, it seemed. "This *man* will take care of the bill," he said, his eyes fixed on Dan. "He can put it on his severance." His loafers hammered the wooden floor, and he never looked back.

Dan apologized to the waitress, then gazed at Seattle.

Happy Birthday to me.

"I just can't get over how marvelous the tree looks from here," Walter said for the third time, running out of things to talk about. At one end of the table, Robyn was playing a game of Trouble with Margaret and Evan. The dice bubble popped incessantly against the clashing sounds of big band music, pumping from the family room television. Robyn had hoped Walter's favorite tunes might lessen the awkwardness; or serve as spirited filler for the lengthening gaps of tension-filled silence. Where in the world was Dan?

On the other end of the table, a large white box held a chocolate cake that read Happy 33rd! in green icing. If Dan ever arrived, they intended to hide behind furniture and yell out, Surprise! Evan had rehearsed the process countless times to determine the best place for everyone. Then they would order pizzas, open presents, eat cake and ice cream, and…

Where is he!

"The birthday boy must be having quite a round of golf," Walter said.

Robyn faked a smile. "Well, it was supposed to be only the driving range, but it's hard to know with those two." She swallowed a lump. "I'm so sorry. You've been here for over an hour now."

A warm hand squeezed her forearm. "It's no trouble at all," Margaret said. "Gives me another chance to beat this little whipper-snapper."

"What's that?" Evan asked. Margaret laughed, popping the dice.

"I'll try his cell again." Robyn walked to the hallway, dialed Dan, and plugged her open ear with a finger. No answer; and she'd already left a message. She punched in a text: Where R U? Please call. A sudden cheer erupted from the kitchen. She rushed to the table. "Is he here?"

"No," Walter said, pouring another cup of raspberry ginger ale. "Just another win for the whipper-snapper." He crunched a handful of party mix.

"What's a whipper-snap?" Evan said loudly.

The Bennings roared with laughter. Robyn shook her head and tried to smile, until her phone buzzed with a text: running very late.

Her gut became a rising knot. *He's going to miss his own surprise party, ensnared by Russell's macho banter: Let 'em wait, Danny Boy! Have one more!* She tapped the phone on her chin.

"What's the matter, dear?" Margaret said.

Robyn flashed a half smile, blinking her eyes against emerging tears. "Nothing. Let's go ahead and order the pizza."

"Back in Black" slipped slowly in the dash of Dan's speeding BMW. His beloved car was about to come off lease. At the moment, he'd just as soon turn it into a twisted hunk of metal and guts. Adrenaline gushed through his veins as AC/DC screamed their heavy metal classics, and the car hit ninety. An air horn blasted from a tractor trailer he'd deliberately cut off, heading for the Cameron Street exit, just three blocks from Bell-Knarr.

I'll call my head hunter. Expand the search. Get back in the game.

The lot was nearly empty as he pulled into Jason Middaur's private spot, almost hoping for a fight. His anger was a bonfire in search of dry grass, anything to ravage. He stared at the building, pulling fingers through his hair, when an Audi pulled curbside, near the main entrance. Jonathan Clauser stepped out of the vehicle, popped the trunk, slung a briefcase over his brown leather parka, and keyed into the building. Releasing bated breath, Dan lifted a lager from between his legs, and took a long swig. It was warm, like a gulp of stale memories. He lowered the window, and slammed down the bottle, spraying shards of glass in every direction.

Park on that, back-stabbers!

He cranked the music, louder than before, and drove feverishly away to the sound of "Hell's Bells."

"You're sure there's nothing else we can do?" Margaret asked.

"No, we'll be fine," Robyn said. "Unfortunately, this isn't the first time." She hugged them both. "Thanks for coming."

"Oh, you're quite welcome." Margaret looked toward the family room. "Goodbye, Ev!"

He didn't answer.

"I wish he'd listen to us like he does Sir Topham Hatt," Robyn said. No one laughed.

"Give Daniel our gift along with our regrets for missing him," Walter said.

She looked in his troubled eyes. "More like he missed you."

And with that the Bennings left. Robyn remained at the door until their car was backed safely from the drive. Then she turned off the lights, and cried in the darkened foyer.

His pressed khakis and dark blue rugby did little to repel the moist chill of night. Stiff gusts had exposed his forehead. His arms were crossed, his teeth chattered, and five beers lay like stones in his gut. Orange streetlights shone eerily over the bridge as beneath it black currents silently flowed, reflecting lights from the city in which Dan once thrived.

Down river stood the shadowy silhouette of Metro Bank Park, where every summer young spotlight players pursued baseball dreams. Daniel Crawford had once been a spotlight player, but in a different sort of game; a game in which he'd played a hard-charging executive in pursuit of corporate elitism. Back then he was aware of what mattered in life. Back then he'd truly been a man … almost.

His hands took hold of a cold steel railing that topped the cement wall between him and the river. A rush of wind invaded his ribs. An insanely loud motorcycle ripped past behind him. Was this the spot? Had Kevin climbed this wall, ended life here? Dan leaned forward and imagined the scene: flailing arms, the nauseating smack of a body hitting water, repulsed gasps by stunned onlookers. He extended his toes, leaned farther still, and looked directly down at the glossy current. Amid the twinkle of lights, he saw his own reflection … or was it merely a shadow?

He straightened once more, and stepped back to the sidewalk, shivering and sobering to a parade of haunting memories. It was time to go home.

28

CHAPTER TWENTY-EIGHT

Early Monday morning, and Robyn was alone in her bed. She silenced the alarm, made her way to the shower. Hot water awakened her senses as she quickly pulled a razor up and down each leg. Pants season; no need to be perfect. Her abdomen cramped. Was it starting? Was it finally starting? The cramping subsided.

Showered and dressed, she discovered Dan asleep on the recliner. And despite an initial wave of anger, she was thankful to see him safely home. His slacks were dirty, his hair tousled, and his birthday gift from the Bennings lay open on the floor: a gift card to Dick's Sporting Goods and a hardcover copy of "Tuesdays with Morrie."

In the kitchen, Robyn discovered the cake still untouched in its box. She shook her head, opened the fridge, and rooted for a protein shake. Closing the door, she almost screamed as Evan unexpectedly slide-stepped past her, lifting his homemade birthday card. "Is Daddy home yet?"

"Yes, but he's sleeping on the chair."

Her eyes dampened at the sight of his card: a crayon rendering of the tree house, with Dan dressed like a pirate. A quotation bubble as big as the tree came out of a window to read: Happy Birthday, Daddy! Evan's name was scrawled at the bottom, and only the "e" was lowercase. "Let's get you some breakfast." She walked close and hugged him, hoping no tears would fall.

While Evan sat at the table picking sprinkles from his Pop Tart, Robyn returned to the recliner. "Dan?" She pushed his arm. "Dan," she said louder. He squirmed, rubbed his eyes, and partially opened one of them. She gave him no chance to speak. "I'm leaving for work. Just needed to know you were up. Ev's at the table eating breakfast."

Dan closed the chair, put his elbows on his knees. His head dropped to his palms. "About last night..." He stopped to clear his throat.

"We'll talk about it later. You can count on it." She marched to the kitchen, slung a brief case over her shoulder, kissed Evan's cheek, and walked out the door.

Dan's head was still in his hands when he heard the rapid approach and joyous (very loud!) exclamation: "Happy Birthday, Daddy!" He looked sideways at Evan, with the best smile his splitting headache would allow. Sitting up straight, he took the paper card and feigned amazement, though part of him wanted to rip it to shreds. *Forget that tree house. Get back in the game!* Dan belched and grimaced at the taste of undigested beer. Evan hugged his arm and returned, shoulders slumping, to his sugary breakfast.

"I'm gonna grab a shower!" Dan called toward the kitchen.

After twenty minutes in scalding water and three tablets of Ibuprofen, Dan felt semi-human again. He found Evan in the family room, still in pajamas, watching PBS Kids. "You need a drink?" he asked.

Do I need a drink?

Evan nodded and Dan complied, trying not to stare at the uneaten birthday cake. But its stark white box seemed almost hypnotic, stimulating thoughts of laughter, conversation, mounting concern, and sad farewells. He longed briefly for a do-over, a second chance to relish the wholesome party. But he likewise saw value in his disconcerting night, as if it had been some kind of needed awakening, a jolt of reality. Evan's cup overflowed, snapping Dan back to the moment.

He cleaned the mess, delivered the juice, poured himself coffee, and sat at the kitchen table. Remarks from Russell stampeded his mind while memories of Walter seemed to hover in his chest. He sucked in a mouthful of hot black water, and looked where he always had—across two fields, toward the top of a grassy hill. The sky resembled a dirty elephant. And beneath it, the tree's leaves were now a deep shade of blood. A little wooden house was hidden behind them. And past it all, Dan knew, was a man wearing coveralls, his white moustache littered with sawdust. But was he really a man? Dan's face felt flushed, and his foot began to tap. Walter had certainly made money, but look what he'd done with it: a run-down little farm with an endless to-do list.

"Dad?"

"What!"

He heard the sound of little feet, retreating upstairs.

He hadn't held the chisel since showing it to Robyn. And now, with his palm wrapped around its smooth wooden handle, he debated whether to return it to the mantle or walk outside and heave it. Evan called from the kitchen.

"What now?" Dan said.

"Can you sharpen the brown?"

Dan returned the chisel, walked to the kitchen, and twisted Evan's crayon in a plastic sharpener, finding the process surprisingly therapeutic. "What are you coloring?"

Evan slid a book in Dan's direction. An ice blue snowman and half-colored mouse were playing checkers by a fire. Dan shook his head, dismissing the absurdity. "Be sure to stay in the lines," he said, handing over the now needle-sharp brown. The crayon's tip crumbled as soon as it touched paper. And finally, the garage door rumbled open.

Dan backed against a counter and perused the morning's paper, hoping to appear coy. A minute passed before Robyn entered. She dropped bags of work-related items, bracing herself for Evan's charge, after which they hugged as if dancing. She slipped off her coat, looked briefly at Dan. "I see you've cleaned house."

"Yeah, well, it was long overdue." He scanned some more headlines.

"I smell Pine-Sol but no dinner." Robyn walked past him to the closet, hung up her coat. "What's up?"

"I thought we'd go out. Friday's sound good?"

"YES!" Evan's arms shot up like he'd won Olympic gold.

Robyn drew a deep breath, looking at the floor. "Well, I guess I'd better change." She climbed the stairs.

"I'll be right back," Dan told Evan, crossing the kitchen. "Try the bathroom."

The bedroom was locked, so Dan knocked lightly. He heard drawers being forcefully handled. "What?" Robyn asked as the door swung open. Her suit had been replaced by faded jeans and a rusty brown sweater, and her hair was pulled back. She turned away before he could answer, walking back in the room and stopping near a window, head down and hands on her hips.

"I just want to know what's wrong. If you don't feel like going out, we can just… I don't know, make eggs or something."

Her head shook as she turned to face him. "Don't patronize me, Dan."

"And just how am I doing—"

"Last night at this time I was holding together a house full of people, waiting to surprise you with a birthday party. And I'm not going to—"

"It was Walter and Margaret!"

"That's not the point!" She stormed to the closet, pulled out her sneakers. "You had to have known we were up to something. And you still ditched us for your dad." She sat on the bed, pulled on her shoes. Dan sat beside her, rubbing her back until she stood, turned, and glared down at him. "And don't even tell me you weren't drinking! And driving, for heaven's sake!" She looked at the ceiling and then again at Dan. "You stunk like a bar room floor this morning."

Dan gripped the bedspread, trying to swallow his escalating rage. "Can't this wait?"

Robyn looked him in the eye. "Until when; after dinner? Oh, big surprise: We're going to Friday's, and you just happened to clean house this afternoon!" She drew a few huffy breaths as her eyes narrowed. "I know exactly what you're—"

"You know what! What do you think you know, Robyn?" Dan stood, watched his wife flinch and back away. Her determined expression melted to fear as he indulged the power swelling in his chest. Clenching his fists, he took one step forward. "You have no idea how hard it was to leave everything that mattered to me! To go from a life of purpose to one of cooking and cleaning and playing preschool!" He watched tears gather and spill from her eyes. "So what if I took a night to let loose!"

Robyn wiped her eyes. "I was so proud of you. I thought things were going well."

Dan smashed his tongue between his molars, closed his eyes, and realized what he'd said: "…to leave everything that mattered." He hadn't meant it; not that way. Yet here he stood, overtaken by pride and pain and unrelenting anger. He opened his eyes, intending to apologize. "Think again," he said instead, leaving the room.

Evan was lying on the bottom step, biting his thumb. Dan stepped over him without a word, and for the second night in a row, entered the windy, cold darkness.

The faster Dan walked, the warmer he felt, until the sweating began. October wind hit his face like icy needles. His ears and cheeks burned, and his eyes watered. He was angry but much more coherent than last night, his blood now laced with only caffeine. And after traversing most of Fieldcrest Acres, wisdom prevailed.

I'll sneak in the garage, sit in the car, listen to music. At least, get a coat.

He turned around, backtracking past dozens of houses that were garishly adorned for Halloween. The wind now pushed him from behind, and though easier to withstand, Dan curiously desired its harsh strikes to the face. His rage had splintered in the cold night air, and now wrapped in his tightened gut and folded arms was but a soggy lump of regret. With two blocks remaining, he decided to jog. His sneakers scuffed with rapid cadence as his breathing increased. And then headlights approached, set to high beam. Dan squinted as they passed.

Robyn's Toyota!

He ran toward home. A neighbor's dog erupted indoors, its claws clacking on a window. And like the desperate man he'd become, Dan ran even harder with his driveway in view. By the time he reached it, his heart could keep time for a speed metal band. Drops of sweat had gathered in his eyebrows. With a shaky finger, he pushed the keypad to enter the garage. Then, pressing his car as if about to be cuffed, he gasped for more air than his lungs could ingest.

She had no time to pack. They've only gone somewhere to eat. Or...

"Please, God." His words blew forth in a gusty exhale. "Please, not again."

29

CHAPTER TWENTY-NINE

He'd placed the note on her pillow. She'd read it nine times.

Dear Robyn,

I'm writing words I should've spoken. I only hope you've returned to find them. I can't bear the thought of losing you again.

I'm very sorry for missing the birthday party. It was a loving gesture, and I know it meant the world to Evan. But I'm even sorrier for the way I treated you this evening. Despite what I said in anger, you and Evan are what matter most to me. I'm hurting inside and confused by many things. I suppose that's no secret. Please forgive me, and please stay proud of me.

I know this sounds crazy as cold as it's gotten, but I'm going to sleep in the tree house tonight. Walter doesn't know, so please don't tell him. I need some time to think. And I feel like a part of my heart is in that tree house. The part I most need to find.

Mrs. Martin will watch Evan tomorrow until I get home. It's already arranged. She'll be there by 8:30.

I love you,

Dan

She sat up in bed, placed the letter on her nightstand, and went to check on Evan. Finding him asleep, she caressed his cheek. *I can't believe he's*

turning five this winter, starting school in August. She lowered her head, drew
in her lips. "I think you should get ice cream," he'd said after dinner. "To
cheer you up from Daddy's mean words." She'd fallen instantly to pieces,
her face shaking behind red paper napkins. Minutes later, they ordered
vanilla, and she discovered he was absolutely right: Ice cream did help.

Robyn returned to her bedroom, sat in a chair near the window, and lit a
pedestal lamp. Beside her on the floor, a stack of alumni newsletters awaited
review. But across the room, a folded blue paper called out from her nightstand. She'd always been a sucker for Dan's written words, like the old love
letters still stashed in her sock drawer.

But I won't play the fool; not this time.

She turned off the lamp, crawled back into bed, and by the soft glow of a
nearby nightlight, read the note a tenth time. And once again her body tin-
gled with irrational conviction; a conviction that seemed to congeal with
each reading, as if Dan's words came from somewhere pure and tender
and…untouched by Russell?

Don't be a fool.

She pictured Dan in the tree house, stuffed inside a youth-sized sleeping
bag that hadn't been used since the weekend his fishing hook snagged Russell's cardigan. Dan's nose bled for twenty minutes, and so ended scouting.
She fluffed her pillows and laid flat on her back as words scrolled though her
mind like the Times Square marquis: *Please forgive me… Please stay proud of
me… I'm hurting inside and confused by many things.*

"I know, baby," she whispered, sliding a hand to her stomach.

"I know."

Dan's eyes opened to the sound of climbing footsteps. Leaf-filtered day-
light permeated the tree house as he rolled sideways, squinting toward the
doorway. Pudgy fingers appeared first, gripping a tall Thermos that clunked
on the floor.

Walter's cheeks were red, his hair disheveled, and his coveralls tan. His
mustache squirmed from side to side above shifting lips. "Hope you don't
mind a wake-up call." He maneuvered to sit with his back to a wall, pushed
his hair sideways, and gave his mustache three strokes. "I'll be running the

mower directly. Thought I'd wake you with coffee rather than the sound of that confounded machine." He unscrewed the Thermos, poured coffee in its red plastic lid. Steam rose high in the crisp morning air.

Dan rolled to his back as the wind blew, sudden and stiff, causing the tree house to sway. Leaves rustled from every direction. A few clicked and scratched on the roof, and one flew in the window. "They'll be falling in droves this week," Walter said.

Dan pulled an arm from his sleeping bag to rub his tired face. "I feel like I fell off a very tall building."

Walter chuckled. "Well, I didn't know we needed to build beds."

Every joint in Dan's body ached as he sat. He fussed with his hair, draping it over his forehead. Cold morning air pushed through his sleep-warmed sweat suit as he yawned, stretched, and cracked his back with a sharp left twist. Then he lifted the lid for a sip of hot coffee. "How did you know I was up here?"

Walter's mustache scrunched, his head dropped, and his eyebrows looked like sloppy handwriting.

"Robyn called," Dan said. He took a longer drink. "I specifically told her not to."

"She was concerned. Although she did ask that I wait until morning."

Dan huffed and reached for the back pack he'd thrown in a corner. He took out his phone, checked the time. "I haven't slept this late in years." The tree house swayed again. "Hard to believe the tree actually moves."

"If you can't bend, you're going to break." Walter unscrewed the Thermos, topped off Dan's cup.

"Don't you want any?"

"I've had plenty. Been fussing with the mower for two hours. Which equates to drinking coffee and staring at it, mostly."

Then buy a new one. You've got the money.

Rockler barked twice in the distance, and Dan's stomach answered with a growl of its own. He put down his coffee, took an oatmeal cream pie from his backpack, and ripped off the wrapper. Then his head snapped toward Walter.

"Wait, she called you?" He pumped his fist, chomped half the pie. "She called you!" His exuberant words pushed through sugary mush. He swallowed the bite, chased it with coffee. "That means she read my letter. That they came home." He stuffed in more pie, and chewed like a second-grader.

Walter stared at him without speaking. Then he adjusted his seat, straightening his leg like it was made of glass.

"That knee bothering you again?"

"Oh, once this cold weather sets in, everything hurts. Old bones, is all."

Dan nodded, smiling. "Thanks for the coffee."

"You're quite welcome, Daniel. Just remember to invite your old friend to the next camp out." He cocked his head. "And you can bet'cher bippy I'll invest in an air mattress."

Dan laughed, swallowed more coffee, and looked outside. The leaves were still rustling, they rarely stopped. And with a wisp of wood smoke, the air smelled wholesome and earthy. He looked back at Walter's white hair, rising and falling in the fluctuating breeze.

"I also want to thank you for the book," Dan said. "Tuesdays with Morrie."

Walter looked him in the eye. "You're welcome."

Dan reached for the Thermos and poured what was left. "So why did you pick that one?"

Walter shifted his body. "Well, I found myself touched by it." He stroked his mustache. "And I suppose I see a bit of us in the story."

Dan almost spilled his coffee. "Don't even tell me—"

"I'm not dying!" Walter said. "At least I'm not planning to. I just meant our relationship. An older man...a younger man. Two views on life." A hush fell over the tree house as the wind momentarily settled, and the coffee was warm, at best.

"I suppose I owe you an explanation," Dan said. He put down his cup, flexed his fingers. "My dad called on Saturday night," he continued. "Wanted to see me on my birthday. We were only intending to drive a few balls, grab a quick bite. Anyway, I knew Robyn had something in the works. And I was going to be home in plenty of time but..." He drew a deep breath, took a quick glance at Walter. "There's still a lot I haven't told you. About me...about my dad." He looked out the door, where crimson leaves waved like little flags.

"I'm here when you're ready," Walter said. "And you know the code: what's said in a tree house stays in a tree house." Dan forced himself to share in a sentimental smile. "Your secrets are safe with me," Walter added.

Dan's thumb nail picked at the zipper of his back pack, and emotion writhed like slugs in his stomach. Words never spoken took hold of his tongue, formed on his lips. "My father's mean... abusive, really." He almost trembled. "He's a hot shot CEO in Baltimore. Hard as nails. Made millions, though. Lives in a gated community, buys his way in or out of anything."

Dan's face burned. He felt cemented in place.

"And you were following in his footsteps?" Walter asked.

"I was. Or I am. I don't know, anymore." No longer cold, Dan rolled up his sleeping bag, tighter than necessary. "I didn't have much of a choice."

"We all have—"

"No, Walter. We don't all have choices." He shoved the bag in a corner, then perched on his knees and stared at the floor, his chest too tight to breathe. "With my dad, you either grind your way up the corporate ladder or get kicked to the curb."

He heard movement, felt a hand on his back. "I'm sorry," Walter said.

"And he drinks." Dan's throat constricted. "He got drunk on Saturday. Cut me down for being unemployed. Said a lot of things that were hard to hear. Too hard, I guess. So... I got drunk, too." Dan swallowed hard as Walter's hand squeezed gently on his shoulder. "I stood on that bridge, Walter." His words became stoic, as if drifting on the slow black current he now pictured in his mind. "I looked down at the water Kevin died in, and I became so riddled with questions, so overcome by memories. I kept wondering... Why? Over and over and over. Why, Walter?"

Huffs of despair wrenched forth from Dan's chest as his face dropped into his hands. Walter tried to pull him close but Dan broke free and stuck his head out a window, where the little red flags seemed now to be clapping. He sucked the cold air, felt it lifting his bangs and drying his eyes. Then he pulled in his head.

Walter was kneeling with his hands on his thighs, and slowly rocking. His eyes were bloodshot and moist. His temples swelled as his jaw clenched tight. Dan moved closer, put a hand on Walter's shoulder, and looked at his troubled expression. "I've had enough of this wooden floor," he said. Both men managed to smile.

"Well then help me up." Walter pushed on Dan's shoulders, crouching beneath the roof trusses. "I'll be right back," he said, moving toward the ladder.

Alone in the tree house, Dan finished packing. A few minutes later, Walter returned with two five-gallon buckets, nested together. He pushed them through the door, and said, "Just turn these over, they make great seats." Dan separated the buckets as Walter climbed in. Then they both sat on one, staring at each other or gazing out the windows until another leaf came flipping in like a red butterfly. Dan picked it up, studied its veins. The house swayed again as the smell of smoke increased.

"I can't believe I just confided in you." Dan stared at the leaf in his fingers. "And then cried like a baby." He shook his head. "It's all pretty embarrassing."

"Pain has to escape a man. It's like poison. There's no shame in releasing it. Whoever said men don't cry is the grandest of fools."

"Well, my dad would sure say it." Dan twirled the leaf by its stem. "You know, this stuff I'm telling you… You've got to promise me…" He dropped his head, stroked his cheeks.

"I won't tell a soul. We all need a safe place to talk about life."

"I mean, Robyn doesn't even know some of this." He looked back at Walter, who was crossing his legs. They sat in silence for a minute, looking everywhere but at each other.

"What makes a man?" Dan finally asked. "In your opinion. I'd like to know."

Walter frisked his mustache, lecture style. "I believe a man is wholesome." He spoke slowly, chose carefully. "A man is strong and dependable. He invests his life in things that matter. He also stays humble; recognizes his small place in this world." He uncrossed his legs, his eyes gazing somewhere overhead. "A man also loves, Daniel. Now I don't mean the gushy romance stuff." He looked squarely and sternly at Dan. "A man loves when those kinds of feelings are nowhere to be found, when the going gets tough. And he's faithful to his wife and children."

Dan rested his chin on a fist. "So where does money come in? A man's gotta work, right?"

Walter pushed some fly-away hairs to the top of his head. "A man *provides*, Daniel. Most of the time that includes money, of course. But never at the expense of love…or protection…or leadership." He twisted on his bucket, drew a deep breath, blinked several times. "When a man defines himself as a bread-winner, he ends up—"

"Like my father."

"Not always. Your father hit the bottle, so I'm sure—"

"That's not all he hit."

Dan's eyes focused on Walter's bucket, and his mouth went dry. He folded the leaf and felt it split. Walter stayed silent as a minute passed to the sounds of the changing season.

"He hit me more times than I can remember." Dan's chest locked in place, tears blurred his vision, and his voice became soft and indistinct. "My mom, too. She took so much crap…so much pain…" He covered his mouth. "And so many times," he said through his fingers. "So many times she was only defending me. I'll never stop hearing the sound of her face being slapped. I could take being hit, but…" He uncovered his mouth, and crumpled the leaf. "But hearing him hurt her… Seeing it, seeing her afterward; that was always the worst." He forced a disgusted chuckle through his runny nose, and sucked in the result. "She even had a welt in her casket." He wiped a finger across his lip. "Covered by layers of cruddy make-up."

"I didn't realize she'd passed," Walter said.

"She had terrible asthma. I found her on the stairs after school. I was just a teenager."

"Oh, Daniel." Emotion seemed to catch in Walter's throat. "I'm so sorry."

Dan's fingers gripped his bangs and, for the first time in his life, pulled them up. He felt alarmingly conspicuous, as if his underwear had suddenly dropped to his ankles at a crowded bus stop. "See this scar?" Walter's eyes were sunken and misty as he looked at Dan's head. "I was thirteen, watching through a stairway railing." He released his hair, felt decent again. "Dad was in the kitchen, screaming at mom about credit card charges. She held her ground until his backhand dropped her to the floor. And I remember… I remember him hovering over her, like some deranged prize fighter, still shaking the paper statement." He looked at Walter's repulsed face. "So I ran to the kitchen, took my best shot. He caught my fist like a ball, then grabbed his beer can and smashed it on my head. I landed on mom, bloody-faced in her bosom, and never stood up to my father again."

30

CHAPTER THIRTY

"Thank you," Robyn said across the small round table. "A night away was just what we needed."

"You're welcome. I'm just glad your aunt was willing to stay with Evan." Dan sipped sparkling cider. "That was a long drive for her."

"Marsha gets lonely. The beach is just a sleepy little town, this time of year." She flashed a grin, lifted her glass. "You're quite a different sight than you were on our first date."

"How so?"

"Snapping crabs. Chugging beer. Dropping cheesy lines on me."

Dan laughed. "I was twenty years old and using a fake ID. Nervous, you know."

"You were nervous because you'd asked out such a hot chick." Robyn's lashes fluttered comically in front of her cappuccino eyes. Her hair was loose, with a few strands tucked behind one ear.

"Well then," Dan said. "I suppose not that much has changed." He leaned back, tipped his glass. He would have preferred bottled lager, or at least some wine; the sparkling cider was Robyn's request.

They were dining at Ricardo's, an upscale restaurant overlooking the Chesapeake Bay. Dan had ordered crab again, but unlike the half bushel of spicy blues he'd dismembered years ago, tonight's fare consisted of two lumped cakes for 37 dollars. With steamed wax beans and four tiny red potatoes! Romantic or not, a late night pizza was more than probable.

Gulls circled in the dusky sky and stalked the edges of Ricardo's dock. And the sinking sun brightened sails on the grayish-green water, where evening breezes pushed white caps atop a thousand little waves.

"Are you still proud of me?" Dan's question seemed to still the air around them, and the jazz seemed suddenly louder. He looked at Robyn, watched her chin drop and her chest rise.

"I am." Her glass touched her lips, then lowered again to the table. "We've talked a lot this week. I don't think we need to rehash how much you've hurt me." Her eyes squinted slightly as they squared with his. "You've made some painful mistakes, but I know you're trying. And the changes I've seen in you; yeah, I'm pretty proud of those."

"Not going to work is… I can hardly explain it." He finished his cider. His breathing turned shallow. A plate dropped and shattered in the kitchen. "Glad we've already been served," he said.

Robyn's smile seemed only polite. Her hands slid together, fingers intertwined. "Dan, I understand. I mean, not totally, but enough." She unfolded her fingers, picked one thumbnail with the other. "It's all you've ever known. You're dad pushed business on you, made it your world. And you were very good at it."

"I still am." His tone was defensive. He clenched his teeth, swallowed his pride. "I'm sorry, honey. I get all knotted up inside when…" He shook his head. "It's a tough thing to talk about."

Robyn slid a hand past the votive candle, and Dan took it in his. "You are so much more than a good accountant," she said. Her head tilted as she talked. "Seeing you with Evan. Watching you spend time with Walter. I see things; qualities I always knew were there." Her eyes moistened. "It takes a long time to change. But you're making the effort, and that's half the battle."

"You really think I can be a good father, after what I grew up with?"

"I do." She pulled back her hand, wiped a tear from the corner of her eye. "And you couldn't have picked a better time to start, because Dan, I'm—"

"I'll take this whenever you're ready." A well-dressed young man placed a small, leather portfolio on the table. Dan shuddered at the sight. "Thank you very much," he lied.

"Is there anything else I can get for you?"

"No, I believe we're all set." Dan looked across the table. Robyn nodded, lifting her glass for a final swallow.

"Excellent," the waiter said, turning to leave.

Dan surveyed the bill, stuck in a card, and placed the portfolio near the table's edge. The eager waiter lifted a hand and smiled as he started their way. "I'll have that back to you in just a minute."

"Because?" Dan said.

Robyn's gaze was toward the bay. "I'm sorry, what?"

Dan smiled. "You were saying something about being a dad and timing?"

"Oh, yeah… With me getting the job is all." She lifted a burgundy cloth, dabbed her mouth, and made a third trip to the bathroom.

The parking lot faced away from the water, but the view was nonetheless stunning. Above a tall row of swaying scotch pines blazed a scarlet ribbon and several pink clouds.

Dan gripped the bottom of his steering wheel, slouching in his seat while silently cursing its clingy fabric. Robyn looked his way, and said with a grin, "You don't like the new car?"

"First of all, it's not a car. It's an S. U. V." Dan said the letters slowly, boldly, thrusting some measure of dignity upon the used (certified pre-owned, he insisted) Ford Escape. "And no. I'm not a fan."

"Well, it was noble of you to choose something affordable. I know you miss the Beamer."

A few minutes passed as they watched the sky mute to a gun-metal gray. Dan jiggled the keys in the ignition, and almost turned them. "Can I ask you something?" he said instead. "Do you remember Lawrence Mac-something-or-other? Everyone called him—"

"Pastor Larry," they said together.

"Yeah, that guy," Dan said above Robyn's laughter. He let go of the keys, sat up straighter. "We used to rip him to pieces."

"Oh man; remember those bow ties and sport coats?"

"With the concealed weapon inside," Dan added. "He'd swing that jacket open, and someone would shout, 'Duck and cover!' That red Bible was always gunning for somebody." They laughed together, long and genuine, until it ended awkwardly, as if snatched away by the last sliver of red in the evening sky.

"What brought him to mind?"

Dan's hands slid to the top of the wheel, and his arms stiffened. "Larry never quit. He never quit standing up for what he believed. And the crazy thing is I can still remember some of what he said to people, about spiritual swords and how faith can move mountains." Robyn said nothing, her hand resting gently on his leg. Dan's eyes fixed on the darkening sky. "Walter prayed for me, Robyn. That morning in the tree house. After we'd talked about the party I'd missed and some other things. You know, I used to get so ticked off when someone talked about God. But when Walter prayed, when he mentioned some verses. I don't know… It just felt different coming from him."

She squeezed his thigh. "You knew they went to church, right?"

"Yeah, and so do half the people at Bell-Knarr, but they never preached to me." His tone intensified. "That stuff's private. I mean, believe what you want but don't push it on others."

Robyn's hand withdrew. "Then why didn't you say that to Walter?" Her question hung thick and conspicuous, like the scent of the small yellow pine tree, dangling from the rearview.

"Do you believe in God, Robyn?" He turned toward her, watched her hands push slowly to her knees.

"I guess I do. Somehow. Somewhere inside." She drew a deep breath, released it. "The world just seems so full of suffering." She locked eyes with Dan. "It's hard to fathom."

"I'm sorry I snapped."

Her head tipped and a sad smile lifted as she leaned his way for a kiss. When their lips separated, she whispered, "What do you believe?"

"I'm not sure, but maybe that's the best place to start." He reached for the keys as she pulled away. "There's something about Walter," he added. "I can't explain it, but I admire it. I'd like to be more like him. And if believing in God can help…well… Open the glove box." Robyn complied. "Walter gave that to me."

From on top of the owner's manual, Robyn lifted a small black Bible, and fanned through some pages. "Let's go back to the hotel and give this a read...Pastor Dan."

"Oh please!" They laughed again as Dan turned the keys, grabbed reverse. He swung an arm behind the passenger seat, and said, "Feel like a mocha? I noticed a Starbuck's around the—"

"Dan, stop." Robyn's phone was ringing. "Pull in a second. It's Marsha, I know from the ringtone." The Escape reclaimed its spot. Dan killed the engine, and Robyn stashed the Bible in favor of her phone. She stuck it to her ear. "Hey, Marsh—"

Five seconds of silence.

"Yeah, we're just leav—"

Color drained from Robyn's face. Marsha's voice sounded like television seeping through shoddy apartment walls. Dan caught every other word.

Evan...Ambulance...Blood?

Robyn's eyes closed as the phone slowly lowered, adding clarity to Marsha's desperate, digitized wailing: "I'm sorry, Robyn! I'm so sorry!"

31

CHAPTER THIRTY-ONE

"My name is Daniel Crawford! Evan's father!"

Soft brown fingers covered his own. "Evan's in intensive care, Mr. Crawford. The doctor would like to speak with you before—"

"Is he okay? Is my son gonna be okay?"

The nurse squeezed his hand, took a deliberate swallow. "The doctor's gonna answer that question. You all c'mon and follow me." She released her grip, lifted a clipboard. "Betty you go on and page Dr. O'Malley." Behind sliding glass, a flustered blonde hastily dialed.

Dan trailed the nurse down a long, stark, fluorescent hallway, studying the swishing cadence of her pale pink pants and the silent strides of her chalky white shoes. The air smelled of band aids and antiseptic. And Marsha's story seemed bolted to his brain.

Evan wanted one more try on the pogo stick she'd given him. But he hurried, skipped his helmet, fell straight back on the driveway. From matted hair, blood trickled. It was the only thing moving. Paramedics applied a cervical collar (a big white horse collar, by Marsha's description), strapped Evan to a backboard, and rushed him directly to William Penn Hospital. Marsha talked about holding his limp hand, and feeling nauseated by the sight of his gauze-wrapped head and the tubes injected in his comatose body.

Why did she have to bring that stupid stick!

A tall man in white rounded the far corner. Spectacles hung from his neck. His hair was thick and gray and combed straight back, like the helmet Evan had forgotten to wear. He didn't smile. His steps were swift and determined. The nurse stopped near a closed door, hung the clipboard on a hook. The tall man ignored her, passing right by and extending his hand.

"Doctor Charles O'Malley."

Dan shook hands. "Daniel Crawford. This is my wife, Robyn."

Dr. O'Malley clasped Robyn's hand as his head turned to thank the nurse. Then he dropped Robyn's hand, rubbed his chin, and said, "Your son is stable. Now, I know you're anxious to see him, but I'd like a few minutes to prepare you, to bring you up to speed." His eyes squared with Dan's. "There are some benches just down the hall. We might do well to sit."

No one ever sits for good news.

The benches were chrome with black, vinyl cushions. Dan and Robyn sat together on one, their backs to the wall. Dr. O'Malley slid a second bench forward to face them as he sat. He folded his hands, drew a deep breath. "I trust you've been told about the accident, how it happened."

"We have," Robyn said. Dan squeezed her hand.

"Your son has suffered a significant blow to the back of his head. He has not regained consciousness since the moment of impact."

Tears dripped onto Robyn's contorting face as her chest shook and her breathing digressed to a series of nasally bursts. Dan wanted to pull her close, to kiss her head and whisper affirmations. But instead he rocked, clawing at his own thighs and allowing warm tears to roll freely down his cheeks. He heard Robyn say "thank you" as the doctor slid a pack of tissues from his jacket. She dabbed her eyes, then reached for Dan. He clutched her hand and pulled it to his leg. She slid closer, their shoulders touched.

"Evan has undergone a CT Scan which clearly indicates that he does not have a skull fracture. We've also run neurological tests to confirm that he has not experienced a brain death." Dan's gut wretched at the sound of those words. A trio in pink walked silently past, averting their eyes. "However," the doctor continued. "There is bleeding inside the skull, applying pressure to the brain. That's the reason he's lost consciousness. It's a very serious condition called a Subdural Hematoma."

"I've heard of that," Dan managed to say.

"Okay, well, that just means that the fall caused a vessel to burst in Evan's head. Now, we've conducted an MRI to determine the amount and location of the bleeding." The doctor wrung his hands.

"And?" Robyn said sharply.

"We found what we expected. The bleeding was significant enough to require trepanation; a necessary treatment to prevent or at least minimize damage to his brain."

"So what does that mean?" Robyn asked. "Trepa-what?"

"We were required to drill a small hole in Evan's skull in order to insert —"

Robyn bent forward and wept uncontrollably. This time Dan pulled her head to his chest, wrapped his arms around her shaking body, and looked up into a panel of long, fluorescent bulbs. An image of what the doctor had described pushed violently to mind, refusing to leave.

"I'm sorry, Mr. and Mrs. Crawford. I know that's a hard thing to hear, but it probably saved Evan's life. It was our only choice."

Dan kept his head raised but closed his eyes. Robyn's crying relaxed. She stayed nuzzled to his chest. He rubbed her back, and thought of calling Walter; a matter of when, not if.

"I'll give you a few minutes while I check on Evan." Dan heard whispery sounds from the doctor's shifting clothes, and then opened his eyes.

Robyn's head lifted. "Dan, tell me he's going to be okay. That my baby's going to be fine."

Dan beheld shadows of displaced mascara that darkened her temples and one side of her jaw. He studied her slacks, her embroidered white blouse, and the golden hoops on her neck and ears. It was an outfit intended for romantic dining, an evening alone with her husband. Their first in years. It was an outfit he'd longed to remove from her body, one silky piece at a time, as salty air pushed through the whistling cracks of a bay-front cottage. They would have snuggled for hours, made love more than once.

He slid a hand past her puffy pink eyes, and said, "Let's go find out." She nodded, lips pursed, as together they stood, just in time to see the doctor emerge from Evan's room and begin walking toward them.

"I'm sorry," Dan said. "It's…"

"Hey, no, don't apologize." O'Malley put a hand on Dan's shoulder. "It's our responsibility to be honest, and the truth isn't always pleasant." He looked long in Dan's eyes. "Evan's still stable."

"What's the prognosis?" Robyn asked. "What's going to happen to my baby?"

The doctor released Dan's shoulder. He folded his hands and swayed before speaking. "Mrs. Crawford, children tend to heal quicker and more completely than adults who might suffer a head injury of this magnitude. Their brains are still growing, they repair easier. So in a best case scenario, Evan wakes up sometime in the next…oh…twelve to twenty-four hours, and with no permanent damage. Now, he might experience a temporary amnesia. And he will almost certainly require an extended period of occupational therapy to restore some neurological functioning. He'll also be at higher risk of seizures. Throughout his life, I'm afraid. But generally speaking, he walks away with little or no lasting impact."

Dan slid his arm around the small of Robyn's back. "Tell us the other side, Doc; the worst."

O'Malley pushed his tongue in a cheek. "He never wakes up."

Dan's knees weakened, his breathing stopped. He glanced at Robyn as she covered her mouth and turned bed-sheet white, like she had in the car with a cell phone clamoring in her ear.

"Of course, there are countless scenarios in between those extremes." The doctor pushed his lips together for a second. "Time will tell. We'll certainly do all we can."

"May we see him? May we see our son?" Panic arose in Dan's voice.

"Of course."

They walked to the doorway of room 119. Robyn entered first and moved straight to the bed. Dan saw her hands rise slowly to her face and the tell-tale shakes of more weeping. His gut knotted, his mouth turned pasty. He swallowed nothing, very hard. Robyn's wet face turned toward the doctor. "Can I touch him?" Her question was a crashing wave between sobs.

"Yes," O'Malley said.

She turned, brushed Evan's cheek, and traced his eyebrows. Dan stepped close to the foot of the bed, and pressed a fist to his lips. "Oh dear God," he huffed through his knuckles.

Evan was flat on his back. His head was wrapped like a mummy and locked in place by what looked like the medical equivalent of a "C" clamp from Walter's shop. A thin, yellow tube stuck out of his head like a three-inch fuse. Other thin tubes proceeded out of each nostril, wrapped his ears, and connected under his chin. From there they linked to an oxygen tank. His left arm was pierced by another tube, just below his elbow. Fluid dripped from a plastic bag, hanging on a stand that resembled a rolling coat rack. And wires—*so many wires!*—were stuck to Evan's chest. On a cart near the bed, a flat-screened monitor pulsed like a graphic metronome.

"His eyes are black." Dan's words were barely audible through his clenched fingers. He lowered his fist. "Why are his eyes black?"

"Ecchymosis," O'Malley said.

Just speak English!

"Head traumas such as Evan's are almost always accompanied by a pronounced bruising beneath the eyes. It does not represent a complication of any kind. Just normal, if you will. It'll disappear in time."

A minute passed without words. Robyn continued to caress Evan wherever she could find unmonitored skin. She sniffled, wiping tears on her blouse.

"The yellow tube is what's left from the trep…from the draining process. There is little to no fluid at this time, which is an encouraging sign. He'll need some stitches on the back of his head, but we'll deal with that much later in the healing process." The doctor walked close and leaned over the bed, as if reading something on the computer screen. "The IV is primarily for hydration purposes, but we will include pain medication when necessary." He stood straight again. "And these other tubes and wires you see are standard issue: heart monitor, oxygen, those sorts of things. Right now, everything looks as it should."

"How long can we stay," Robyn asked.

"Well, we'd like you to stay overnight if possible. You can stay here in the —"

"Thank you," she said.

"Well then, I'll leave you folks alone while I notify the nurses that you're in here. If you have any questions or need help in a hurry, just push this button." He pointed to a spot on the wall, then backed out the door, closing it gently.

Dan slid a chair to Robyn and encouraged her to sit. She did, holding Evan's limp hand and looking at his peaceful, racoonish face. Dan massaged her shoulders, kissed the top of her head. Then, like a dagger to the chest, he remembered Evan in his bright new cap, smiling like the sun and pitching rocks like an ace reliever. Dan's head bobbed as pulses of pressure leaked from his skull. His lips curled. Tears fell on Robyn's hair. She stood to embrace him, clawing his back as together they wept, surrendering to the grotesque awareness that their final hugs and words to Evan may have already taken place. Casually, deceptively, like a simple matter of routine.

32

CHAPTER THIRTY-TWO

In a hospital waiting room, Dan held his phone to his ear, standing in a corner like a disciplined pupil. "Margaret, it's Dan. May I talk to Walter?"

"Well, of course, Daniel. Are you okay?"

"No."

Silence.

"Just a minute."

He knew Margaret had covered the receiver of the old rotary dial phone, and still he heard her shout twice for Walter, hastening him to the kitchen. The phone changed hands. Walter spoke quickly, seriously. "Daniel, what's wrong?"

Dan's mouth opened but no words came. He took a big swig from a sweaty can of Sprite, and pictured Walter's pinched expression. "Evan..." He bit his bottom lip, then swigged again. CNN droned from a television, high in an adjacent corner.

"Daniel!"

"He fell on the driveway. He's hurt...really bad." Nine words, squeezed from his chest.

"Where are you?"

"William Penn Hospital." Dan finished his Sprite, crushed the can in his fist. "He's in the ICU. They drilled a hole..." He broke down and cried, in the hidden way of a man too embarrassed to feel. He sensed eyes upon him and dared not turn.

"What is it?" Margaret demanded in the background. "Walter, what's going—"

"Just a minute, Margaret! Daniel, we're coming. Give us an hour."

Dan gained the composure he needed to lie. "No, that's not why I called, I just..."

"I won't hear it!" Walter cleared his throat. "I won't hear it. We'll be there as soon as we can."

Dan consented and ended the call. His forehead fell against the corner as he imagined Margaret, her tight gray curls shoved in folded arms, her dripping face just inches from the farmhouse table. Then he imagined Walter preparing for urgent departure, strong and assertive, fear and sadness rammed down the barrel of his chest. Oh, how Dan hoped it were true! He couldn't bear the thought of a blubbering Walter, gimping around the house, stroking a soggy mustache. A Walter as weak and broken as he was.

Dan stood straight and turned around. He pocketed his phone, wiped his cheeks with his shoulders, and watched a room full of heads go slightly askew. Then he sat on a paisley cushion, averting his eyes. He should return to Evan's room, but Marsha was there now, comforting Robyn with sappy clichés and an overdose of hugs. *To ease her own guilt, no doubt.* He wanted to shove that pogo stick where...well...where Marsha's thick frame saw no rays of coastal sunshine.

Standing again, he shoved a hand in his pocket to check for more change. Although unreasonable, soda seemed somehow to settle his nerves and increase focus. He found only two dimes, two nickels, and one mysterious, crinkly wrapper from the last time he'd worn his charcoal Dockers. But the machine took bills, and... *Walter's coming.* The anticipation in Dan's chest was like a sip of spiced rum as his shiny black loafers clapped the hallway, in search of the nearest vending area. But then his phone vibrated, stopping him dead in his tracks.

"Dad?"

"Yeah, hey, I need a favor. You free tomorrow?"

"No..." The truth felt barbed.

"Oh, c'mon. I'm on an early flight to Boston. Those numbskulls need another bail out."

"I can't, okay?"

"Just listen! You might be able to—"

"Evan's in the hospital!"

There was a strange, silent unease, like the sky was falling.

"What happened, Danny?"

"Robyn's aunt brought a pogo stick. He fell on the drive...and he..." His father's breathing intensified, and Dan sensed him straining—for once—to stay quiet. "Dad, he's unconscious. There's no guarantee..." He couldn't finish.

"And you don't call to tell me this?" The question had a serrated edge.

"I was going to..." Dan paused to consider the dishonesty, how best to spin it. "Things have been crazy, very tough... We haven't even been here that long and—"

"Where?"

Oh no! Why did I open my mouth?

"Where, dammit!"

"William Penn Hospital. They have an advanced pediatric—"

"I'll be there in an hour. Those schmucks in Boston can suck it up another day."

"Dad, you don't have to—"

"Don't tell me what I should or shouldn't do, Danny! He's my grandson and I'm coming!"

"Right." Dan's consent was guttural, an obligatory groan shoved through his teeth. The call ended without a goodbye. His heart felt like a wad of over-chewed gum, devoid of any particular flavor; just a malleable mass, ready to be discarded. He passed several closed doors and a row of parked wheel chairs before finally reaching a vending area, where another can of Sprite clunked its way through metal guts.

Dan placed his empty can in the waste basket, then closed the door as gently as possible, as if a sudden click or thump might awaken Evan.

Let him sleep. Let him heal. Please God, if you're really there...

Marsha sat on a stool in the far corner, her thick frame packaged into black denim jeans and a heather gray sweatshirt, embroidered with seagulls. Stringy, perm-in-a-box hair hung just below her jaw like an overturned bowl of Ramen Noodles. Dan gave her a nod before kneeling beside Robyn, still sitting by the bed, holding Evan's hand. "No movement?" he whispered. Robyn's head shook. "I called Walter. He and Margaret are on the way. They insisted."

"I'm not surprised." Her voice was hollow.

He didn't mention Russell; no need to introduce another trauma just yet. He stood and placed a hand on Evan's bandaged forehead, then traced his eyebrows with a finger.

Please move, buddy. Twitch a finger… a toe…

"Maybe we should pray?" Robyn said.

Dan pondered the question as it hovered between them. He moved his hand close to the tubes in Evan's nose and felt a slight exhale, a sign of life. He felt another….another…another… "I don't know how," he finally said. "I'm not sure what to say."

Marsha sniffled from her perch in the corner. Dan noticed she was rubbing her eyes. Then he looked down at Robyn, saw her diamond-clad hand sliding smoothly, endlessly over Evan's limp body. She looked up for a moment, with a forgiving glance that also lacked hope.

Dan stepped away from the bed, pulled his fingers through his hair, and stared. At blipping screens and dripping bags. At tin blinds deeply set in a boxed window where he would soon place flowers and cards and whatever else people might send. And he wondered: Can sentimental verbiage or artistic bouquets really ease any pain? Can they do anything to lessen the sea of regret in which he'd spend the rest of his pitiful life, longing for second chances to laugh and tickle and savor the precious feel of Evan's soft little fingers? He stared at his son, motionless, connected to life by a web of tubes and wires. Was Evan dreaming, running, arms outstretched through an endless meadow? Was he sifting through clouds, looking down on places that had filled him with wonder for almost five years? For only five years! Was he nearing pearly gates? Were they opening?

And then Dan's stare turned inward, searching for memories of times he'd cherished his son, looked upon him with awe, relished his innocence, chased his fleeing toads, inspired his heart. Searching for those moments when he'd actually fathered. Walking backward through time, Dan stared. What else could he do?

33

CHAPTER THIRTY-THREE

"Mr. Crawford?" He'd dozed off unexpectedly, in a chair near the door. "Mr. Crawford, there's a Mr. Benning in the lobby to see you." His eyes lifted like rusty trap doors. "I'm sorry to wake you, sir. But the gentleman insists on seeing you."

She was a tiny nurse, and her hand had felt like Evan's when it touched Dan's shoulder. He stood, stretched his arms, and stuck his head out the half-open door, holding its frame for support. "Miss! Miss Nurse." She turned with a smile. "Who is waiting for me?" he asked. "You didn't say who....at least I don't think so."

"Well, I guess you weren't quite awake." She took a few steps in Dan's direction, slipping a note from the pocket of her shirt. "Let's see... It's a Mr. Benning. Walter Benning." Dan drew a deep breath, sighed in relief. "But you'll need to visit him in the lobby," the nurse added. "Only family members are permitted to see Evan."

"But Walter is..." She raised an eyebrow, and Dan let it go. Pulling back in the room, he sat again, rubbing his bleary eyes. "Walter's here."

Robyn stood to face him. "Margaret, too?"

"I would assume." Dan flexed his jaw, furrowed his brow.

"You can both go," Marsha said. "I'll stay here. But if you don't mind, who are these people?"

"They're the neighbors who own the farm," Robyn said, sounding slightly upbeat. "Where the boys built that tree house. Remember me telling you?"

"Oh, that's right." Marsha slapped her thighs and walked to the chair near the bed.

Dan stood, pulled Robyn to a hug. "A little walk will do you good," he whispered. Her head nodded on his chest. "We won't be long," he told Marsha, who looked back with a sour smile. "You know, it wasn't your fault," he added. "What happened to Evan was an accident…nothing more." Robyn looked up, mouthed a silent thank you. Marsha only nodded, wiping her face.

Leaving the room, Robyn took his hand as they walked toward the lobby. And Dan felt like a fog had lifted. His unplanned nap had restored some vitality, enough to forgive Marsha, at least. Or was that only a dismissal? A pardon?

Wait! Tell Robyn about dad!

Too late.

"Hey, sweetheart. How are you?" Margaret's voice was like a sad hymn. Robyn trotted to her waiting arms.

Walter stood behind them, wearing tan slacks and a forest green coat. Dan walked close, extended a hand. "Thanks for coming, it really means—" Walter embraced him, and Dan's emotions exploded anew. He squeezed with equal gusto as they swayed. Tears leaked from Dan's eyes. And then…

"Danny?" The question stung like an angry hornet.

Dan stood at attention, wiping his face and avoiding Walter's gaze. "Yeah, hey, you made it."

What a stupid thing to say.

Russell wore faded denim, woven loafers, and a sleek gray trench coat, tied at the waist. "My apologies, son." He massaged Dan's shoulder. "I should have the decency not to interrupt a hug." Removing his hand, he looked at Walter. "Russell Crawford."

"Walter Benning." He looked like a dough boy, shaking Russell's hand.

"And this must be Mrs. Benning."

"Margaret." She took Russell's hand with tears on her face, sniffling and trying to smile.

Robyn's hand clutched Dan's as his father moved toward her, reaching for her shoulders, inclining his head. "Robyn, my dear, I am so dreadfully sorry." Her nails nearly broke through the skin of Dan's palm. "You'll forgive me for being a little unsure of the details."

Dan swallowed a brick. "Why don't we all sit? I can explain the situation."

Robyn dropped Dan's hand as she slipped from Russell's grasp, and immediately moved toward the Bennings, resting her head on Margaret's shoulder. Russell's eyes locked on Dan as his smile vanished. He sucked his teeth, tweaking his face in a show of contempt.

Dan surveyed the lobby and walked toward a cluster of chairs overlooking the hospital's lighted courtyard. He sat with his back to a wall of windows. To his left sat Walter, with an empty chair between them. Margaret and Robyn arranged their chairs to face Dan while Russell hung his coat and declared that he'd stand. Then Walter, still seated, squirmed out of his coat, revealing a V-neck sweater just as tan as his slacks.

"Robyn and I were away for the weekend." Dan began, lowering his eyes. "Robyn's Aunt was at our house with Evan. She called around dusk." He pictured the sunset, thought of budding romance...the dropping phone... Robyn's face, ghostly pale...

"Dan? Honey?"

"Evan was playing on a pogo stick, without a helmet. He fell backward..." Dan leaned forward, folded his hands. "Split his head open, lost consciousness." He heard gasps and garbled breathing. "So Marsha called 911. And the ambulance brought him here. They ran scans on his head. There's no skull fracture, but they decided to drill a hole to relieve pressure, drain the fluid. It probably saved his life."

Margaret sobbed, and Dan sensed Walter moving toward her. But he didn't look up. Like a detached reporter, he'd allowed the facts thus far to punch forth like a ticker tape. He couldn't look up now, inject himself with emotion. He had to keep reporting. "So anyway, the procedure went well. But Evan has not regained consciousness. He's hooked up to a thousand things, and his head is locked in some kind of sci-fi device. The doctor said he could potentially wake up within the next twelve to twenty-four hours, but..." The ticker tape jammed. Dan bit his lips, tilting his head away from Russell as tears squeezed past his compressed lids.

"He may never wake up," Robyn said.

Dan's eyes stayed closed. And while his mind gave image to the sounds around him, he dared not look. A strong hand landed in the center of his back. "Can we see him, Danny?"

Dan shouldered his tears, then opened his eyes to the sight of pristine leather loafers. "You can," he told Russell's shoes. "But until Evan wakes up, it's family only."

34

CHAPTER THIRTY-FOUR

Robyn's hands were wrapped around a cardboard cup of dreadful decaf, cut with cream. "Thanks again, guys. This is comforting."

Margaret's hand touched Robyn's forearm. "You're very welcome, honey. Are you sure you won't have something to eat?"

Robyn forced a smile. "No, thanks. I'll be lucky to keep this down." She took a slow sip. "I'm so sorry you can't see Evan. You're more like family than that..." She shook her head. "I'm sorry."

"Nonsense. You're exhausted. We're just happy to be here for you." Walter shifted in his high-backed chair and then elbowed the round wooden table. "We'll see that little rascal soon enough." He winked.

They all leaned back, putting cups to their lips. It was after 9:30 and the small cafeteria was empty save a custodial worker in perpetual slow motion. "Dan showed me the Bible you gave him." Robyn stared at an overhead light. "Before Marsha's call, we were watching the sunset, and Dan talked about God, said you've been sharing things with him." She looked at Walter. "I think he's hearing you. I think something's getting through."

Walter's mustache lifted. "Well, it certainly does my heart good to hear that." He sipped from his cup, then smacked his lips. "They serve better coffee to prisoners, I'm guessing." They all laughed, but only a little.

"Daniel sure resembles his father," Margaret said. "They're both so dashing. What does he do, Robyn?"

"He's a CEO. Works in Baltimore, mostly."

"Well, I would have guessed as much. So debonair."

Robyn pitied Margaret's ignorance, and likewise envied it. "He certainly can be."

"So Daniel's been reading?" Walter's intonation felt like a rescue.

"I can't say for sure," she answered. "But he asked me about... I don't know. Religion, I guess. It's just not like him."

"You know the Bible teaches that someone only seeks spiritual things when God is at work in their lives." Margaret's eyes were wide and bright. "I'll bet Daniel has just come to a time..." She drank coffee at the sight of Walter's stern expression. "Well, it's true," she then mumbled, returning a look of her own.

"There is a season for everything," Walter said. "It may well be a time in Daniel's life when spiritual matters are of greater concern. He's certainly made some significant changes."

Robyn sat quietly, allowing Walter's words to permeate her thoughts. "I asked him to pray, but he didn't know how. That's what he said." Walter and Margaret made eyes at each other.

"May I pray with you?" Walter asked.

"I'd like that."

She watched their heads bow before lowering hers. Walter spoke of love and grace and power and purpose and then: "Evan is healed in the name of Jesus..." Robyn's hair stood on end, her heart beat faster. "Amen," Walter said.

Robyn took a long, bitter drink, feeling warm all over and strangely compelled to sprint through the halls, burst into 119, and rejoice at the sight of Evan's fluttering eyes and dopey smile. "Mommy..." he would moan, trying to sit.

"Thank you," she said, sliding from her chair. "For everything, I mean. I just... I really need to be with Evan. I hope you understand." Her words were hurried, almost dismissive.

"We'll be right here," Margaret said as Walter nodded.

Robyn was a speed walker trying not to run. Cool air rushed past her face and blouse. She felt alert, awake, and eager beyond reason. She'd never had a panic attack but now wondered, jettisoning past nurses like an all-pro tailback, if that might indeed be the case. Her mind rolled over and over with images of Evan, awake and smiling.

In the name of Jesus…

She reached the door, thrust it open.

The lights were dim. Marsha had resumed her perch. Dan sat alone near the bed with his hands behind his head. And Russell paced near the window, a cell phone stuck in his ear. The heart monitor blipped… blipped…blipped. Evan was still and silent, adorned with tubes and wires and gauze. Nothing had changed. Except behind his left ear, where a few red drops now dotted the pillowcase.

"Jesus," she whispered, unsure how she meant it.

"I'll get there when I get there!" Russell plugged his open ear with a finger. "What? No, I have a family emergency."

Robyn's jaw tightened; everything tightened. Her head shook rapidly, almost vibrating as she marched forward, gripped Dan's arm. "He's not supposed to be using a cell phone. It says so right on the wall!" They were venomous words, more hissed than spoken.

"I know. But it's just a quick call to straighten things out with—"

"I don't give a crap if it's the President of the United States, Dan! He could interfere with this equipment!" Her muffled rant edged closer to shouting.

"Is there a problem?" Russell snapped his phone closed.

"No…" Dan began. "I think we're all just getting a little—"

"Yes there's a problem! Get off the phone! Go outside and call!" Robyn stared at Russell like he'd put Evan in the bed. She saw his eyes narrow, his nose curl. He was ready to kill her. She felt ready to die.

"Whoa…" Dan stood between them. "Our son is clinging to life, here." Robyn saw his hands trembling. She dipped her head, snipped her bottom lip, and sucked away the steely liquid.

Russell stomped toward the door, slamming it shut as he left the room. The noise startled everyone. Except for Evan.

"Dad! Wait! Hold-up!"

"*Shhhhhh!*" said a doctor, glaring over the chart in her hands.

Seeing Russell march left and out of sight, Dan jogged, turned the blind corner, and... *Thud!* Strong hands pounded his chest, gripped his shirt, and pinned his back to the wall. Shirt buttons popped and clicked on the floor. Russell's eyes were arrows, his upper lip curled. "Look at me, you little punk." His words were cold and quiet. "It's for the sake of my grandson that I walked away from that smart-mouthed little—"

"That's my wife!" Dan's words erupted from unchartered depths. His heart became an unbalanced tire.

With two fistfuls of pinpoint oxford, Russell lifted Dan's heels and pushed his shoulders tighter to the wall. "NOBODY speaks to me the way she just did! Especially a woman!"

"What's going on here?" A female voice, resounding in the hallway. Russell released his grip, took two steps back. The short, black nurse kept her distance, talking on a two-way radio.

A bespectacled male rounded the corner. "This an ICU, sir." His eyes were on Russell. "You can't—"

"I know what it is!" Russell scowled, looking at Dan. "And I was just leaving."

Two uniformed men entered the hallway near the female nurse. With a gait of authority, their polished shoes knocked loudly on the floor. "What seems to be the problem here, gentlemen?"

Don't talk like big shots, you idiots! Not in front of my dad.

Russell turned to face the approaching men, appearing ten inches taller than both. "There's no problem," he said. "Just a discussion. Now, if you two distinguished officers will excuse me..." He tried to move around them. The nearest guard grabbed Russell's left forearm. Russell stopped walking, his right hand forming a fist at his side. He looked at the man, flashed a haunting smile.

The second guard spoke to Dan. "Has this man hurt you, sir?"

Dan shook his head; had there ever been a more loaded question? "I'm fine," he said. "We both got a little carried away." He looked at Russell. "Exhaustion got the better of us, but it's over now."

"Are you men visiting a patient?"

"My son. He's in 119. I was just on my way to the lobby."

The first guard, still holding Russell's arm, said, "And you, sir?"

"I'm leaving. And I won't be back."

The declaration pelted Dan's conscience. "Dad… You should stay." He looked at the floor, horror-stricken.

Have I encouraged the wolf to remain in the pasture?

"Fine," Russell said. "But I need some air."

Dan heard loafers pounding, fading in the distance.

"Now there can be no more of this commotion. Is that understood, sir?"

Dan chuckled through his nose at the guard's rebuke. "I understand," he said, lifting his head.

The two men nodded, their mouths turned down, trying to look tough. Then they walked away, as did the nurse. Dan was alone. He leaned against the wall, ran fingers through his hair, closed his eyes, and exhaled toward the ceiling.

"Daniel?"

"What? Yeah…" Dan lowered his hands, opened his eyes, and beheld his beige-clad friend. "Walter, what are you doing back here? I've already gotten in trouble."

"So I gathered." Walter's mustache moved from side to side and then up, like his chin. "I saw security rushing from their posts, so I strolled to the end of the corridor."

Dan dropped his head with a sigh. "What did you see?"

"I saw the reason your shirt now lacks two buttons."

"I'm embarrassed." Dan laughed a little as his eyesight blurred. "Man, I didn't know I had so many tears in me." He drew a finger across his cheek, and raised his head. "I think I hate my father, Walter." An internal pressure nearly cracked his ribs. "But right now… I can't deal with hate or…"

"Come with me." Walter stepped forward, took Dan's hands. "The coffee in this place isn't fit for a rat. I'll buy." He winked, his sand-colored teeth peeking out from their wooly, white blanket.

Holding cups of recycled cardboard, Dan and Walter stood shoulder to shoulder in the lobby, staring through the wall of windows. Margaret sat in a chair behind them, rifling through back issues of People magazine. Russell's coat still hung on a nearby rack, but he'd yet to make another appearance.

It was almost eleven, and like the glowing fountain in the dimly-lit courtyard, thoughts gurgled endlessly through Dan's tired head. He'd explained the hallway argument twice to Walter, who'd since grown unusually quiet.

"It means a lot to have you here." Dan watched his reflection, saw his own mouth moving. He sucked in more coffee, hoping the caffeine might justify its flavor. "I'm not sure I can make it." He watched a reflected Walter tip his cup, his head nodding as if lost in thought. "Where is God, Walter? I mean, how can you—" Dan pinched off the question, drew a deep breath.

"Pain enters all of our lives," Walter said. "We never know when or how it's going to come. Many times it happens through no fault of our own."

Dan stared through his reflected chest at the churning fountain outside.

"Jesus never promised a problem-free life, Daniel. Quite the opposite, I'm afraid. But it's our faith in Him that gives us the grace and strength to endure, you see? Where is God, you ask? He's right here. Right here in our midst."

Dan's head swung toward Walter, their eyes met. "You really believe that? Even after all your years in higher education?"

"With all of my heart."

"I just can't... I mean..."

Walter put a hand on Dan's shoulder. "Let God show Himself to you. Take a step in His direction, and let Him show you." He glanced, mustache twitching, at Dan's half-empty cup. "Now, are you ready for a refill?"

Fatigue-driven laughter spilled from Dan, and when Walter followed suit, Margaret tried unsuccessfully to calm them with exaggerated throat clearing. The next voice they heard, however, sobered both of them instantly.

"So we've cause for celebration?" Russell's question was a gavel to the back of Dan's head.

"Laughter's wonderful medicine for a despairing heart," Walter said, turning.

"That it is, Mr. Benning. That it is, indeed." Russell smiled and winked at Margaret, but her head only dropped into a magazine. Dan wondered what she'd seen, or what Walter might have told her. "So what's the source of this humor, Walt?" Russell moved closer. He smelled like cigars.

"The coffee," Walter said. "It's the laugh-or-cry variety, and we've all shed enough tears for one night. Care for a cup?"

"No, thank you." Russell shot a look in Dan's direction. "I grabbed a drink while I was out." A wet, murky wave of anxiety lapped at the walls of Dan's chest. Walter turned his back, feigning interest in a stack of books. Russell looked at Dan, devoid of forgiveness. Dan looked down, as he always had.

And then came a squeal; shrill and distant and... in motion?

All heads turned to see a woman, trotting, hands folded over her face, brown hair bouncing and swaying on the shoulders of a white blouse. Margaret dropped her magazine, stood to her feet. Walter moved behind her.

"He's awake!" Robyn shouted through her hands. She opened her arms and nearly tackled Dan. He stumbled backward as she squeezed his chest, weeping upon it. "He's awake" The words were pulsations amid a sequence of sobs.

Evan's awake. He's... AWAKE!

Dan's skin felt covered by a million fizzing bubbles.

35

CHAPTER THIRTY-FIVE

It was standing room only in 119. Doctor O'Malley and his staff had been examining Evan for thirty minutes. The IV now dripped pain medication, and all the tubes and wires were still connected. But Evan's eyes were partially open. He'd moved his fingers and toes. Muttered Mommy and Daddy and, to everyone's surprise, Rockler.

"You're a very fortunate family," O'Malley said, shining a small light in Evan's eyes. He clicked off the light, put it in his pocket, and turned to Dan and Robyn. "To be awake this soon... Well, I have to be honest; it's fairly unusual." He smiled big and extended a hand. Dan shook it heartily, returning the smile.

"I think it's the power of prayer," Robyn said.

"A help, no doubt." O'Malley's tone lacked conviction. Releasing Dan's hand, he scribbled on a chart near the door. "Evan will stay in the ICU until at least sometime tomorrow afternoon." He turned, glancing at his watch with a grin. "Much later today, I should say." At this everyone looked at the institutional, black-and-white clock on the wall: 12:15 am. "Now, Mr. and Mrs. Crawford, you're welcome to stay the night with Evan, but it would be best if everyone else left." He scanned the room as heads tipped in agreement.

Russell moved to the door.

"Heading to Boston, after all?" Dan asked.

"If I can catch a later flight."

"Well, don't forget your coat in the lobby."

Dan offered his hand. Russell gripped it briefly and nodded to the room. "You'll let me know how things go tomorrow." His bravado rang false, drawing only murmurs in response. He looked at Evan. "We've got ourselves a little fighter." The Bennings smiled weakly.

"He's quite a boy," O'Malley said, approaching Russell with a tired smile. "Do drive safely." The doctor gave a departing wave before walking away. Russell followed, closing the door. And the room felt a thousand pounds lighter.

Robyn hugged Walter. "Thank you for praying."

"You betch'er bippy."

Marsha stepped forward. "Hi. I'm Marsha, Robyn's aunt." Her words were long and overdrawn with enthusiasm.

The Bennings introduced themselves. "May we buy you a snack on our way out?" Walter asked Marsha. "You've been in here for hours."

"I'd really appreciate that."

"Daniel? Hungry?"

"Yeah, I am actually. For the first time all night."

"Well, let's hope the food in those machines is better than the coffee." Walter looked at Robyn. "I imagine you'll be staying right here, young lady." Her smile lit up the room. Words appeared to catch in her throat. She hugged him again, Margaret too. "We'll be by tomorrow afternoon," Walter said.

The tired foursome walked to the lobby and feasted on assorted Lance crackers. Dan also had a Baby Ruth. Their conversation popped with witty remarks, made all the more funny by fatigue. But then Marsha mentioned the accident, causing caramel and peanuts to lodge in Dan's chest. "Yeah, he loved watching kids use pogo sticks on the promenade this summer. And I just wanted to surprise him with one of his own, you know?" She bit into a cracker, cupping her hand to catch the crumbs.

"Well, it was hardly your doing," Margaret said, inclining her head toward Marsha.

Dan forced down the candy, but his teeth remained clenched. *We've resolved this. Why is she dredging it up again?*

"He must've hopped on that thing for an hour," Marsha continued. "Evan the frog, I called him. And he had his little helmet on the whole time." Her voice cracked. "But then we were cleaning up, you know? It was near dark. And his helmet was already on a shelf when that landscaping fellow came walking up the drive. Just some guy handing out flyers, was all, but that boy got to showing off and—"

"What did you just say?" Half a Baby Ruth was now crushed in Dan's fist.

"You mean about the landscaper?"

"What was his name?"

"I don't know, Dan. After Evan fell, it got—"

"What did he look like?"

"Daniel?"

"Just a minute, Walter." Dan's eyes stayed tight on Marsha. "What did he look like?"

"Well, I mean…" She twisted her torso, shook her stringy hair. "He was a bigger guy. Not tall but thick. His head was mostly shaved. I can't really remember much else."

"Was he scruffy, unshaven?"

"Dan, I don't—"

"Did he have thick glasses?"

"Actually, yes, now that you mention it."

"Daniel, what's wrong? Why the interrogation?" Walter looked tense, almost angry. Dan only stood, searching for composure.

"Do you know that guy?" Marsha asked.

"I'm not sure. No, not really." Dan rubbed his face. "Man, I'm tired."

"He stayed with us while I called 911. I think he was as scared as I was. The police arrived first and told him to move his minivan. He never returned."

Dan palmed the little round table. "What color was the van?"

Walter stood. "Oh, for pity sake, Daniel!"

"I'm not sure," Marsha began. "Some sort of dark red, I think."

Dan shoved the table, marched across the room, and heard Walter following. "What in the blazes is going on?"

"He's stalking us, Walter."

"Who?"

Dan wheeled to face him. "I can't remember his name."

"Daniel, you've just been through a traumatic experience. And you're exhausted. Surely you're being irrational."

Dan considered Walter's words as he sat in a chair, positioned near the wall. He folded his hands, looking up at the voice of reason. "Maybe you're right. But there's been this guy. We went to a restaurant one day, right? He sits in the booth next to us, and I swear to you, Walter, he acted so weird. Paid too much attention to us. And then a few weeks later, he shows up in my driveway. Says he's a landscaper looking for business. And he was weird then, too. Pushing to know things, getting too personal."

"Coincidence," Walter said.

Dan propped his head on his fingertips. "But he came back. After I clearly told him not to. And now I find out he drives a maroon van. Which is another story, I guess." He twisted in his chair, looked up at Walter, and noticed Marsha and Margaret listening from afar. "So I'm leaving your house one night, and this minivan is parked along Rake's Mill. Just pulled over in the dark, no flashers or anything. I almost side-swiped it! And then it follows me, all the way into the development." He tipped his head and opened his palms. "Walter, it was a maroon van."

"Well, you've the start of a good novel." Walter smiled. Margaret chuckled. Dan's face burned, his eyes narrowed. "Daniel, it's suspicious." Walter's tone turned consoling. "I don't mean to dismiss it. But it's after midnight, and your son has just survived a life-threatening injury. Can we simply thank God, tonight…" His mustache twitched. "…and turn Perry Mason on this landscaper another day?"

Their eyes united in a moment of silence.

36

CHAPTER THIRTY-SIX

Evan's welcome-home had been a grand occasion, and rightfully so. He'd stayed only one day in the ICU, followed by one week in a regular hospital bed. His recovery rate, as the doctor put it, was remarkable.

His head was shaven and striped in the back by a row of purple stitches. Three additional stitches closed the hole above his left ear. His eyes were still bruised, but the blackish color had receded. And though some pain remained, a strong prescription kept it in check and helped him to smile.

Robyn and Dan had served trays of deli sandwiches, fruit, vegetables, and succulent deserts (all compliments of MCC, along with helium balloons and a marvelous bouquet of flowers). Marsha had driven all the way from the beach. And of course, the Bennings were there. Other guests included some of Robyn's colleagues, a few neighbors, and even her parents via video chat from their Arizona retirement community. Russell, thankfully, could not attend.

Presently the house was emptied of guests. Two sacks of garbage waited near the door, and stacked in the fridge were small, precarious mountains of leftovers. Evan was napping upstairs.

In the family room, Robyn's head was at rest on Dan's leg, and she was almost asleep, thinking back on Walter's prayer. She'd never understood how people could believe in a God who controls all things. A God who lets four-year-old boys smash their precious little heads. A God who created a world so full of pain. Yet it was in the midst of deep pain that she experienced His presence. Walter's prayer had made a difference. She was sure of it, even if the doctors were not.

Dan coughed and shifted his body, preventing the sleep she'd been inches from grasping. Her mind shifted also. Instead of prayer she now thought of the tree, pictured it proud on the hillside. Unlike her husband, she'd never chosen to ogle the distant white oak. To Dan it seemed larger than life, like an epic story concealed behind bark, mysteriously coursing through the veins of a million glossy leaves. But had the tree beckoned him? Led him to Walter? Introduced him to a chisel?

From there she thought of life … and love … and then sleep found her.

Dan shuffled past his small SUV before shoving two bags in a pail already full. Unsuccessful, he emptied the pail, poking the bags to release trapped air. And that's when he saw it: a small white rectangle stuck inside the pail by a nauseating adhesive (trash juice, Robyn called it). His face warmed. His muscles tensed. What were the chances?

He pulled keys from his pocket, leaned in the pail, and scraped the rectangle loose. It tore slightly before flipping to reveal its identity: a cheap, inkjet business card. Most of the words had smeared in the trash juice. The largest were discernable: Hake Landscaping.

Butch Hake!

The name bit like a mosquito. How could he have forgotten? Leaving bags on the floor, Dan walked outside to where the air was icy but calm. He slid his phone from a pocket and Googled Hake Landscaping. Three hits, in Vermont, Oregon, and North Carolina. He added "PA" to the search. No results were found.

PA White Pages!

He typed Butch Hake. Zero results. He changed it to "B" Hake. The results were plentiful but none said Butch, and none were in McKinley. Could it be a nickname? Dan tapped the phone on his chin as adrenaline swept through his body. He hadn't thought much about the landscaper—

stalker!—since that night at the hospital, when Marsha connected him to the scene of the accident.

Dan dialed information and waited for an answer. "McKinley," he said, followed closely by, "Hake Landscaping." His words were firm and well-articulated. "Can you check a larger area, please?" Several seconds passed. "So you're telling me there's no Hake Landscaping in the entire state?" He ended the call. What was it Walter had said in the hospital; turning Magnum P. I. or something?

Perry Mason; that's it! But who's Perry Mason?

Cold air prickled his skin in spite of his surging adrenaline. And a sinking feeling crept into his stomach. He pocketed the phone, finished garbage duty, and headed inside for a cup of hot coffee. Robyn was upstairs, tending to Evan's regimen of constant rest. They had moved an old TV/VCR combo to his room, and unboxed dozens of Thomas and Winnie the Pooh tapes that Robyn purchased at a yard sale. Dan thought the movies would never be viewed and had emphatically said so on the day she'd brought them home. *Live and learn.* He poured a cup, sat at the table, and had scarcely begun to ponder Perry Mason when his cell phone rang.

"Walter. I was just gonna call you."

"Great minds think alike, or so says the cliché."

"You go first," Dan said.

"They're forecasting beautiful weather tomorrow. Assuming Robyn's still at home, I thought you might enjoy some time outdoors. After lunch, perhaps?"

"You have no idea. I'll walk over in the early afternoon, if that's okay?"

"Wonderful. Now what's on your mind, Daniel?"

"Perry Mason."

Walter laughed. "Another Hallmark marathon?"

"What? No, not that." Dan's serious tone diffused Walter's laughing. "You said we could go Perry Mason on that landscaper. Remember?"

"Ah, yes. The stalker with a green thumb."

"I know who he is now, or at least who he claims to be. I found his card."

"Well then give the man a call and talk things through, Daniel. I'm sure it's just a simple matter of—"

"He doesn't exist. I've done some looking. There's no Hake Landscaping anywhere close. And the name he gave doesn't exist locally, either." Dan sipped his coffee. "I think he flat out lied, Walter."

Walter said nothing at first. Dan heard scratching whiskers and a lengthy inhale. "Daniel, is it possible this man is hard-pressed, performing work on the side? Did he leave a phone number?"

"The card was stuck in trash jui… Never mind. The card was too damaged to read any numbers. I could barely make out the name."

"Why would this man be stalking you?"

"Maybe it isn't me, Walter. I mean, Robyn's attractive."

"Got that right," Robyn said, laughing.

Dan turned to discover she'd entered the kitchen, quiet as a cat. "And just who are you talking to?" she asked.

"Walter."

"Well you're not telling him anything he doesn't already know." Her intentional loudness rousted more laughter on Walter's end of the phone.

"This isn't a joke." Dan's voice was stern. "What if it's Evan? What if this guy is some creepy child molester?"

Robyn's face sobered. She raised a finger to her lips.

"I think I should call the police," Dan said.

Brow furrowed, Robyn sat in a chair at the end of the table.

"And what will you accuse this man of?" Walter asked. "Do you know how many maroon minivans are driving around? And Marsha was merely guessing at the color, if you ask me. There's no guarantee this landscaper followed you home from my house. Which leaves you with what; a restaurant encounter? It's thin, Daniel, at best."

"So you think I should let it go?"

"I do," Walter said. "At least for now."

"I'll see you tomorrow afternoon."

Dan ended the call, and looked away from Robyn. It bought him only seconds. "What's going on?" she said.

"That landscaper guy was here when Evan fell."

"What do you mean?"

Dan faced her. "Marsha said he showed up when they were outside hopping on the driveway. Apparently the bum was just following up on his prior visit."

"Now why wouldn't she have told me that?"

"I have no idea. Scared, I guess. Or maybe it just seemed irrelevant."

"I thought you told that man not to come back."

"I did! I know I did!" He took a drink of coffee, hoping to drown careless words. "I found out he was here after Evan woke up; when we all went to the hospital lobby. Marsha felt the need to rehash everything, but she included more detail, mentioned this landscaper guy. And I overreacted. At least, Walter seems to think so." He looked in her eyes. "I'm sorry I kept it from you. I didn't want to dampen your joy. And when I thought about it further, it did seem like just a coincidence."

Robyn rubbed her face. "And now?"

Dan drew a deep breath. "He doesn't exist. The man, his business; they're fake. I think." He explained everything to Robyn: the card in the trash, his efforts on Google, the call to information, his conversation with Walter.

"So Walter thinks this guy is drumming up side work, under the table?" she asked.

"He suggested it. But he also admits the whole thing is suspicious."

"Are you going to call the police?"

"I haven't decided. Walter suggests waiting."

"But Dan, what if—"

He grabbed her hand. "I know…I know. We'll stay alert. But it could very well be nothing." Their eyes locked. He caressed her hand. "Honey, I trust Walter's judgment."

"Me, too," she admitted, pulling him close.

37

CHAPTER THIRTY-SEVEN

From the tree house window, the leafless forest looked like a road map on the blue horizon, and the fence row, once lush and diverse and brimming with life, was now nothing more than a blurry, contiguous gray.

"You're a life saver," Dan said. "And that's final."

Walter's chin was tucked with his eyes at half-mast. "Nonsense. I only prayed. It was God who answered."

"I'm not only talking about Evan's life." Dan backed into a corner, and looked out at a twist of black branches. "You may well have saved mine." He heard Walter getting settled on an overturned bucket.

"You've brought joy to my life as well, Daniel. I'd say it was all meant to be." Dan looked at Walter, watched him flexing his mustache as if scrubbing his nose.

"I used to dislike God," Dan said. "Hearing about Him, at least. But you've gotten through to me. Somehow."

"So you believe?" Walter stared with beckoning eyes.

"I don't know. I can't lie to you; you're too good a friend." Dan sucked his top teeth. "But I'm considering it. The Bible, I mean. And for me that's a first." He studied Walter, beheld his plaid, woolen coat. "You're a good man, you know that? I don't know what I would've have done in the hospital. I don't know what I'd do *period* without you." He grinned, prepared to ask about coffee, until Walter's head fell awkwardly forward.

"I haven't…" Walter cleared his throat, longer than necessary, like a moved man in a crowded theater.

Dan flipped a second bucket, and sat down beside him. "Hey, man. I didn't mean to be sappy. I'm usually not, believe me. You wanna grab a cup inside, warm up a little?"

"It's not you." A tear splashed on the plywood floor. And Walter's head stayed down. Dan became a statue, a petrified man on a cold, hard bucket.

"I haven't been forthright with you, Daniel." Walter's head turned but stopped short of eye contact. "What do you say we take those coffees for a walk?"

Steam rose from holes in the lids of their stainless steel mugs. Their boots swished in fallen leaves and overgrown grass. Their pace was slow, methodical, as if the journey superseded destination. And Rockler lagged somewhere behind, sniffing everything.

"I try not to think about my past, Daniel."

"Why's that?"

Walter slowed the pace further, took a sip, and glanced at Dan. "For the same reason I steer clear of a hornet's nest, I suppose." He grimaced, then stopped. "Confound that blasted knee. I should've listened to you and stayed indoors."

"Wait, you mean you have … a dangerous past?"

Walter took several steps before responding. "Dangerous, perhaps; but only to me. If I think about my mistakes … well …" He breathed deeply, sighed like the wind.

Dan took a drink, trying to make sense of Walter's confession. "I see a couple stumps ahead. Maybe you should rest that knee a minute?"

They sat on rings of wood, aged charcoal gray. Distant smoke mingled with the aroma of autumn earth. Dan frisked his four-day whiskers, glad they were there on this frigid second of November. And though his coffee had cooled to a notch below warm, he forced another swig, waiting for Walter to speak.

"I was just a boy when my daddy died." Walter seemed to be looking deep into the forest, perhaps farther. Dan watched him briefly before turning his eyes to the serrated edge of a brown, brittle leaf. Rockler raced in crunchy circles behind them, and finally lay down. "He took a bullet in the arm," Walter added. "A second one grazed his neck. He lost a lot of blood, too much. Died on Korean soil."

From the corner of his eye, Dan saw Walter moving and frisking his mustache. They both sniffled, and Walter continued: "A few years later my mom remarried. She had to, I guess. Or so she always said." He took a long drink, wiped his mouth with his sleeve. "That man kicked me around like a dog, Daniel. Called me things I dare not repeat. I finished high school and got out of that house."

Dan felt as rigid as the stump beneath him. But he felt likewise moved, in deep and shadowy places, where traumatic memories still primed the pumps of indefinable rage.

"I took a job in logging." Walter's laugh was short and sarcastic. "My goodness; I worked like mad. It was what I needed, though. Chopped away my anger, I suspect. Drank it away too."

Dan's mug nearly cracked in his hands.

"Plenty of unsavory fellows saw logs for a living, Daniel. Not all of them, mind you. But enough. And I'm afraid I became one." Dan's jaw pulled tight. His breathing came in small, stiff bursts, as if forced from a punctured life vest.

"I needed to feel like a man, but chose all the wrong paths," Walter said. "Young and stupid is what I was. Deceived, too. So I took to tipping the bottle every night." He drew an audible breath. "And I also took hold of a desperate young woman. Moved in with her...and treated her like dirt." He drew a raspy breath as he balanced his cup in the leaves. "We somehow lasted a few years, Katherine and me. But then I walked out...and I never looked back. I cut logs a while longer, until—"

"Did you hit her?" Dan's question seemed to shush the forest. Walter, too, said nothing. "Did. You. Hit her?" He looked at Walter, and stood. "You know what, just forget it. Your silence says enough."

"I was a different man then, Daniel."

"Don't give me some lame excuse!" Dan stepped forward, holding his cup. "After all the preaching!"

Walter stood and winced. "You don't know the rest of the—"

"I don't care. I trusted you. I thought…" Dan dropped his head and nearly bit though his lip, feeling like a boy with freshly skinned knees. He turned his back on Walter, and crunched leaves under every retreating step.

"If you'll just let me finish!"

Dan walked farther from the desperate voice, his thickening rage suffocating reason.

"Daniel!" The plea was louder, more direct. "There's more to the—"

Dan wheeled. His stainless steel mug flopped through the air with speed and accuracy. Walter lurched right as the mug flew past him, hit a tree, popped its lid, and splashed black liquid in every direction. Staggering, Walter encountered the stump and fell, palms first, to the earth. Rockler was there in a matter of seconds.

As Walter pushed up with the hands that had cushioned his landing, Dan could only stare, motionless and disoriented. His guts felt like a pint of curdled milk. His hands began to shake, and he thought of his mother the entire walk home.

38

CHAPTER THIRTY-EIGHT

Sitting in the loveseat, Robyn watched Evan push trains around a plastic track. His hair had grown out to about a half an inch (Lil' Hedgehog they affectionately called him) since arriving home from the hospital. Two weeks of in-home occupational therapy had produced wonderful results. No significant neurological damage; that was the latest prognosis. He still slurred a sentence here and there, and took longer to process information at times (delayed cognition, the therapist called it). But these things were only temporary. Starting school next fall would be no problem. He'd have an elevated risk of seizures, the doctor had cautioned. But somehow, however uncharacteristically, Robyn believed that prayer had negated such concerns. It was a quiet, inner assurance unlike anything she'd ever felt before.

Evan dropped to his belly. His stocking feet kicked briskly in the air while his head rested on the carpet, watching trains pass at eye level. The chuffing sounds, whistles, and sincerely-toned gibberish he spoke between engines warmed Robyn's heart. Evan would be an excellent big brother. She smiled, placed a hand on her midsection.

And Dan was a better father now. Still far from perfect, he'd come a long way in a short amount of time. Of course, he'd been more than a bit crotchety since coming home from Walter's last Saturday, but she hadn't pressured him for answers; mood swings were a part of Dan's make-up unlikely to change. And despite what may have transpired between Walter and Dan, he'd continued to meet her needs: talking to her, encouraging her, even cooking real dinners four out of five evenings! He just, under the surface, seemed depressed. Until this morning; when something seemed to click. A new glint, an enthusiastic swagger; exactly what Robyn had been hoping for.

Time to break the news!

"Honey? What'cha doing?" Her tone was playful, inviting.

Dan was in the kitchen, shuffling papers. "Oh, just sorting through some old files. Junk, really."

"Well, I'd like to talk to you, when you have a minute."

He entered the family room, smiling. "I need to talk to you, as well." He sat on the floor, rubbed Evan's head. "What's up, Lil' Hedgehog?"

"Don't!" Evan griped, ducking.

Dan laughed, then looked at Robyn. "Curious, aren't you?"

"About what?"

He joined her on the loveseat. "About why I'm looking through work papers."

His answer put a check mark on her heart. "I didn't know you were. I thought it was bills or statements or something." She adjusted her posture to face him fully. "Does this have anything to do with your cheerful mood this morning?"

Dan chuckled and nodded. "My dad called last night. You were already asleep. I know his calls are usually mood breakers, but this was a good one."

The air felt warm and close as Robyn fought for composure. Her emotions rose and fell like an old country road. Had her prince fallen victim to another poison apple?

There is nothing good in Russell Crawford. How dare he steal this moment!

"He's lined me up with an amazing job opportunity," Dan said.

"What?" she whispered through quivering lips.

"Listen." He gripped her arms. "This at-home thing has been great for us. For me. But we're talking about an executive position that'll almost double my previous income. It might even include a company car, certainly stock options." Her chin dropped; he raised it with a finger. "Robyn, it's too good to pass up."

"After all your time with Walter … ?" A single tear ran down her cheek.

"Walter's not…" Dan's words had turned intense. She watched his eyes narrow. "He's no superman, okay? And his advice isn't always…supportable."

"What about my job? MCC has been so gracious to us."

"Well, that's true. But I assumed you'd like to be here again, in light of Evan's condition."

"What, Daddy?" Evan stood and walked toward them, placing a hand on Dan's leg.

Robyn watched her husband lie through his toothy grin. "I said, 'Which is Evan's favorite engine?'" Evan ran to pick up Thomas.

"I can't… I don't understand," Robyn said. "I thought you were—"

"I'm sorry." He faced her again, still smiling. "Now, you had something to tell me?"

She turned her eyes toward Evan and saw him approaching, blue engine in hand. "I just thought you might like to get pizza," she said.

"Great idea." Dan pulled Evan close. "The job's not official, but there's no reason we can't celebrate early."

39

CHAPTER THIRTY-NINE

The Ford Escape cut fresh tracks in a dusting of snow before rumbling to a stop, near Walter's front porch. Dan beeped the horn twice, stepped out of the vehicle. Margaret opened the screen door, motioning toward the barn.

When he reached the top of the barn's grassy ramp, snow was caked on Dan's hikers. He kicked them together, dropping brown slush on the pure white ground. Stepping into the barn, he saw dimly lit bulbs, mounted to rafters. A stiff breeze caused the barn to creak in a hundred different places. "Walter?" He walked farther, stopping near the table saw. The barn felt almost warm inside, and its greasy aroma seemed strangely comforting. "Walter? You in here?"

"I am now!"

Dan's heart skipped as his body convulsed. Turning toward the door and gripping his chest, he said, "Holy crap! You scared the daylights out of me."

Walter's head was topped with a gray stocking cap. He smiled vindictively, closing the door with his foot. "It was an opportunity too good to pass up."

An interesting choice of words.

"Margaret didn't realize I'd come in for coffee," Walter added. "And when she told me you were out here." His countenance stiffened. "Well, I'd half a mind to stay hidden."

"I can't blame you," Dan said. "Listen, about last weekend, I was…" He pushed sawdust with his foot. "I hope you can forgive me?"

"You bet'cher bippy." He handed Dan a steaming, stainless steel mug. "Consider yourself lucky; Rockler found the lid."

"Where is the little fellow, anyway?"

"Curled up in front of the fire, apparently smarter than us." They laughed though the mood remained brittle with unanswered questions.

"Are you making something?" Dan said.

"No, just rooting out winter supplies. Snow shovels and the like."

They both drank coffee. "The snow's sure pretty for only a dusting," Dan said.

"A skiff of snow can do wonders for a barren landscape."

More drinks. Sporadic eye contact. Nervous tapping.

"Walter, I've decided to work again. I don't have a position yet, but a promising opportunity has opened for me."

Walter rubbed his chin with a leather work glove, and adjusted his cap. "I'll bet the view from the tree house is delightful with snow."

Dan smiled and shook his head. "Walter, it's cold and windy and…"

You're nuts. You're avoiding the subject.

"Let's cover the windows with plastic, rig up a space heater. We'll talk as we work."

"I can't believe you," Dan said.

"Seems to me, I've heard that before." Walter patted Dan's shoulder. "There's a clear plastic tarp in the house, brand new. Margaret'll get it for you. And while you're at it, bring my new space heater. It's still in an Amazon box. I'll gather some tools and meet you, directly."

"I can see you've given this no prior thought."

Walter's mustache pushed forward, scratching his nose. "A house as special as ours should not be seasonal."

The hole-cutting blade pierced cleanly through the wall. Dan silenced the driver. "Okay. Send it through." From outside the tree house, standing on the next-to-last rung of a large, folding ladder, Walter fed a bright yellow cord through the freshly cut hole. Dan plugged in the space heater, turned it on. "We've got heat!"

"Turn it off for now," Walter said. "Seal the hole with some of that Gorilla Tape."

Dan heard the ladder snap closed. And by the time he looked out the window, Walter was already lugging it back to the barn, favoring one knee.

I could've done that. Stubborn old man.

Dan used pieces of tape to seal the yellow cord. Then, with arms wrapped around his shivering knees, he sat in a corner and closed his eyes, thinking of tactful ways to hasten his departure. But as minutes passed his mind surrendered to a disturbing trail of fabricated images: a frightened young woman, sitting alone in an antiquated kitchen, an ice cube melting on her fat and bloodied lip. A husky young man, standing in a corner, his palms pressed against adjoining walls. His head is turned down, and he is huffing in anger. And then he turns. A brown mustache conceals most of his mouth. His thick eyebrows pinch together as he grabs a brown jug from a nearby counter. "That'll teach you! You bet'cher bippy it—"

"Sleeping on the job?" Walter's voice was a raspy alarm clock. With a plastic tarp tucked under one arm, he crawled in the tree house. Dan could hardly look at him. "Let's get these windows covered, fire up the heater." Walter unfolded the tarp, cut it in half. "Hold this in place, Daniel."

Against contrary breezes, Dan positioned half the tarp over one window. Walter used a staple gun to affix the corners before driving staples around the entire frame. A few minutes later, the second and final window was finished in the same manner. They covered all the edges with tape. And though the tarps flapped and snapped, they did stop the wind.

After a short period of tidying, Walter closed the door and started the heater. Their bucket seats were cold at first, but the convection-style heater had them and the whole tree house toasty warm in no time. The men said nothing as heavy shadows darkened their world. Dan stared through the tarps at millions of snowflakes, suddenly swirling like an impenetrable cloud. Then, as abruptly as it began, the snow squall stopped, yielding to afternoon sunlight.

"Follow your heart," Walter said.

Dan felt his face contorting with irritation. "What?"

"If taking this job is something you truly desire, and for the right reasons
—"

"I didn't ask for your advice."

"You came over."

"Yeah, to *tell* you about my decision; not to hear some nugget of direc-
tional wisdom. Not anymore." Dan looked away. His feet began to tap. The
silence that followed was long and hollow and offset by tarps, whapping in
the wind.

"You're being unfair," Walter said.

"Am I?"

"Daniel!" Walter sounded like a scolding father.

Dan lunged to his feet and banged his head. "Dang it!" He rubbed the
rising knot.

Walter stood also, his wispy white hair stopping inches from the truss
peaks. He stepped toward Dan. "I hit her once, Daniel. One time. In an
angry, drunken stupor. But there's more to the story."

Dan stared into Walter's determined expression, and they both sat.

"A year or so after I walked out on Katherine, the owner of a hardware
store caught me with a package of drill bits in my coat pocket. He promised
to keep it between us if I'd let him explain Jesus to me. So what could I do?
We talked that evening in the back of his shop over a bottle of Coke-a-Cola.
I'll never forget it."

Dan continued to rub his sore head. Walter's eyes grew more distant
than determined. "Mr. Guthrie was the store owner. And there was something about his simple tale of restoration and forgiveness. He put a Bible in
my hands, even allowed me to keep the drill bits. Turns out we'd talked for
over an hour. But I'd hardly noticed… or cared."

Walter wiped his eyes, straightened his hair. "Well, I continued logging,
but in a different town. Made a fresh start. Lightened up on the drinking,
too. Lucky for me, I had a foreman who noticed and took a particular
interest. He'd eat lunch with me on the trunk of a fallen tree or sitting in a
skid loader. He believed in me, you see? Saw me trying to better my life, and
decided to be a mentor. And it wasn't long before he shared *his* faith in
Jesus. I guess I knew then God wasn't fooling around. He was going to get
my attention."

As the story unfolded, Dan fought to retain his resentment of Walter and the permission it afforded to dismiss their friendship, chalk it up to nothing more than an unexpected diversion, an offbeat chapter in his life of executive destiny.

"Before long, I'd moved in with his family. I'd never seen such love, such respect. He treated his children with tenderness. His wife, as well. And they loved me like one of their own, Daniel." Walter cocked his head, tucked in his chin. "I came to the Lord a month or two later. Surrendered my life. And God changed my heart. Of course, most of the changes took time, but not all. My language cleaned up, almost overnight. And my desire for the bottle, well... It was miraculous how that disappeared. Never touched it again. Came to detest it, in fact."

Walter paused, secured eye contact, and leaned forward. "I've seen what alcohol can do, how it changes some people, goads them toward wickedness. God rescued me from its destructive influence, Daniel. And I'm eternally grateful."

"Did you ever forgive him?" Dan asked.

"Beg pardon?"

"Your mother's second husband."

"In time, but it was awfully hard. He ditched her not long after I left. We never heard of his whereabouts after that. I'd visit home on occasion, but not nearly enough. My mother had friends and relatives to look in on her. I was 32 when she passed."

Walter looked at the floor and shuffled his boots, nodding his head for no discernable reason. "Unforgiveness is a beast, Daniel. We hold on to it and think we're condemning those who've hurt us. But all it does is claw us to death, ravage our insides." He looked squarely at Dan. "When I finally forgave that man, that's when I really found freedom. I'll never forget the harm he caused. It was dirty, low-down wickedness and nothing more. But, Daniel, Jesus has forgiven me of the same."

40

CHAPTER FORTY

Broadmore Glen was one of Russell's favorite courses. They were to meet in the clubhouse for coffee and mimosa prior to tee time. A cold day was forecast, but at least winter rules would apply.

VP of Finance Javier Sanchez was to accompany Paul Andrews, the CFO for Conway Distribution, a publicly-traded corporation based in the Harrisburg area. Paul had worked with Russell until making the leap to Conway, and now he was searching for a senior director. With Russell by his side, Dan needed only to shoot a respectable round of eighteen holes.

A few pars, some astute conversation…

It was 11:13 pm, and the kitchen was dark save the glow of Dan's laptop. He sipped coffee, staring at Conway's online portfolio, determined to memorize it and thus diffuse any shanked drives or wayward putts. But amid the facts and figures and business lingo, Walter's story loomed.

Unforgiveness is a beast.

Wind splattered the window with a swarm of flurries that ticked and hissed on impact. Dan gulped coffee and continued reading: For over a decade, production in the area of accounts payable has—*I called Walter my best friend*—exceeded expectations overall—*I have a wife and a son at home because of him*—while work efficiency ratings have steadily…

What in the world?

Dan closed his laptop, and in near pitch darkness, he stared toward the tree. Then he stood and walked closer, his heart in his throat, as the flickering light in the distance intensified.

"Robyn!" He ran in the garage without closing the door, threw on his hikers and a heavy brown coat. "Robyn!"

He heard feet shuffle briskly on the kitchen floor. "What!" she said, reaching him.

The garage door clanked into motion. "Call Walter first, then 911!"

Robyn pulled her robe tight. "Dan! What's—"

"The tree is on fire!"

Dan's feet pounded the frozen soil, and he couldn't determine if the tears on his cheeks were spilled by the wind or the panic driving him forward. His legs burned like the tree, now engulfed in flames.

Reaching the hilltop, he conceded to walking as the crackling fire lit up the ground. Waves of heat touched his cheeks, and plumes of smoke gushed toward the barn. He circled downwind to Walter's front porch, flung open the screen, and pounded the locked door. Sirens sounded in the distance.

"WALTER! MARGARET!"

The door opened. "I'm here," Walter said, stepping onto the porch. "Just had to get dressed." He stuck his head back inside. "Margaret! You get bundled quickly and get outside, in case the house goes!" The men dashed from the porch and rounded the house. Its bricks were an eerie shade of orange, and every window reflected the inferno.

"I've put the hose away already!" Walter shouted, running for the barn.

Dan chased him. "Let me get it!"

Walter stopped and with winded breath said, "It's just left of the door." He reached in a coat pocket. "Here's the key. I'll head to the cellar and connect water to the outside bib."

Dan sprinted to the barn, his back turned to the advancing smoke. He unlocked the padlock, and dropped the key in the snow. *Forget it, move!* Shoving the door open, he searched to the left, toppling shovels and rakes and whatever else got in his way. "Walter! I can't see!" The sirens drew closer. "WALTER!" He kicked in the darkness, desperate to strike rubber.

"Daniel!" Walter's voice was distant. Dan ran out the door, and then pulled his coat up and over his nose. "Get out of the barn!" Walter shouted. "It's on fire!"

Heart pounding, Dan ran toward the house and the sound of Walter's voice. He slipped on the grass and went down hard, soaking his pants in the melting slush. Standing again, he saw Walter and Margaret, near the back door, motioning him forward. Margaret kept Rockler at bay on a leash as swirling red lights sped down Rakes Mill Road. Fire trucks turned in the drive. Within minutes, firefighters swarmed the flames.

"I'm so sorry," Dan said.

"The garden hose would've been little use," Walter managed.

"Are you the homeowners?" The fireman's question was pointed and aggressive.

"Yes," Walter said, struggling to compose himself.

"Is there anyone inside the house or barn?" He held an ax in one hand.

"No."

"We're gonna need you people to stay back and let us work!" He ran toward the action, became part of it.

Trucks and ambulances continued to arrive. Hoses were unfurled, connected to pumpers, and massive showers smothered the tree as branches dropped, one at a time, to the ground. The tree house was barely discernable amid the flames, and what remained of its structure eventually plummeted when the main trunk split and crashed like charcoal. Several trucks pulled behind the house, where a hook and ladder elevated fire fighters above the burning barn. Others attacked from ground level. Mobile floodlights lit up the scene; for three tearful spectators and one trembling brown mutt.

The relentless wind was an agitated enemy, bent on fanning the flames, including those thought to be extinguished. Two trucks sprayed nearby brush to prevent wind-driven sparks from igniting the forest. In less than an hour, the barn collapsed to a drenched pile of wood and tin and memories. It smoldered for hours. An impending, unavoidable death.

The first thing she noticed was his ashen-gray face. His hair hung ragged, his eyes were bloodshot, and as he walked closer, she noticed muddy sweats and crew socks stained black. Slowly and stiff-legged, Dan moved like a soldier who'd lived through combat.

But he doesn't look injured. And thank God he's alive.

He sat beside her at the table, folded his arms, and dropped his head. He smelled like sweat and soot. "Tell me this is a nightmare." His words sounded spoken from a cave.

Robyn covered her mouth as a tear escaped. "I'm so sorry."

"Does Evan know?"

"No. I kept him upstairs. He woke up when you shouted but I told him you went to help Walter with something. He was drowsy enough to buy it; went right back to sleep. With the medicine he's on he can sleep through anything."

Dan's head lifted then nodded, as if relieved. He slid his chair back and turned to face her. "I'm so insanely tired."

She stared at him, pitied him, wanting to release him to shower and slumber. But it was after midnight, and his phone was still face down on the table, right where he'd left it. She'd worried for hours and had to know. She had a right to know. "How bad was it?"

Dan sat up straight, frowned, and sucked his top teeth. "The barn went up, too," he finally said. "Everything's destroyed. The tree. The tree house." His face pinched. "The whole barn collapsed. I mean…"

Robyn leaned forward, gripping his arms. Their heads tipped, their foreheads touched, and together they cried. "How did it start?" Her words were but sniffles.

She felt his forehead twisting. "Investigators are coming back in the morning. They suspect the space heater." He lifted his head, looked in her eyes. "But I know we unplugged it."

Robyn wiped her face. "So no one was hurt?"

"No. Just heartbroken. I think it was the hardest goodbye I've ever had to say. I mean, Walter…" Dan cocked his head, knuckled his lips.

"I'll stay home today," Robyn said. "I've had a lot of time off lately, but I think they'll understand. I can burn up some comp time." She almost slapped herself. *What stupid words!*

He looked long in her eyes. "That heater; it was just convection, no kerosene or anything. And I know we unplugged it."

Robyn did her best to form a sympathetic smile, but her mind took a hairpin turn. How quickly life can change. A day—*only a day*—had passed since Dan shared his decision to go corporate again; since he imposed staying home on her, casting showers of sparks upon the dry, brittle grounds of what had been positive change. Her stomach soured, and she nearly shared the awkward analogy with Dan. But tonight was tragic, a devastating loss. Family dynamics could wait. They should wait. And yet they festered, churning beneath talk of the fiery facts, lurking behind their sentimental exchanges.

How quickly life can change... or be lost forever.

"Honey..." she began. "I... I'll make you a sandwich." She walked to the fridge, pulled out a Gatorade. "Here, start with this."

"Thanks." Dan twisted the cap, downed half the bottle. "Did my dad call?"

41

CHAPTER FORTY-ONE

It was ten before noon on Monday, and as luck would have it they were seated in the exact same booth. This time, however, the booth across the aisle stayed empty, as did most of Friendly's. Dan picked at his fries but couldn't stomach his cheeseburger. Imprinted on his mind were images of fire, and they were about to be shared with Evan.

Robyn pulled diet soda through her gurgling straw as the waitress arrived with Evan's ice cream: a vanilla mouse with Peanut Butter Cup ears and licorice whiskers. "Whooaaa!" he shouted. The waitress giggled as she left with Robyn's cup.

"Hey, sport," Dan said softly. "I've got something to talk to you about." Evan nodded, shoved in a bite. "You remember last night, when Daddy had to help Mr. Walter?"

"You were screaming." Evan's words sounded suctioned.

"Yes, I was. That's right. I was pretty frightened."

Robyn slid her arm over Evan's shoulders. "Why?" he asked, inserting another spoonful.

Dan shot straight: "The tree was on fire. The tree house, too."

White liquid dribbled from the corners of Evan's mouth. "Did you put it out, Daddy?"

"No, I didn't," Dan said. "Evan, it's all gone. The tree burned down. And Mr. Walter's barn did, too."

Robyn's mouth turned down, and Evan stopped eating. He blinked a few times, as if pondering the shocker, and then asked, "When will he build a new one?"

Dan guffawed, elbowed the table, and rubbed his face. "You know, I'm not really sure about that Lil' Hedgehog."

Where's the weeping? The heart-wrenching emotion? I should have told him at home, over a bologna sandwich!

"Honey, I'm sorry," Robyn said, giving Evan a sideways squeeze.

"Did you start the fire, Mommy?"

Oh, for the love of…

The waitress arrived, placed a drink on the table. "Here you go. Will that be all today?"

"Yes," Dan said, and the waitress retreated. "You know, Evan, while we're sharing news, I might as well tell you: Daddy has a job interview on Saturday morning." He sensed Robyn squinting, and nibbling her lip. She softly kicked his shin.

"What's an in-view?" Evan licked ice cream from a Peanut Butter Cup.

"It means I might get another job. At an office, like before." His tone was condescending. "It means I've decided to stop staying at home every day, buddy. And start going to work again."

A hush fell over the table. Evan returned his candy to the dish. His bottom lip pushed forward as his body slumped, and his buzz-cut head came to rest on Robyn's chest. He looked like a baby bird. "What?" Dan said. "You're done with your ice cream?"

Evan nodded, his eyes glistening. Robyn kissed his hair, near the smallest scar, and Dan felt like he'd swallowed his cheeseburger whole.

42

CHAPTER FORTY-TWO

The afternoon air was cold but calm; no more blustery wind or iron gray clouds or three-minute white-outs. There was also no tree house, no barn. Shoulder to shoulder, Dan and Walter surveyed the rubble. Traces of smoke still lifted from the deepest piles, and amid the embers and ashes, power tools, metal implements and even a blackened tractor stood like heroes. But they were dead just the same.

"Talk to your insurance company?"

"Yep." Walter's clipped reply was laced with pessimism.

"Is there a problem with the policy?"

"I have no idea what was in there, Daniel. I never bothered to take inventory or assess what I had." He looked away. "Insurance will cover the barn, but…" He stroked his mustache. "I'll have to fill it with new memories."

They stood in silence, as if beholding the ruins of an epic battle.

"I know we unplugged that heater," Dan said.

"Well, they've no less determined it the cause. Sawdust smoldering in the coils, or something. Seems to me we did have that rascal pretty hot."

"Then why didn't the fire start earlier?"

"Daniel…" Walter inhaled deeply. "My heart aches too much to think about it."

Dan nodded. "So where do we begin?"

Walter smiled. "With a cup of coffee." His expression sobered. "There's not much we can do. A contractor can finish the demolition, truck it all away. I just need some companionship today."

"I understand." Dan looked beyond the rubble, toward the tree line. His eyes swept left to right, stopping on the Norway spruce which, in the barn's absence, looked somehow larger and almost protective, like towering guardians of the grassy path. The protruding rocks seemed altered as well, appearing less like tombstones and more like a proud row of monuments.

He turned to face the tree's charred remains. "You know, I'm sure gonna miss—"

His heart hammered.

Behind the ashes was a rotund man with whiskered cheeks. He wore a camouflage beanie, a brown canvas coat, and horn-rimmed glasses, obscuring his eyes.

"Walter, that's him."

"Who, Daniel." His voice was hushed and tentative as he turned toward the tree house rubble.

"I can't be sure at this distance, but I think it's the stalker."

The uninvited man began to walk around the smoldering pile.

"Can we help you?" Walter's call was loud in Dan's ear.

The man leaned forward, picked up some sort of shard. "I never meant to burn that barn." He threw the remnant back to the ground, and wiped his hands on his jeans. Dan's skin prickled from head to toe. The fire was arson, and this was surely Butch Hake.

Walter stepped forward. "Are you crazy?" Dan scolded. "Stay back." His fists clenched as he scanned the ground, desperate for anything with which to defend himself.

"My apologies, sir," Walter called. "But I'm afraid I don't understand."

Dan forced a breath. His chin began to quake as enormous thoughts collided, causing him to bolt toward the fallen barn, where he remembered spotting the charred remains of what appeared to be a small garden spade. He kicked away a blackened beam that covered most of the tool, and found that it was indeed a spade. He wrenched it free, thankful to discover it warm not hot.

"Daniel?" Walter's voice was careful and controlled.

"What?"

"Stop it."

Spade in hand, Dan stomped his way to Walter, and said, "That creep started the fire." His words were venomous hisses. "And he's been messing with my family for months."

"He could have a gun. Now just stay calm."

"Then yell for Margaret. Have her call the police."

"She's not home." Walter spoke in a snappy whisper.

Fear diluted Dan's anger. "I have my cell. Just let me get behind you and —"

Butch Hake approached... closer... closer... and stopped five yards away. Dan remained quiet, still gripping the spade. "I only meant to burn that tree house," Butch said. He removed his glasses, rubbed an eye with his shoulder.

"Did you start this fire?" Walter said. Butch Hake scowled like a provoked bull. He put on his glasses, and spat on the ground. "Who are you?" Walter added. "Why did you—"

"What is it, old man? You wanna know my name?" He shoved his hands in his pockets, and his breathing turned audible. "What's it matter, now?" His gaze dropped. "I always believed you was a drunk; some selfish 'ol bastard didn't want no kids." He motioned Dan's direction, then locked eyes with Walter. "Turns out I was wrong."

"But why would you ever think—"

"'Cause my mom told me! That's why!"

Walter lifted a hand to his mustache, as if pondering, or connecting dots. "Your mother?" he said through his fingers.

"Katherine Grimes."

"You can't mean..." Walter seemed to choke. He lowered his hand from his face to his chest, and then slowly took a knee on the soggy lawn. "I had no idea." His words were muddled.

Dan knelt beside him, keeping an eye on Butch. "Are you okay? Is it your heart?"

"I think this man is my son."

"Don't call me that! You might'a planted the seed, but you ain't no father."

"She never told me. I never knew."

Butch sniffled twice, shoved a finger under his lenses. "She didn't want you to know. Said you was gone and I was better off for it."

Dan tossed the spade aside, and stood tall before Butch. "You've been stalking my family. Why?"

"A man grows up without a father and he don't quite feel complete. Mom died a few years back, but before she did she told me his name." He nodded toward Walter, who was attempting to stand. "Turns out we aren't that far apart; 'bout forty-five minutes." Walter brushed off his behind, and the trio of men stood face to face. "I wasn't figurin' on meetin' him or nothin' like that," Butch continued. "Just wanted to see the deadbeat. I don't know why, maybe that… What do you call it; closure or something?"

"How touching. What's that got to do with me?" Dan asked.

"I started spying," Butch said. "I know it ain't right; ain't even legal. But I did it, and I saw you and him, all buddy-buddy and stuff. And I thought: I've been wrong all these years; my dad's a decent guy. He's even got a son to take my place." He spat again. "Then I got freakin' pissed, Mr. Crawford." He squared shoulders with Dan. "I grew up dirt poor with a single mother working three thankless jobs."

Dan stepped toward him. "I told you he wasn't my father!"

"Which only made it worse!"

Dan drew a fist, but Walter hustled between them. "Daniel, don't!"

"Forget this sob story crap, Walter; it doesn't justify anything. This guy burned down the barn and he's going to jail!"

"I'm sorry!" Butch Hake's apology seemed to silence the world. "Honestly, I am. And I have some skills to help make it right."

Dan shook his head, gripped his hips. "I don't believe this. This isn't happening."

Walter turned toward Mr. Hake. "You became jealous of my relationship with Daniel?"

"I seen you guys buildin' that tree house, puttin' your arms around each other. I can't tell you how many times I wished for a daddy like that; cryin' in bed after gettin' called a fatso all day." He removed his glasses, sucked in snot. "I been out'a work the last few months. And I used the time to do more than drive by. I knew it was wrong to spy, but I ain't a bad guy. I was just too scared to knock on the door. Knowin' you didn't want nothin' to do with me, anyway."

"I never knew. She never told me, Mr. Hake."

"Grimes. My name is Kevin Grimes."

Dan's gut knotted at the sound of that name. Another Kevin. An even bigger schmuck.

"Kevin," Walter said. "If I had only known…"

"Well, you never came back to find out. Never."

"I was a different man then. I just… By the time I got my life on track, years had passed. I assumed she'd moved on, wanted no part of me. I thought I was doing right by both of us. If I had only known…" Dan heard the tears in Walter's words, and watched as he wiped them away.

"I was watchin' from my van yesterday," Kevin said. "Had a few shots 'a Jack to knock off the chill. And then I lost my mind. Over everything, from way back. I never felt such anger. Figured I'd just destroy that tree house. It don't make no sense lookin' back. Guess I was drunker than I thought." He kicked the grass. "When I seen the barn go up…" He drew a breath, dried his stubble with his shoulders. "I barfed on the side of the road, smashed the bottle, and got the heck gone. I felt like I'd killed somebody. Still do. But I really ain't a bad guy, Mr. Benning. I know I seem crazy comin' here. But I needed to make things right."

"I'm overwhelmed," Walter said through his folded hands. "I think we'd better sit down and talk."

"Are you kidding me?" Dan said.

Walter turned, lowered his hands. "Daniel, I don't—"

"Don't *Daniel*, me." He motioned toward the rubble. "That was our tree! Your barn! Your tools!"

"And I've made no decisions!" Walter stepped closer. "I've made no decisions, Daniel; nor am I of mind to. Now I don't expect you to understand how I'm feeling, but you will respect me enough to let me handle this. We're both hurting. But sentiments aside, this is my property… and apparently my son."

"How do you know he's not making this up?"

"Daniel, look at him! Put a mustache on his lip!"

Dan watched Kevin light a cigarette, take a long drag. "What'd you do, flip a butt in the tree house?" Kevin forced smoke through his nostrils. "Where'd you hide?" Dan continued. "In the corn? The woods? Come to think of it, you probably kicked the dog, didn't you?"

Walter's head swung toward Kevin, who only looked away.

"Can't even look at your old man now, can you?"

"Daniel! That's enough."

"Forgiveness can't be this big, Walter."

Walter gripped Dan's arms. "You mean mine… or his?"

Dan allowed the question to resonate before shaking loose and walking away. "Daniel!" He turned, slipping in the wet grass.

"No police," Walter said.

Dan glared a final time at both Kevin and Walter.

"No police," Walter repeated.

43

CHAPTER FORTY-THREE

A nightlight softened the darkness as they lay on their backs, holding hands beneath the covers. Robyn listened, though she'd heard it all before: Butch Hake was actually Kevin Grimes who was actually Walter's long, lost son. He'd spied on them, kicked the dog, and started the fire in a drunken fit of jealous rage. And, oh yes: Walter was an idiot. She disagreed with the latter, of course. But Walter's life was now doubtless inverted, changed forever. But what about Dan's?

"I knew there was something freaky about that guy the first time we saw him. Didn't I tell you?" Dan asked.

"You're quite perceptive, dear." Her tone was cajoling.

"I can't stop wondering what they talked about. After I left, I mean. For all I know they could still be hashing things through."

She shushed his intensifying voice, and said, "Give him a quick call. At least you'll know he's okay."

"I don't want to talk to him. And he's not okay, Robyn. He's nuts."

"Oh, c'mon; you love that old man and you know it!"

She wanted to comfort him, to hear his concerns and help him to process this inconceivable turn of events. But the winds of change now seemed to be blowing in the wrong direction, and bitterness simmered in her heart. For days her mind had felt swollen by thoughts of pompous golfers, bundled in sweaters, sipping silver flasks, and wooing her bone-headed husband away from his newfound commitment to family. So many changes had transpired in Dan, but they were green, fragile. None felt anchored. And now he seemed doomed to regress, slip into old patterns, resume a self-absorbed stride. Abandoning Walter was the nail in the coffin that she and Evan—*no, the children and her!*—would be tasked with kicking open.

Or dropping six feet under.

She withdrew her hand from Dan's and tried to relax as the darkness grew evermore pressing. "How can Walter forgive that man?" Dan said. "Even if he is his son?"

"I don't know. I'm sure he must be shocked to find out he's a parent after all these years. I can't imagine how Margaret must feel."

"I couldn't do it," Dan said with assurance.

"Well, I guess you don't have to."

"Unforgiveness is a beast." Dan whispered.

"Excuse me?"

"Oh, it's just something Walter said. About not forgiving people. How it really eats us up inside." He rolled to his side, facing her. "I just…"

Robyn kept staring up, waiting for more. Spears of light from a passing car interrupted the darkness. "Do you believe him?" she finally said.

"I'm hurting, Robyn." His voice was sincere. "Walter's been like a father. And for a while, I wanted to be like him."

"You still can be." Hope sprung to life, rode on her words. She turned her head in his direction. "You've been through a lot. It's gonna take some time to—"

"He used to drink. And once he even hit Kevin's mother."

"I had no idea. When?"

"Years ago. Before he got all religious; turned over a new leaf or whatever."

"Does that bother you?"

"Yes, it bothers me. What do you think?"

"I think you'd better watch your tone." She looked up again. A minute passed in silence. "Okay, I'll bite: Why, Dan? Why does it bother you so much?"

"Because he acts so goody-two-shoes. All sentimental and wholesome and down-on-the-farm. But it's all phony. Isn't it? I mean, he was a drunk, a jerk. And now he wants to chisel the hell out of me?"

"But he's obviously different now. Are you so dense? Why can't a changed man encourage others to do the same?"

Dan threw back the covers, sat on the edge of the bed. "I don't need this. I swear, I don't need this."

"What, Dan? What don't you need?" She paused, lowered her voice. "A wonderful friend? A loving old man who thinks the world of you? Or maybe you'd prefer a wife who doesn't think for herself. Maybe that's— "

"It's too much like my dad!" He stood, walked into the darkness. "Walter's story hits too close to home. There, I said it."

Robyn's heart was in her throat. She sat up straight, pressed her back against the headboard, pulled her knees close, and waited. A prayer sprung to mind: *God, please help my husband. Please save my family.* It was simple and frantic, but a prayer nonetheless.

"It wasn't a baseball bat," Dan said. She could hardly hear him. His form moved closer, and sat where her feet had just been.

"What do you mean?"

Dan gripped his bangs, held them aloft. "It wasn't a baseball bat."

Robyn tapped the bedside lamp to its lowest setting, and beheld the waxy, branch-like scar embedded in her husband's forehead. She knew in an instant that Russell was to blame.

"He knocked Mom out on the kitchen floor. I defended her, so he put me down with a beer can to the head." He released his hair. "I fell and bled all over her." He looked away, and his voice became eerily calm, as if disembodied. "He hit her all the time, Robyn. Me too. And yet for some pathetic reason I still care what he thinks. How sick is that?" He walked to the bathroom and closed the door.

Robyn curled blankets in her fists as she pictured the scene: a shaking boy, bloodied by his father, clinging to his motionless mother, and Russell hovering over them, eyes like fiery darts, a satisfied smirk creasing his cheeks as he mutters profanity, cracking open another beer. Kicking off the covers, she walked to the dresser, and gazed in her mirror. A decade of marriage, and she'd never heard this story? How badly had her husband been abused?

"Mom." It was Evan's familiar call, long and droned. She practically raced to his room, rubbed his hair, and kissed his cheek. He'd had a bad dream, and she felt like she was in one. Minutes later and no less disturbed, she returned to her bedroom.

Dan was sitting in a chair, bare-chested, arms folded. His complexion was pallid, his expression disengaged. "Can I get you something?" she asked.

"A sweatshirt."

She opened the closet, grabbed the first one she saw. He stood to put it on, and their eyes met. For several seconds she held his gaze, until he dropped to his knees and hugged her stomach.

If only he knew; would it make any difference?

She ran fingers through his hair.

I'll tell him this week. No more excuses.

Head spinning, Robyn drove away from MCC.

Three days had passed since an act of arson rocked the known world. Dan had yet to speak with Walter, but she'd called Margaret on two occasions, learning Walter and Kevin had spent hours in productive conversation. Kevin's wife was named Brandi, and the Bennings were now officially grandparents to a five-year-old boy named Jake.

Despite three redneck zingers, Dan had said little in response to the news. Instead he'd driven twice to Conway Distribution, gauging the commute and, as he labeled it, getting a vibe. When Robyn arrived home yesterday, she found him dressed in khakis and a blazer for no apparent reason. And during dinner, when Evan asked him to go to the farm, Dan's curt reply was like a squirt of cheap cologne.

She pulled in the garage, and killed the engine. Entering the kitchen, Evan clamped her legs, insisting she come to the family room. "You did great, Lil' Hedgehog!" she said of the farm he'd created with blocks, logs, and plastic animals. He smiled, rubbing his lengthening crew cut. She unloaded her purse and briefcase. "Where's Daddy?"

"Upstairs."

"Okay. I'll get changed, and then..." She thought about mentioning the special news. "I'll be right back." She trotted to the bedroom.

Dan was in the chair, his laptop open and humming. "Did you know Conway employs over three hundred people?"

"Nice to see you, too." She stepped out of her heels.

Dan scribbled notes on a steno pad. "Good day?" He was wearing his best jeans and a striped, purple oxford. With a silver pen, he tapped his chin.

"It was okay." She finished changing. Her pink and gray warm-up suit swished with every step toward the door. She closed it gently. "Can we talk?"

His eyes glanced up. "Yeah."

"Without the computer?"

He drew a long breath. "Yeah, okay." He closed the laptop, placed it on the carpet. Standing, he stretched and made momentary bug eyes. "What's up?" The silver pen was now clipped to his shirt pocket.

This isn't ideal, but nothing has been. The interview's Sunday. It's time to tell him. Past time!

Robyn walked close, held both of his hands, and smiled sadly at the bangs she could now see through. "I want you to help me." It was the first line of a rehearsed scenario.

Dan's head tilted, his eyebrows scrunched. "Okay...?" He sounded annoyed.

"I want you to be with me when Evan hears the news."

Please ask what news. Please ask what news.

"And what news might that be?"

His expression turned smug, but he'd asked the right question. She paused for effect, her eyes moistening. "That he's going to be a big brother."

Dan's face went blank. "You mean..." He laughed. "I can't..." He laughed louder. Robyn dropped his hands and hugged him. As he rubbed her back, she heard him sniffle. "Are you sure?" he asked.

"Yes," she said, without letting go. "I've known for weeks, but finding the right time to tell you... There was so much going on, and I didn't want to overwhelm you."

Wow! I didn't even rehearse that part.

He tightened their hug, kissed the top of her head, and said, "Let's go tell him." She backed away, nodding and wiping her eyes. Dan's smile was full and genuine.

They descended the stairs.

"Guys, look!" Evan shouted, adding a pig pen to his sprawling complex.

"That's cool, bud," Dan said, sitting down on the loveseat. "Now come on over here and sit on my lap. Your mom and I have something to share with you." His delivery was smooth, full of wit, like that of a seasoned executive.

Evan climbed on his lap, and Robyn sat beside them. Holding Evan's hand, she noticed hers was shaking. "Ev," she said. "You're going to make a wonderful big brother." From the look on his face, no connection was made. She looked at Dan, who gave a quick nod. "Honey, Mommy's going to have a baby. You're going to have a little brother or sister."

"What'cha think about that, sport?" Dan wrapped an arm around Evan.

A smile spread on Evan's face. "Good, I guess." He thought a few seconds. "Can you make it a boy?"

Robyn laughed as tension escaped from her body. "I'll do my best, but no promises." She caressed his cheek. "God will make that decision for us." It was the first spiritual thing she'd ever said to her son. Her chest and face felt suddenly warm.

"Can I play farm now?"

"Sure," Dan said, helping Evan slide to the floor.

Holding hands, they watched their son build. Robyn rested her head on Dan's shoulder, he palmed her stomach, and every care in the world felt washed away. "Another mouth to feed," Dan said with a chuckle. "I'd better shoot well on Sunday. Which reminds me: Let's call Dad, share the good news."

Robyn's eyes squeezed shut, and the world once again felt soiled.

44

CHAPTER FORTY-FOUR

Dan's Ford traveled the crushed-stone lane, rumbling more than rolling, almost causing his teeth to chatter. But he wouldn't be visiting Walter as much, and certainly not in this heap.

I'll lease another Beamer. Or maybe an Audi…

He parked behind the house, rapped the back door. Margaret answered. "Robyn told you I was coming, right?"

"Yes, she did. Walter's sitting by the fire. But I'm afraid he's a bit under the weather this morning."

"Oh, hey, I'll reschedule. I didn't realize…"

"He'd like to see you."

Dan stepped inside, removed his coat, and folded it over a kitchen chair. Margaret's popcorn curls seemed tighter, freshly styled. She wore dark blue jeans, pleated in front, and a purple sweatshirt with floral prints. "Here we are," she said, passing Dan a mug, full and steaming and mixed with cream and sugar. "Hot coffee, Daniel style."

He smiled, sipped, and motioned with his head. "May I…?"

"Of course; take it with you. I'll be preparing lunch, directly, if you'd like to stay."

"Thank you, no. I have a lot to do at home."

Dan walked to the family room. Walter was sitting in a chair with a blanket on his legs, reading glasses low on his nose, an open book propped on his stomach. His eyes appeared closed. A fire crackled in the fireplace.

"Knock-knock," Dan said.

Walter closed the book, sat up straight, and removed his glasses. "I understand…" He cleared his throat. "I understand you've something to tell me?"

"Yeah, I wanted to—"

"Come in first, Daniel. Get comfortable."

Wooden planks creaked as Dan crossed the room. He sunk into a Victorian sofa, positioned along a wall, opposite the fireplace. "I hear you're not feeling well?"

Walter pulled his blanket higher. "Oh, just a blasted cold is all." He coughed as if prompted. "Nothing too contagious, but do keep your distance." He lifted a mug, took a long swallow.

"Robyn's pregnant," Dan said. "I wanted to tell you in person."

A muffled gasp came from the kitchen. "She's already dialing," Walter said. "You should've whispered." They laughed briefly, until their smiles faded and their eyes returned to the flames.

"I also wanted to tell you that I have my golf-game-slash-interview tomorrow morning," Dan said. "It seems like a sure bet, so I won't be having much free time."

Walter drank again, glancing at Dan. "Who's the lucky employer?"

"I'm not at liberty to say."

"I see."

"Well, I'd better get going, let you rest." Dan heard clicks from the hallway as Rockler entered the room, turned a few circles in front of the fire, and lay down on a denim-covered pillow, embroidered with his name.

"Congratulations," Walter said. His mustache wiggled and scratched his nose. "On the baby and the job. May you find much joy in both."

Dan nodded, took a final sip of coffee. Then he stood, walked toward the door, and heard Rockler's tags behind him.

"You know, time heals nothing," Walter said.

Dan stopped, exhaled forcefully. *Forward or backward?* For a disconcerting moment he saw value in neither.

"I neglected my past," Walter continued. "Called it water-under-the-bridge. But I've healed more in three days of talking than I ever did in thirty years of forgetting. You see, the strange thing was: I didn't know my heart was still broken. But it was; buried under years of better choices." He coughed and grumbled and cleared his throat. "Now, you can walk out my door if you want to. Act like you're no longer hurting. But I know better."

Dan turned around. "So what if I am?"

"Then you might have an ounce of understanding for what drove my son's behavior."

"I have been—" Dan bit his lip, lowered his voice. "I have been hurting my entire life, Walter. Do you hear me? My entire life. And not once have I burned down a building."

"Walter?" Margaret entered the room. "Everything okay?"

"Yes," Walter said. "Now why don't you go visit Robyn and talk about the baby. We know you overheard."

"I'm not sure I feel comfortable leaving," she said.

"We'll be fine. Daniel and I have some things to discuss."

Margaret consented, walking briskly to the hallway closet. "There's hot coffee in the carafe!" she hollered on her way out the door.

Walter broke the subsequent silence: "Daniel, we've become too close to end this way."

"Well, I don't know what else to say."

"Then why not listen?" Walter motioned toward the sofa. "After you top off our cups."

Dan huffed, shook his head, and said, "You're unreal; you know that?" Yet he fetched the carafe all the same from the kitchen, and brought it to Walter's side table. Steam rose as he poured hot java. The fire snapped loudly behind him. "So I hear you're a grandfather."

"Jake," Walter said. "He's a little rough around the edges, but cute as a bunny. I hope you'll meet him someday."

"We'll see." Dan sunk into the sofa once more. "This thing's like sitting on a marshmallow."

Walter chuckled. "I'm glad you're here, Daniel." His eyes were directed toward the fire. "I know you think I'm a fool for pardoning Kevin. And I understand; we worked long and hard on that tree house, and the tree itself was very special to you. I'm terribly sorry."

"It wasn't your fault."

"Not directly, no."

"Walter, you can't possibly be taking the blame for this?"

Walter pushed air from one cheek to another, as if chewing Dan's remark. "Not blame, Daniel. But I'm accepting accountability for the life I neglected. I've vowed to do all I can to right the ship. And it starts with forgiveness. If I push a criminal record on this man—my son—he'll be lost to me forever. But if I forgive him, if I accept his remorse; well, only then may I ask his forgiveness of me."

He looked squarely at Dan. "I'd give up ten barns for that, Daniel. For one chance to be a proper father to my son, I'd do anything." He sipped his coffee. "Like the old prof in that book I gave you, I'm on the way out, Daniel. And…" He coughed again. "Now don't get me wrong; this isn't some terminal illness. I hope my closing chapters take twenty years or more. But like I've told you, I'm sixty-eight years old, and from where I'm sitting I can tell you plainly: It's people that matter. In the end, they're all you'll care about, too. No man ever lies upon his death bed saying, 'bring me my tools; let me see them one last time.' No indeed, it's his loved ones he craves. One more minute, you see? One final hug, one final chance at words unspoken." A tear rolled down Walter's cheek. "I'm going to do everything in my power to be a great father. And grandfather." He reached for Dan's hand. "And friend."

Dan held Walter's hand, pleased to discover it warm to the touch. "You're the best friend I've ever had." It was all he could say without crying.

"Now, there's another book I gave you," Walter said.

"The Bible?"

"You bet'cher bippy." Walter smiled as another tear fell. "You'll find what I'm saying is in there also. Nothing matters more to God than His love for people."

Logs shifted in the waning fire, and Rockler's head lifted as the sparks settled. Dan and Walter drank coffee for more than a minute. "You know," Walter finally said. "It'll sprout again in the spring."

"What?"

"The tree."

"You honestly think so?"

"Its roots are still in the ground, and there's a bit of the trunk left. I figure you'll see some shoots poking out by the end of April."

Dan squirmed in his marshmallow seat. "But I certainly won't live to see it fully grown again."

"Perhaps not, but you might find that watching young growth develop is … well … an even greater masterpiece; that it speaks to you in ways the old tree never could."

Dan pondered the idea, watching the fire die slowly. "I really should be going."

"Your family awaits."

"Yeah, there's that, and I should hit the driving range. You have no idea how important golf can be in my line of work."

Walter's mustache fluttered. He was hiding a smirk.

"What?" Dan asked. "You got something against golf?"

"No, it's just … They're calling for snow tonight, Daniel."

45

CHAPTER FORTY-FIVE

They sat by a window overlooking a fairway that was topped with an inch of wet snow. Flurries still swirled in the watery sunlight, starting to emerge. Their phones lay face-down amid assorted fine glasses and a cloth-covered basket full of sugary muffins.

"So he literally writes 'head down' on his golf balls, right. And shoots a round of seventy-six!" Paul Andrews shook what remained of his second mimosa before swallowing it. "Now he's got half our members using Sharpies on their Titleists, but they couldn't shoot seventies to save their sorry behinds." Russell mimicked Paul's bold laughter.

"What do you average per round, Dan?" said Javier Sanchez.

Dan sensed his father staring. "Well, it's not anything that begins with seventy." He smiled. "I've shot in the eighties at times. I don't play as often as I'd like."

"He's been going for dad-of-the-year," Russell said, elbowing Paul.

"Is that right?"

"Yeah, well, I've been at home a few months now, waiting for the right opportunity. It's given me plenty of time with my four-year-old son."

"So you'll be adding stay-at-home-dad to your resume?" Javier said, glancing at Paul and Russell.

"Well, not exactly." Dan faked a laugh. The men made eyes at each other. Russell motioned for the waitress, and ordered a round, their third of the hour.

"From what I've seen. And *heard*…" Paul tipped his head toward Russell. "There's little need to embellish your resume, Dan."

"Thank you, sir. I only wish we could've shared time on the links."

"Well, you might have bettered my score. And then…" Paul winked, and everyone laughed.

When the waitress arrived with another tray of mimosas, the conversation finally turned to business. Dan was given a chance to share answers (all rehearsed) to standard interview questions. He likewise boasted his already advanced knowledge of Conway's financial profile. "I believe this young man knows more about our company than you, Javier," Paul Andrews jabbed at one point. Russell stayed quiet and withdrawn, like a nervous prosecutor studying the defense's key witness. And indeed this conversation, in a haughty fairway country club, surrounded by wealthy, brunch-eating patrons, felt like a courtroom drama.

With Dan's life hanging in the balance.

About thirty minutes into the interview, talk turned to policies and office protocol; closing remarks, Dan figured. But no offer was extended, only subtle hints and suppositional remarks. And like a wrong turn down a one-way street, Paul abandoned the interview to tell tales with Russell. Yarns of comedic incompetence by long-forgotten colleagues.

Javier said little during this time. He occasionally smiled or gestured in an effort to align himself with the brass. But in the midst of their hoarse laughter and muffled obscenities, he'd become a third wheel to two corporate leaders, bent on killing drinks and trampling memories. Like Kevin Clark's. Paul had asked Dan about Kevin, earlier in the morning, when nervousness prevailed and every man volleyed his best quips and witticisms. It was then, amid Bell-Knarr small talk that Kevin's memory surfaced, only to be promptly dismissed. Now, however, listening to his father and Paul cutting up the schmucks-of-old, Kevin Clark's image—around the office, in the downtown bar, plummeting to his death—became a fog in Dan's mind, stirring his emotions.

Was it the alcohol? The abrupt manner in which Paul had disengaged from the interview? Regardless, Dan's stomach churned as he traced the rim of his glass with a finger, and then fidgeted with a spoon.

"You like sports?" Javier asked him; the start of a quieter, sideline conversation.

"You bet'cher bippy," Dan said. "Wow. That just slipped out." Dan chuckled to himself, looking out the window. "I have a friend…" He couldn't finish the thought.

So Javier continued, "That Bowl Championship is so hard to understand. To me, anyway. But man I love the hype this time of year."

Dan turned to look at Javier's argyle sweater and round, gold spectacles. "Do you get to many games?"

"Nah, I'm at work most Saturdays, at least part of the day. There's always an eight o'clock game, though." Dan nodded, looking away again.

When the waitress arrived, Russell requested a round for all but Dan declined, asked for a soda, and endured verbal jabs from his three companions. Then, like flashlights from heaven, sunlight pierced through the clouds, causing parts of the fairway to shimmer.

Russell turned toward the sudden brightness. "If we sit here long enough we might play nine after all!" He seemed to be squinting, with a hand above his eyes.

"You're nuts, Crawford; I couldn't hit a softball after the drinks we've just had," Paul said.

Russell faced him again, muffled a belch. "Well, you don't have to hit a softball, Paul; we'd be playing golf!" He laughed, loudly, drawing looks from other tables.

As the near ruckus subsided, Dan stared at the brightening fairway. "Did you ever use a chisel, Paul?" he said, sounding almost cocky, still looking out the window. Spikes of heat invaded his face as he became suddenly, shockingly aware that a line had been crossed in every sense of the expression. Through awkward silence he willed himself closer to the point of no return. "A chisel," he repeated, looking directly at Paul. "You know, the tool?"

"No, I can't say I have, Dan."

"What's your point, Danny?" Russell finished his drink.

Dan folded his napkin, watched his finger press the seam. "It's an amazing tool, really. You see, it precisely removes small slices of wood, and at just the right places."

"So you've been watching a little PBS while sitting around the house. Is that it?" Russell breathed a disturbing snigger. "What's this got to do with our conversation?"

Paul laughed, Javier followed suit.

"I wish I could explain it," Dan said. He looked in Russell's eyes, saw the shut-up-this-instant message they conveyed. Then he looked at Paul Andrews, at his double chin and glassy, dilated eyes. "Funny thing is, Paul; once the material is chiseled away, you can't put it back. I mean, I suppose you could try, little by little, some glue here and there. But it'd look pretty ragged, no doubt." Dan's ears drummed. Looking down, he realized his napkin was torn in two places.

Russell exhaled like a freight train, and spoke through gritted teeth. "Danny, I swear you'd better get to the—"

"Russ, hey, it's okay," Paul said. "About time we cool the jets, anyway. Sober up a bit. Are you a wood worker, Dan?"

Dan looked up. "No, sir. But my best friend is."

"Well then, perhaps he can make something to adorn the shelves of your new Conway office."

Dan forced a breath through his clenching jaw, and his eyes dropped again.

"Danny!" Russell kicked his leg, forcing him to look up.

Paul Andrew's hand was extended over the table. Dan's arm rose for a second, but then came to rest on the table. Paul's smile receded as he withdrew his hand. "I'm honored," Dan said. "But I'll need some more time to make my decision."

Stunned silence.

Dan sipped his soda. The other men shifted in their seats, straightened their place settings. Russell ordered scotch, and Javier broke the ice: "You know, speaking of wood, those trees look gorgeous with the snow and sunlight." He motioned out the window, beyond the ninth green, to where snow clung and sparkled on the limbs of two trees. Everyone looked, except Russell. His eyes remained locked and loaded and aimed at Dan's skull.

"Can you imagine all the golf those trees have seen?" Javier added, laughing, desperate to lighten the mood. "I wonder how many times they've been plunked?"

Paul swallowed hard. "Yes, Javier. If trees could talk. I think we get it."

Hairs stood on end all over Dan's body. "A tree can say plenty." He squared eyes with the inebriated CFO. "They can talk, Paul. I sure think so." And with this he stood, offered thanks to his hosts, and walked away.

"Danny!" It was Russell's voice, gruff and commandeering.

Dan continued walking.

"DANNY!"

The entire club fell silent, except for the screeching legs of a chair thrust in motion and the unyielding claps of Dan's oxfords on the hardwood foyer.

46

CHAPTER FORTY-SIX

Robyn stood near the sliding glass door, watching Evan. He was supposed to be resting, but the first measurable snow of the season had fallen, and the afternoon sun made it perfect for packing. Of course, there wasn't much snow to pack, and grass was poking through in most places. But it doesn't take much snow to excite a boy's heart.

And thank God his heart is still beating.

She planned to help stack and then adorn the snowman with a scarf and floppy hat, lying beside her on the carpet. But for now she wanted only to watch, distantly, with a warm mug in her chilly hands. Dan had been gone all morning and part of the afternoon. And she knew the snow had confined the men to drinking and schmoozing.

Crawling in his bibs and a bright blue cap, Evan strained to move a thickening snowball, his exertion forcing Robyn's hand. She slid open the door. "Ev, stop! I'll be out in a minute and we'll push it togeth—" The garage door rumbled into motion.

Robyn walked to the kitchen, tabled her mug, and rolled her head against the mounting tension in her neck. Breathing deeply, she leaned against a counter, just as she'd planned, shoving fingers in her pockets and trying to appear cool…which lasted all of ten seconds.

"Robyn!" Dan's shout began before the door was halfway open.

"Robyn!" He made a beeline toward her, and then kissed her mouth. Her arms wrapped around his black woolen parka until the kiss ended.

"Dan, what in the…"

"I screwed up," he said. "I walked away from the job and… But that wasn't the screw-up. It's just… We don't have much time, okay? You have to take Evan; go to Walter's or… Anywhere! You have to leave." His jaw quivered, and then his head hit her shoulder.

Her spine tingling, she ran fingers through his hair. Her mouth felt like cotton. "You're really scaring me. What in the world is going on?"

He stepped back, clutching her arms and looking in her eyes. "I know I'm hard to live with, Robyn. I have crap on the inside of me that I can't…" He looked away, shook his head, and looked back in her eyes once again. "I love you. You and Evan and the precious little child alive in you. You all deserve better. I want to be better."

Time seemed to stop as a single tear rolled down Robyn's cheek. Dan caught it with his thumb, and she trembled at his touch.

"Dan…" She was lost for words.

"The past few months: almost losing you, meeting Walter, Evan's accident. Even just being at home more. It's caused something good. I'm still confused. And God knows I act a fool sometimes. But I don't want to lose it, Robyn. Whatever's happening in me, I don't want it to end." He flashed a sad smile, and then pulled her close and kissed her head.

"But why do we have to leave?" Her words were muffled by his coat.

"I've crossed my dad. He's drunk and angry and… I think he might come here."

She pushed away and stood up straight, heart racing. "Then come with us!"

"No. I've run away for the last time." His eyes turned steely and distant, as if looking through walls.

"What?" She shook her head, wiped her eyes. "Dan, he's a…" She held her tongue.

"He's a monster." It wasn't defensive, and it wasn't a question.

Robyn stayed silent for several seconds. "I'm terrified," she finally whispered.

"Then listen to me. Gather a few things and go. He might not come, but let's play it safe."

"You can't ask that! Not after you waltz in here and..." She wiped another tear, looked at the floor and then up again. "You melted my heart, Daniel Crawford. And now you want me to leave you in harm's way, to wait two fields away, scared to death, worrying what's going to happen to you? I haven't gotten over the true story of your scar, and now..." She threw up her hands.

"We'll have our phones." His tone was urgent. "Now let's go. He probably left the club soon after I did, if he wasn't kicked out."

"Oh, come on!" She licked her bottom lip, placed her palms on his chest. "Baby, this doesn't make sense. It's completely unreasonable." Her tone softened. "Don't misunderstand, I am flattered by what you did today, and I'll stand behind you one hundred percent, but don't ask me to—"

Evan rushed in, eyes wide and grinning, clumping snow over half the kitchen. "Grandpa's here!"

Robyn's knees weakened, her stomach convulsed. "Come upstairs, buddy," she managed to say. "Let's get you into some dry clothes."

"But I want to finish the snowman." It was a whiny response. "I want to show Grandpa."

"You've done enough for one day. Remember the doctor's orders." She tried to smile but her teeth stayed clenched. A car door thumped.

"But my boots always go in the gara—"

"NOW!" She tilted her head, raised two hands, and searched for an ounce of composure. "To your room. Now. Please." Evan dropped his head as he trudged toward the stairs.

Dan removed his coat, fussed with his hair.

"Dan?"

"I'll be okay, just—" They heard a melodic rap on the door. "Just stay upstairs."

Robyn folded her hands, drew a deep breath, and walked away, her stocking feet turning soggy with boot-slush. Running upstairs, she spotted Evan on his bedroom floor, wriggling out of snow clothes. Then she heard the kitchen door open, and the sound of Russell's voice drizzling through the floor boards: "Well I'll be; if it isn't the big-shot tree whisperer." His vindictive laughter could have peeled the paint.

"Evan!" It was a frantic whisper. "C'mere. My room!"

"But I can't walk in these—"

"Stop whining!" She rushed in the room, scooped him in her arms. Wet bibs dangling, he grabbed her neck and giggled as she crossed the landing, plopped him on her bed, and locked the door.

Please, God… Help us.

She grabbed the landline phone from Dan's dresser, crying as she dialed.

47

CHAPTER FORTY-SEVEN

In a brown leather jacket, Russell stood by the fridge. "Please tell me that's not your heap parked in the garage. What tree told you to buy that?"

"I needed to trim a few expenses," Dan said, standing near the table. "I just… You know what, I don't owe you an explanation."

"Oh, you owe me one hell of an explanation!" Russell looked toward the hallway. "Where's the family? I saw the little one run in here."

"They're upstairs. Away from you."

"So I'm the bad guy?"

"You're drunk."

"And you're about to choke on your own teeth." He opened the fridge. "Where's your beer?" He rummaged the bottom shelf, found a bottle, twisted the cap, and took a long swallow. "Domestic sewage," he said with a scowl.

"It's my last one. You can have it. I quit."

Russell wiped his mouth with the back of his hand, and walked toward the table. Dan's head pounded, his gut tightened. Standing face to face, he stared in his father's hollow eyes, and inhaled his sour, smoky exhaust. "You shouldn't have come here."

"I put myself on the line for you, Danny Boy. Got you in front of top execs, assured them of your competence and superior work ethic." Dan flinched when Russell's spittle hit his eyes. "And not only do you turn down the job of your dreams, you have the audacity to act like a pompous little fruit loop. I cannot believe…" His right arm lifted. "That a screwy little mess like you ever came from my loins." Cold beer lapped into Dan's hair, cascading his face and the back of his neck. "As if I needed one more reason to believe your mother was a—"

Dan thrust a fist into Russell's ribs, then shoved him backward. He fell on his rear, rolled to an elbow. "Get out of my house!" Dan's eyes burned with beer. "You're not welcome here, anymore!"

Russell recovered to a seated position, and began to chuckle. Then he stood…and flipped the table. Robyn's tea mug shattered on impact. Holding two fists in Dan's direction, his lips curled, his nostrils flared. "I'm gonna beat you like a drum, boy."

"Daddy!" It was muffled call, from somewhere upstairs.

Evan! Be quiet, buddy!

Dan pictured Robyn, her hand pressed over Evan's mouth as they huddled together in a bedroom corner, shaking with fear.

"Sounds like somebody wants his daddy." Russell said. "How's about a little visit from Grandpa?" He dropped his fists, walked toward the hallway.

"Don't even think about it!"

Russell kept walking.

Dan lifted a chair. "I said, STOP!"

Russell raised his arms to buffer the blow, but it wasn't enough. The chair struck his head. Wood crashed and cracked on the floor as Russell staggered, then fell. From a split lump above his eyes, a red line lengthened down the bridge of his nose. He reached for the neck of his empty beer bottle, and then warily stood, raising the bottle over his head before thrusting it downward on the edge of a counter. Shards of glass showered the kitchen.

Get him out of the house!

Dan wheeled, ran to the family room, and opened the sliding glass door. "Out here, you coward!"

Russell charged like a rhino.

The sun-spiked snow was blinding on top, slushy beneath. Dan's oxfords were squishy by the time he reached the field, but it hardly mattered; he lost his footing and slid as if stealing second base. Icy wetness filled one leg and soaked half his shirt. Heart pounding, he attempted to stand, and saw Russell gaining, his broken bottle shining as brightly as the snow.

Dan tried to run but fell again, on his chest this time. He rolled to one side, just in time to see Russell take a stab. He dodged right, and the bottle stuck in the muddy sod. Dropping to his knees, Russell jerked it free, and took two reckless swipes in Dan's direction.

Dan crawled away backward. A siren sounded in the distance. "They're coming for you," he said, attempting to stand.

"Let'm come." Russell stayed hunkered down, gasping for breath. Blood on his cheeks had joined the stripe on his nose, and the lump on his head had turned purple.

"Daniel!"

Walter stood in the field, wearing nothing but khakis and a red flannel shirt.

"Well, looky who it is." Russell managed to stand. "Welcome to the party, Old McDonald!" He held the bottle like a six-shooter.

"Walk away, Daniel." Walter cleared his throat, and nearly coughed up a lung.

Russell sneered. "What it's gonna be … *Daniel?*"

"Walter, you shouldn't have come," Dan shouted, his eyes still on Russell. "You're sick."

"Nonsense. Now walk away. No good can come from this."

Dan stepped sideways, eyes still on his father, until he felt Walter's grasp from behind. "The police are coming," Walter said in Dan's ear. "I came as soon as Robyn called. It was faster by field than by car. But my knees are killing me."

Russell stepped closer to them. "So you're gonna walk in and save the day? Is that it? You're corn cobs aren't that big, Porky."

"Back away, Daniel." Walter moved in front of Dan, holding both arms down, shielding him from Russell.

"Walter, don't! Just get out of the way."

"I'd listen to the boy, Walt, and get out of my way." Russell switched the bottle to his left hand and, lunging forward, slapped Walter with his right.

The fleshy smack all but turned Dan's stomach. Walter stumbled to his left before falling in the snow.

With a guttural growl, Dan rushed his father like a blitzing linebacker, and slammed him to the slushy earth. Russell's hands opened on impact, but the broken bottle stayed well within reach. He groped for it, until Dan arched upward and punched him in the mouth. Now it was Russell who growled, but Dan only pressed harder with his knees, and then struck his father again.

"Daniel!"

Disregarding the plea, Dan lunged to his right, gripped the bottle, and stuck it to his father's throat.

"Go ahead," Russell said, his lips split and bleeding.

Pointed glass dimpled Russell's neck.

"DANIEL!"

Dan's upper lip felt slimy. His hands started shaking.

"DAN! NO!" It was Robyn's voice, from somewhere near the house.

"You're a wuss, Danny Boy. And you hit like one, too."

Lights flashed from a police car in the drive, and Dan pulled the bottle from his father's throat.

"Don't ever call yourself my son." Russell said, turning his head to spit blood on the snow. "I don't ever want to see your sorry ass again."

"No problem."

Dan crawled away from his father, and tossed the bottle in front of two fast-approaching officers, gripping their holsters. Then, as ordered, he lifted his hands, stood to his feet, and stepped farther away from his drunken, defeated old man. A short time later, with official statements given, Russell was seated in the back of a squad car, hands cuffed, while Robyn stood crying near a large, forgotten snowball.

Dan's chest felt full of wet sand when a familiar hand came to rest on his shoulder. Weak and trembling and no longer cuffed, he fell into Walter's arms, where the setting sun felt warm on his face.

48

CHAPTER FORTY-EIGHT

The Bennings antique knocker was beset in a wreath of holly. Dan rapped it three times. Robyn stood beside him, hand-in-hand with Evan. They heard footsteps approaching.

"Well, hello there," Margaret said, smiling as the door swung open.

The farmhouse had become a winter wonderland. Electric candles shone in the windows. The aroma of pine and nutmeg mingled with wood smoke and the smell of polished wood. Looking in the living room, Dan saw a towering Christmas tree, trimmed with white lights, maroon balls, and dozens of crocheted ornaments. In the dining room, train tracks still topped the table. But now they encircled a golden runner on which stood the largest collection of nutcrackers he'd ever seen. The chandelier burned dimly above them.

"Margaret, you've outdone yourself," Robyn said. "And it's still three weeks until Christmas."

"Well, thank you, honey. I love to decorate. We've been collecting these things for years."

"Seventeen totes and counting!" Walter called from the family room. Everyone laughed, but tension hung thick in the festive air. Dan pulled off his gloves and shoved them in a pocket of his parka. By the time he looked up, Margaret had stepped aside to reveal the young woman who'd been standing behind her.

"I'd like you all to meet Brandi Grimes."

"Hi," Robyn said. "Nice to meet you." They shook hands.

Brandi's face seemed stretched but otherwise becoming. Soft brown hair fell a few inches past her shoulders, and her bluish eyes were mildly distorted behind a pair of marbled brown glasses. A Santa Claus broach was fastened high on her sweater, and a little boy clung to her black denim jeans. His hair was dark and long and wavy.

"This shy guy is Jake," Margaret said, tickling the boy's chin. "Say hello, Jakey." He said nothing, only lowered his head.

"This is Evan," Robyn said, almost pushing him forward. "He's four. And this is my husband, Dan."

Dan only smiled. Brandi nodded at him, flashing a row of crooked teeth. "Kevin's in the other room," she said, glancing backward, dipping her chin.

Margaret buffered the resulting silence by piling their coats on a chair near the Christmas tree. Returning to the foyer, she said, "What's that, honey?" although Dan had heard nothing.

"He wanna see my twain?" Jake said, still clinging to his mother.

"Well, I've got news for you," Margaret said. "Evan was actually the first engineer to ever operate that train." She winked at Evan, put her hands on her hips. "What do you say, Ev? Feel like watching the train go 'round?" Without waiting for an answer, she walked in the dining room. Everyone followed and stood by the table.

"Let me see here…" Margaret squatted, fumbling with wires.

"Let me guess," Robyn said. "Jake's this quiet all the time."

"Yeah, right," Brandi returned. "He's loud, mostly."

"There we are." Margaret groaned as she stood, and then the train started buzzing. It picked up speed as it passed the mesmerized boys and chuffed behind a battalion of nutcrackers.

"Choo-choo!" Evan said, as it neared them again. The women shared in an edgy sort of laughter, and Dan walked away to the "other" room.

A fire burned in the fireplace. Walter was lounging in his usual chair while Kevin Grimes sat waist deep in the Victorian sofa, his beefy arm propped on its wood-trimmed back. His face was clean-shaven, his head freshly sheared, and with black glasses and a red crew sweater, he looked almost presentable. He didn't smile, and he barely made eye contact.

He looked almost as troubled as Dan.

Rockler was the first to say hello, springing from his pillow to prop paws on Dan's slacks. Dan scratched the dog's ears, again and again and...

"Merry Christmas, Daniel." Walter stood to shake hands. His eyes flickered, and his mustache looked bigger than ever before. "I'd like to properly introduce you to my son, Kevin Grimes."

Rockler dropped to all fours and returned to his pillow, and Kevin stood. Dan stepped forward to put his sweaty hand in a grip that felt exactly like Walter's. "You like that Ford Escape?" Kevin asked.

"I'm learning to." Their hands released.

"Buddy-a-mine had one. Said it was alright, but he'd rather have an Explorer. More room, you know?"

"I'll keep that in mind."

Kevin wiped his hands on his jeans. "I guess we got off to a pretty bad start."

Dan's throat drew as tight as his fists. Walter closed the door.

"I mean... I know I messed up royally, man. I just..." Kevin looked down, opened his arms.

"I forgive you." Dan's sudden proclamation startled even himself. He drew a deep breath, and noticed Walter frozen in place. "I don't want to," he added. "I think it's only fair I be honest. There's still a part of me that wants you behind bars." He dropped his head with a defeated chuckle, then groaned as he turned toward the door.

"I'm real sorry for what I done, Dan. And I'm sorry for all you been through. That was a terrible bad injury your boy had. Shoot, I shouldn't have even been there. But once I started the snoopin' routine—scam, I guess—it was hard to stop. Again, I'm sorry." For several seconds Dan heard only Kevin's belabored breathing and the crackle of flames. "I also heard what happened with your dad," Kevin added. "That's really a bummer, man."

Dan death-gripped the door knob, and more seconds passed without words. "I know my son's accident wasn't your fault," he finally said. "You shouldn't have been there, but..."

There's no way we're discussing my father.

There came a knock on the door. "Walter? We'd best be going."

Dan released the knob and turned around.

"Yes, dear." Walter said with embellished compliance, kneeling at the hearth, rolling his eyes.

Kevin slapped his thigh and laughed like a skidding tire, and despite the coils in his throat, Dan couldn't help but grin. "You know, Kevin," he said. "You've got an amazing father."

The room fell silent.

Kevin looked at Walter. "I'm startin' to realize that."

"So do you, Daniel." Walter's mustache tweaked as he pointed up.

Dan laughed at first but then earnestly nodded, and echoed, "I'm starting to realize that."

"I ain't never been to no church before. Just for weddings and funerals."

"Well, that makes two of us, Kevin," Dan said.

Walter walked past them, opened the door. "The concert begins in thirty minutes, men." He looked at each of them in turn. "We run Margaret late, and we'll all be hitting our knees."

49

CHAPTER FORTY-NINE

Behind the old brick church was a modern addition that presently housed all the action. Adults mingled as their sugar-filled children dashed from one corner to the next, aimlessly running and loving every second of it. "Watch out for the Christmas tree!" a different mother warned every couple of minutes. Aligned folding tables held pot-luck desserts, including seven trays of box-mix brownies.

Margaret had introduced Robyn and Brandi to every other woman in attendance. Evan's cheeks had been reddened by affectionate pinches. Smiles and laughter mixed to an almost musical quality. A music that softened for Dan as he exited the banquet room; and faded as he walked the corridor; and then stopped entirely when he entered the sanctuary, closing its doors.

The main lights were off but smaller ones, near the front, cast a glow on the altar and pulpit. Brass organ pipes also captured the glow, reflecting it onto the choir loft, where an hour earlier men and women and children, their faces replete with joy, had sung Christmas hymns to the forty-couple people in attendance.

Now it was truly a silent night.

Dan walked behind the last pew, sliding his palm on its smooth, varnished surface. Reaching the aisle, he turned and sat, resting his hands in three different spots before folding them safely in his lap. Then he pictured a coffin, half-open in a garish parlor, and a fourteen-year-old boy, choking back a swollen wad of nothing. His mother had talked about Jesus sometimes, but with a tone of inquisition that Dan readily dismissed or criticized. And yet here he was, two decades later, seeking similar answers and wondering: Had she reached a conclusion before—

The door creaked. A white mustache entered the darkened sanctuary. "Daniel?" Four chandeliers awakened slowly overhead, as if controlled by a dimmer.

"I got lost on my way to the bathroom," Dan said.

"So I see." Walter closed the doors, began his approach. "Although I can hardly call this a wrong turn."

Dan slid sideways on the pew, making room for Walter to sit. For more than a minute the men remained quiet. "Where's your regular seat?" Dan finally said.

"Fourth row, middle," Walter said pointing. "I imagine they'll etch my name on that pew before long." They laughed for a moment, and then more silence ensued.

"My dad's moving to Texas." Dan's eyes stayed forward. "He wiggled out of any major criminal charges, but the stock-holders pressed his resignation anyway."

"Why Texas?"

"Old connections. Men willing to turn a blind eye. But he won't be CEO."

"Texas is a long way from Baltimore." Walter's tone held assurance, optimism.

"Yeah, well… It's not Seattle, but I'll take it."

Walter's arm fell over Dan's shoulders. "It's hard to believe you'll have a baby to care for next summer."

"You're telling me." He looked at Walter's knees. "I'll need plenty of coaching."

"I'll buy you plenty of books." Their laughter was warm and loud and free, until the doors opened again.

"Seems like the social's been moved," Margaret said, entering. Robyn, Brandi, and the boys followed.

Robyn stopped behind Dan, rubbed his shoulders. "You haven't been struck down, I see." She kissed his cheek, then scolded Evan for running in the church.

"That goes for you, too, Jakey!" Kevin said, entering the sanctuary. "Slow'r down, boys!" Dan turned to catch Robyn's eye. They sucked in their lips and giggled through their noses.

"Did you tell him," Kevin said, closer now.

"No," Walter said.

"Tell me what?" Dan looked at Robyn. She turned up her hands and appeared still to be fighting off giggles.

"Alright," Margaret said, seeming annoyed. "Ladies, let's take these boys to the bathroom before we leave; give the men a chance to discuss their little secret." She walked toward the door. "C'mon boys!" They charged. "You men get the lights on your way out." Robyn patted Dan's back before leaving the sanctuary, boys in tow.

"So, what's going on?" Dan asked Walter.

"I didn't mean to spill the beans," Kevin said, sitting two pews in front of them, turned sideways and looking back.

"Nonsense; he'd hear soon enough." Walter stroked his mustache, raised his chin. "Daniel, I'd like you to help us build a new barn."

"You have got to be kidding. *Build* a new barn?"

"You bet'cher bippy. My insurance will cover the cost of materials, and Kevin here is a skilled carpenter, even dabbles in masonry."

"I was union for a while," Kevin added.

Dan shook his head. "Guys, I don't know. I mean, that's a huge undertaking."

"Daniel." Walter softened his tone. "We'll be building much more than a barn."

Dan clenched his teeth, felt pressure in his chest.

"What's that mean?" Kevin asked. "We gonna throw up a new tree house or somethin'?"

Walter winked at Dan. "Not exactly." He turned to face Kevin. "But I don't see why a custom-built barn can't include a loft that's…what do they call it, nowadays…a man cave?"

"'At'll work!" Kevin said, his plump cheeks creased by an ear-to-ear smile. Dan could hardly contain himself. *If Robyn were here…*

"Kevin," Walter said. "If it's not too much to ask, I'd like another moment alone with Daniel."

"That's fine." Kevin pushed himself up and out of the pew. "I'd better help out with the wild child, anyway." He walked the aisle. "I mean, Jake, now," he added, looking back at Dan.

"No worries," Dan said, raising a hand.

When the church doors closed, Walter cleared his throat and turned his gaze forward. "Is this when you ask me to pray?" Dan said. "To give my life to the Lord, or however you say it?"

Walter breathed deeply. "I do hope you see Him in me, Daniel. In my life. In my story. When the day comes you're ready to make that decision, I'll be honored to pray with you." He paused several seconds before shifting gears. "Tonight I simply want to tell you how proud I am of you. I know how hard it must be to face Kevin, to accept him and forgive his actions." Dan said nothing as he wrung his hands, staring at numbers on the wall near the loft. "God knows, he's rough around the edges," Walter continued, his voice escalating.

"It'll take time," Dan said. "But I'm willing to try."

"No boy ought to go through what you did, Daniel. I mean…" He pulled at his slacks, fumbling for words.

"I'm sorry my father hit you."

Walter looked at Dan. "I should say likewise." His mustache turned down. "I'm just glad it's over…and that you dropped that bottle."

Tears clouded Dan's vision as murmuring voices drew near to the door.

"I also want you to know…" Walter turned his body, looked squarely at Dan. "That I've come to love you like a son."

Dan looked up, determined not to cry. Then he turned toward Walter and broke down just the same. "Thank you," he managed. Their teary eyes locked as the doors burst open. Dan wiped is cheeks, then swung his head left.

"We are now the last people in the building," Margaret scolded. The boys, in their coats, ran circles around her. Robyn stood in the background, lips pursed and eyebrows raised.

"Well," Walter said in a hushed sort of way. "Shall we join our family?"

Dan faced him once more, and smiling like the sun, whispered, "At'll work." They laughed like children as the chandeliers dimmed.

"Honestly," Margaret said. "We'll meet you at the cars. And hurry up; these kids need to get to bed."

Dan followed Walter toward the doors of the sanctuary. "You really think it'll sprout again? The tree, I mean."

Walter stopped walking, put his hands on Dan's shoulders, and looked long in his eyes. "Daniel, I believe it already has. In both of us." His moustache twitched, the two men embraced, and Daniel Crawford's heart felt right as rain.

FastPencil
http://www.fastpencil.com